DARK ECHOES OF THE PAST

DARK ECHOES OF THE PAST

RAMÓN DÍAZ ETEROVIC

TRANSLATED BY PATRICK BLAINE

amazon crossing

This is a work of fiction. Names, characters, organizations, places, events, and incidents are either products of the author's imagination or are used fictitiously. Any resemblance to actual persons, living or dead, or actual events is purely coincidental.

Previously published as *La oscura memoria de las armas* by Lom Ediciones in Chile in 2008. Translated from Spanish by Patrick Blaine. First published in English by AmazonCrossing in 2017.

Published by AmazonCrossing, Seattle
www.apub.com

ISBN-13: 9781542046916
ISBN-10: 1542046912

Cover design by David Drummond

Printed in the United States of America

DARK ECHOES OF THE PAST

1

The worst was not having anything to do. Or almost nothing, because every now and then I went to work lighting a cigarette, changing the cassette in the tape player, and wetting my right index finger to turn the pages of the book I was reading, all the while listening for the knock that might come on my office door. Sometimes I also tried to communicate with Simenon, and when the boredom was strangling me, I would leave the apartment and go down to Anselmo's newsstand to talk about the week's horse races and the best animals we had seen run throughout our long-lived passion for horses and betting. My principal occupation, with no clients arriving at the office—and what allowed me to keep moving through life (along with the occasional good bet)—consisted of reviewing lengthy and boring books on politics, sociology, economics, and other occult sciences that purported to explain the erratic behavior of human beings since their first steps on Earth. The reviews were published in the bulletin of an organization with the pompous name of the Institute for International Research, and I couldn't care less if anyone actually read them. With a bit of patience, I had managed to get through my first fifty years—a late age to change professions in a country where the passing years weighed like a criminal conviction upon anyone looking for work. An old university friend had gotten me the reviewing job.

I was OK, but I don't know if I'd say I was happy. At night, while I tried to get some sleep, I thought about my investigations over the last few years, and a tiny prick of pain close to my heart made me recognize that I missed running around the city trying to chase down fragments of truth that were as ephemeral as the shooting stars that sometimes crossed the dirty sky over Santiago. Once or twice a week I got together with Griseta, whom I had met thirteen years ago when she was a university student needing a place to crash for a few days. Since then, too much water had passed under the bridge. Pleasant and stormy moments, breakups and reconciliations. In spite of so much pain and happiness, all I had to do was look her in the eyes to know that what we had was real, and that gave us that little bit of peace we needed as one day piled onto another.

I didn't have much to do, and this, among other things, made me think about a dream that came to me some nights as soon as I put my head on the pillow and closed my eyes, trying to wipe out the events of the day, the humming on of the hours, the dry leaves of boredom scattered about my desk. It was always the same, as if it were the text of a scriptwriter trying to perfect a key scene. Always the same, the spitting image, reiterative and brutal, like being punched in the dark: I was standing at the edge of the ocean with my feet buried in the sand, staring at the line of the horizon where a wave had begun to form. A handful of seagulls flew over my head, the ocean ceased to roar for a moment, and I could hear the resigned beat of my heart. Soon the wave approached, sinuous, agile, gray, with a crest painted in mystery. Serpent wave. Rapacious wave. I wanted to escape and I couldn't. In the dream, I opened my eyes and I couldn't recognize where I was. Mystery, all mystery and shadows. My desire to flee didn't matter. The wave always ended up reaching me. It was like the past, my past and the past of many others. A wave, the ocean, its fury of enigmas and truths confused among the remains of shipwrecks.

I spent a good bit of my time nodding off with my elbows on the blotter of my desk or smoking with a lost gaze that went far beyond the window overlooking the Mapocho River and the La Chimba neighborhood. The area was inhabited by the inebriated phantoms of Rubén Darío and Pedro Antonio González, poets I had read in my university years while feigning interest in the useless pronouncements of my Roman law professor. But that all belonged to the past, and the only thing reminiscing did for me was awaken a slight nostalgia for the agility and shoulder-length hair I'd had when I was twenty. My hair was still thick and abundant, but the gray that tinted it made me remember the indefatigable march of the pages in the calendar. It didn't really bother me, except when I thought about how life was a handful of sand slipping between my fingers.

I got off the carousel of memories and left my apartment to take a walk around the neighborhood. I nixed the idea of using the elevator and took the service stairwell instead. On the way down, I thought about the little that I knew about the other residents of the building. I remembered Stevens, the blind neighbor who'd helped me solve a case involving a group of bomb makers. And some girls who'd delivered friendly service in a massage parlor until it was closed down due to the protests of a dozen neighbors who were far too interested in preaching at men with sore backs. As for the rest, the majority of my neighbors were a series of masks without names that I crossed paths with when entering or exiting the building. Just the same, I didn't have any complaints about them. Some afternoons I would hear arguments or annoying music coming from their apartments, but neither one made me want to restart the Trojan War or barge into the hall to shout about my right to silence.

As I ambled through the Plaza de Armas, the painters who spent the day selling landscapes and caricatures to tourists began to pack up and say goodbye to one another. The plaza was a small oasis of green in the middle of the thousands of gray buildings in downtown Santiago. On the western corner of the Portal Fernández Concha, two men smoked and appeared to be studying the pedestrians hurrying by at the end of their day. As I was passing, I glanced at them with mistrust and walked on until I had reached the base of the Mapuche Indian monument. Nearby, an Adventist preacher repented his alcoholic past, and two raggedy girls sold bouquets of violets. It was the same show as always, and it extended all the way to the Mapocho River in a confusion of filthy bars, strip joints, and alleys that served as hiding places for crooks keen on robbing the drunks who stumbled down the sidewalks.

My walk took me to the Don Quijote Winery, where I drank a glass of wine and entertained myself by listening to the conversation between two patrons who had spent a lot of time in the company of Bacchus, and who found it difficult to see any farther than their reddened noses. Afterward I went back to the office to review one of the books awaiting me on my desk. As I was entering the building, the doorman stopped me. He was a short, pale man who had been hired recently and who was attempting, by all means at his disposal, to win the favor of the residents.

"You have some missives, Mr. Heredia," he said, passing me a dozen envelopes.

"Missives?"

"Letters," the doorman clarified in a tone of voice containing a hint of compassion for my possible unfamiliarity with a word that, so far as I could remember, I had seen only in the dusty old pirate books that I'd read in my youth.

"The mailman doesn't go up to the apartments anymore?"

"I receive the correspondence here and deliver it to the addressees personally."

"Very efficient," I said with a trace of sarcasm. "What's your name, friend?"

"Félix Domingo Vidal."

"Feliz Domingo."

"Félix, with an *x*. Like *xenophobe* and *xylophone*."

"Xipe Totec and Xochicatzin."

"Xerox and *xeroderma*."

"Xochipilli."

"Félix, with an *x*. Don't forget, Mr. Heredia."

I said goodbye to Feliz Domingo, and as I was going up in the elevator, I looked over the envelopes. Most of them were mailings from financial services offering earthly paradise in return for abusive interest payments over eight or ten years. Of the rest, one contained an invitation to subscribe to a magazine about astonishing crimes; another, a letter and a check from an old client who was thankful for my services and apologized for the delay in sending my fee. The check wasn't huge, but it was enough to pay the rent on my apartment, buy a few books, take Griseta out for dinner and a movie, and save a few bills with Andrés Bello on them in the snakeskin wallet a Mexican friend had given me. The last envelope was addressed to someone named Desiderio Hernández who lived in apartment 707, two or three doors down from my office. I thought about going back down to the first floor to show the efficient Feliz Domingo his error, but it seemed too far away, and I preferred to fix the mistake myself.

As I came out of the elevator, the hallway seemed darker than normal, and it gave me a small amount of pleasure to see the acrylic plaque that advertised my name and profession. The plaque was discolored at the edges, but the phrase **HEREDIA, PRIVATE INVESTIGATIONS** looked as brilliant as the first time I'd seen it. I arrived at the door of apartment 707 and pressed the doorbell beside it. I waited, and after a few seconds, I heard the sound of a deadbolt being unlocked with some difficulty. Then I saw the face of a man. His cheeks were perfectly shaven and a bit stiff, as if they were covered by a layer of wax. Above his lips was a well-trimmed black mustache. He looked at me with mistrust and didn't seem at all enthusiastic about my presence at his door.

"Mr. Desiderio Hernández?" I asked, already regretting my improvised job as mail carrier.

"What do you want?" asked the man, hard and cutting as a knife.

"The doorman gave me my mail, and it seems like he must have put one of your letters with mine by mistake. Since we're neighbors, I thought I would bring it to you, and—"

"Give it to me," Hernández ordered without offering me a chance to finish my explanation.

I passed him the letter, he checked that it hadn't been opened, and, without saying even half a word, he closed the door. Again I heard the noise of the deadbolt and struggled to repress my desire to kick in the door.

"Friendliness is in short supply these days," I said aloud, heading toward my apartment.

As I prepared my coffee, I forgot about the incident. Living in the same building with other people is just another sign of the capricious fate that links us to strangers, sometimes by strong bonds and other times by threads as ephemeral as a greeting in passing. Nothing to worry about, unless one happens to be a nosy neighbor or a writer interested in other people's problems.

I made myself comfortable in my desk chair, and after lighting a cigarette, I opened the closest book, whose title—*The Incidence of Educational Levels in Urban Environments*—assured me hours full of yawns.

"Do you agree?" I asked Simenon.

"Agree with what?" asked the cat, who was hunting a black-winged moth.

"We haven't had much to talk about lately," I answered him with a raised eyebrow.

2

Boredom was eating away at my skin like voracious bacteria, and I was still stuck on the first page of the book I was trying to review. It was as seductive as a drunk's breath the morning after. I had to look for a new client or I'd end up in the loony bin or howling like a dog at the moon. But it wasn't easy. Nobody was knocking on my door, and to make matters worse, listings for private-detective agencies were multiplying in the yellow pages. Some even had the audacity to put flyers under my door offering services like stolen-vehicle recovery, documentation of infidelity, supervision of nannies via microcameras, internet investigation, and thorough background checks. Bad times for a detective who could only offer his clients the indecisiveness of his nose and the certainty of his doubts.

The ring of the telephone interrupted my woes. I put it to my ear and recognized the quiet voice of the Writer, my friend who dedicates himself to writing novels based on the stories I tell him over drinks at the City or Rimbaud.

"How are the muses treating you?" I asked. "Are you still writing about me, or have you found something better to work on?"

"Neither one, Heredia. I'm going through a rough patch and I really need one of your stories. Anything, even if you don't think it's that interesting."

"Nothing. I've got nothing for you, Writer. It's been two months since so much as a spider came into my office. I haven't even been able to tilt against windmills like the skinny old knight from La Mancha who just celebrated his four hundredth year of life and keeps going with the same energy he had in his younger days."

"They just asked me for a piece for an anthology of short stories, and I was counting on you to help me out."

"I'm afraid you'll have to use your imagination."

"In that case, buy me a drink. My pockets are as empty as your office."

"Change careers. Sell hot dogs or candied peanuts. Not many people are interested in writers and their books. Most prefer to spend their money on hamburgers and french fries. Some people can't be pulled back from the cliff. They'll end up fat and dumb as a doornail."

"I thought about writing a novel about horse racing, with you in it. What do you think?"

"It's hard to come up with an original ending to that one. In racing you win or lose, and everything else is secondary."

"You're more apocalyptic than ever. Hopefully, the next time we talk, you'll have a good story for me."

"Read the paper, go to a bar, walk the streets. I'm sure that at any time, and in any part of the city, there is a story worth telling."

Griseta walked into the office, came up beside me, and kissed me on the lips. I remembered the first time she had appeared there. She had been around twenty years old. Her lips were painted a provocative red. Her hair was cut close to her head, emphasizing her features, as though she had stepped out of a Renaissance painting. Dressed in black, she possessed the beauty of a virgin who has just been seduced. She was wearing tight jeans and a John Lennon T-shirt. Her brother, Juan Ordoñez, was an old classmate of mine from the university. After fighting clandestinely against the Pinochet dictatorship, he joined up with the Sandinista guerillas in Nicaragua. He died in a battle against the Contras. At some point he had told his sister about me, and said she could go to me for help if she needed to.

Griseta had come from Talca in central Chile, and she wanted to find a job and begin studying psychology at the university. She'd asked if she could stay at my apartment for a couple of weeks. I said yes without imagining that, after a few days, I would have to admit that I had fallen in love with her.

It had been a long time since I had seen her dressed in black, like when we met, but her short red hair still gave her the young, attractive look that had captivated me the first time I saw her.

Now she was accompanied by an older brunette in a blue suit. "Virginia Reyes," said Griseta, introducing me to the stranger.

I pointed toward one of the seats in front of my desk, and the woman sat without speaking. I observed her closely. Something in her expression made me repress the desire to light a cigarette. On the side of her nose she had a couple of small moles. Her lips, lightly painted red, were surrounded by little wrinkles.

"Virginia was my high-school math teacher," said Griseta, in what I sensed was the start of a long story that she was going to tell me for some reason that would eventually become clear. "We haven't seen each other since I finished school, and a couple of months ago we met in the supermarket. We decided to get together for lunch the next week, and the day before, she called me to tell me that her only brother had died."

"I'm sorry," I said instinctively, without managing to convey a sad-enough tone in my voice.

Virginia Reyes replied with an understanding smile. She adjusted her blue skirt and looked kindly at Simenon, who had just jumped onto the desk and gave the impression of being interested in the conversation.

"Griseta told me that you're a private detective, and that you investigate all sorts of crimes."

"Sometimes, when I can, or if the occasion presents itself, I do the work you're talking about," I said, at the same time asking myself whether I could summon the energy to continue listening to the woman's story.

"Well, perhaps you can help me," the woman responded.

"What's the story?" I asked in the weary tone of an information-booth worker.

"My brother, Germán, was killed. Two men waited for him outside of his work and shot him. He died right there without anyone to help him."

"A street robbery is something the police know how to investigate. They put their informants to work, and it won't take long for them to figure out who did it."

"My brother's murder wasn't the product of a common robbery. I think they faked a robbery to throw off the police."

"What makes you think it was faked?"

"They didn't steal anything from him, and he was carrying his monthly salary and a watch that he inherited from our uncle."

"Maybe they were inexperienced. Maybe they panicked and ran. It wouldn't be the first time that happened."

"That's what the police said. But a week before he died, my brother told me that he thought he was being followed."

"Who was following him?"

"Germán had seen a couple of men in a bunch of places he used to go to. And also in the street outside the house. What I am sure of is that he was afraid."

"I thought those times were in the past," I said. Everyone knew that, during the seventeen years of Pinochet's dictatorship, his secret police routinely chased, tortured, and assassinated those who wanted Chile to return to democracy. It had begun in September of 1973, after the government of Salvador Allende was overthrown by a military coup encouraged by the CIA and Chile's conservative political parties. Today, few people dared deny that those crimes had been committed. The only ones who did were the military men who'd committed them and the civilians who'd supported the repressive government. "In any event," I told Virginia, "I'd recommend that you seek the help of a lawyer and take the case to the tribunals."

"I doubt they'll care now that he's dead. My brother had seemed strange lately. He would come home and close himself in his room. If he did have a problem, I think it might have been something that was happening in the home-improvement store where he worked."

"What are you thinking about, specifically?"

"Theft, some problem with a coworker. I don't know exactly. The only thing I know for sure is that the police didn't pay as much attention to his death as they should have."

"How old was your brother?"

"Sixty."

"Married?"

"He got married when he was twenty-five years old, and got separated four years after that. He didn't have any kids and didn't get into another relationship for a long time. About two years ago, he dated a woman and they lived together some of the time. Her name is Benilde Roos. She works as a nurse in a medical center."

"What does she think about all this?"

"I don't know. I saw her at the funeral and she didn't look like she could think about anything but her grief. I haven't seen her since then. We were never friends. As far as I can remember, she only came to my house once."

"Did your brother have any friends? Someone he would have trusted?"

"None that I ever met. I know he used to go to meetings at some club or society that he didn't talk about much."

"Your brother was a man of few words."

"He said what he needed to say, to me and my daughters. When Griseta told me about you, I tried to think of what I could tell you concerning my brother, and the truth is that there isn't much. We were seven years apart. Germán was from my father's second marriage, and except for the natural affection between a brother and a sister, we weren't really that close."

"How did you find out he had been killed by two men?"

"There was a witness, Darío Carvilio, a coworker of Germán's. He gave his version of the events to the police."

"Can you help Virginia?" Griseta asked.

I looked out the window at the sun hitting the horizon and didn't say anything.

"I can pay you," Virginia added, reacting to my apparent disinterest.

"I wasn't thinking about my fee, ma'am. The main mystery seems to be your brother."

"What do you mean?" asked the teacher.

"If we discover the cause of his fear, we might be able to figure out who killed him. That's assuming, of course, that it wasn't just a botched robbery."

"So you'll take the case?" asked Griseta, impatient.

"I can ask some questions, but that doesn't mean I'll draw any conclusions that are different from the police's," I said. After a pause to look out the window again, I asked the teacher the name of the place where her brother had worked.

"The León Lumberyard. It's on the Avenida Vicuña Mackenna. Germán worked as a cashier there."

"I'll also need to find Benilde Roos and look over your brother's belongings."

3

"Thank you for helping Virginia," said Griseta. "She's a good woman and she didn't know where to turn. That's why I gave her your name . . . I hope you don't mind."

The teacher had gone, and Simenon was the only witness to the embrace that brought us together as the afternoon gave way to the first shadows of night.

"Don't worry about it. Reviewing books was killing me. It'll be good for me to smell the air in the streets. The best part is that at the end of the road there's a beautiful damsel waiting for me who's proud of my deeds."

"Damsel? We live in the twenty-first century, and I'm not the girl you met years ago. It's time for women to stop being other people's prizes."

"I didn't think I'd get my head bitten off for a little joke."

"Better to stop the macho caveman before he starts."

"Quijote wasn't the only sad old guy with a right to be a bit crazy," I said, kissing Griseta. "And the chick from El Toboso wasn't exactly in the flower of her youth."

◆ ◆ ◆

Virginia Reyes received me in the living room of her house. It was a small, poorly lit room with two chairs, a coffee table with several ceramic ashtrays on it, and a picture frame that held a collection of portraits that I guessed depicted her, her husband, and their two daughters. She offered me a coffee, and while she served it, she reiterated her regret for her lack of communication with her brother. Nothing that she hadn't already said in the office or that seemed unforgivable in any way. I asked her to show me Germán's room, and as we moved through the hallway, she told me that her husband had died six years ago, and that her daughters were university students studying education and social work.

"Germán's things are exactly as he left them," she said when we came into the room, whose most attractive feature was a window through which the backyard could be seen. There were roses, gladiolas, daisies, and other plants whose names I didn't know growing there. The furniture looked shabby. There was a bed with a bronze headboard, a double-sided wardrobe, a wooden seat, and a desk with a few books and a radio that looked like it would be more at home in a museum.

"I'd prefer to go through everything alone."

"However you'd like," she answered, a slight note of annoyance in her voice.

The first thing that caught my attention was the framed picture on the nightstand—a brunette with a grim face, and a bald man with a bushy gray beard. I imagined that was Germán and his girlfriend. I took the picture out of the frame and put it in one of the inside pockets of my jacket.

Inside the wardrobe, I found a wrinkled suit, two shirts, and a discolored tie. There were also some scuffed shoes and a pile of newspapers. None of these objects grabbed my attention, and there wasn't anything of interest in the nightstand drawer either. Some aspirins, a couple of pens, a bit of loose change, and a book of popular maxims. I closed the nightstand drawer and looked at the books that were on the desk, most of them political essays by authors I had never heard of and a few novels by Eric Ambler. In the desk drawer, I found a box with some yellowed postcards, a few sports magazines, and a savings book from BancoEstado with a paltry sum recorded in it. As I was leafing through one of the magazines, half a flyer fell out. It showed the picture of a fat man with thick glasses and neatly cut hair. Above the photo, the text said: *Werner Ginelli, Torture Doctor*. I looked at the flyer for a moment and then put it back in the drawer. I sat on the bed and lit a cigarette that I smoked slowly, trying to imagine the feelings of the man who had lived in that room.

Later, back at the office, I put the picture of Reyes on top of my desk and began writing in my notepad my impressions from my visit to the sister's house. The only thing I felt confident writing was that Germán had been a lonely man who, except for the existence of Benilde Roos, lived with a certain self-denial, eliminating anything superfluous from his surroundings. An ascetic lost in the capitalist jungle.

I called Marcos Campbell, a journalist friend who sometimes helped me with investigations. After listening to his complaints about having too much work, I asked him if he remembered seeing anything on a doctor named Werner Ginelli when he was covering human-rights violations during the dictatorship.

"The name doesn't ring a bell."

"Can you check your archives?" I asked, remembering that the journalist obsessively saved his articles and reports, along with secondary sources.

"I can't do it right now," Campbell responded, and after an instant of silence, added, "A number of doctors participated in torture during the dictatorship, and some of them had their licenses taken away by the medical board. What kind of mess are you caught up in now, Heredia? Are you still poking around in the past?"

"It's not my fault there are so many ties between the past and the present. History can't be left behind, especially when the picture is drawn in blurred lines," I responded, and after a brief pause, I told him about my visit to the teacher's house.

"It's nothing more than a flyer that he could have picked up in the street or that someone left at his house," said Campbell when I mentioned my discovery in Germán Reyes's room. "Maybe he cleaned his desk before dying, and what you found are a few pieces of paper that didn't make it into the garbage."

"My imagination might be playing tricks on me," I said without convincing myself, "but just the same, I'd appreciate it if you could look into your archives."

"Nothing is free in this life, Heredia. You'll have to buy me two or three drinks."

"I apologize for calling so late," I said after the teacher picked up the phone. "But when something sticks with me, I try to find an answer as quickly as I can."

"Don't worry about it. I was watching one of those stupid TV shows that my husband used to like. Pretty girls, nasty language, and no brains in their heads. But I'm sure you didn't call to hear me complain about the TV. Do you have any news?"

"I want to ask you a question, Virginia. Your brother, before he died . . . did he clean up everything in his room? I don't mean sweeping and dusting. Did he go through his documents? Did he throw away a bunch of papers?"

"Why would that matter?"

"Did he or didn't he?"

"He had piles of magazines and newspaper clippings. One afternoon he threw it all away. It made the room look so much better. I couldn't have been happier."

"The papers that he threw away, did he throw them in the garbage or take them somewhere else?"

"He went down to the dumpster with seven huge plastic bags."

"In my office, you said that your brother was being followed. Do you think this purge had anything to do with him being afraid?"

"Ever since I talked with you I've been asking myself if I was right to believe what my brother said without questioning it. Maybe I got ahead of myself."

"What do you mean?" I asked.

I heard her breathing harder on the line. "There's something I didn't tell you when we talked in your office. Germán was detained after the military coup."

"That would justify his fear."

"Probably. He couldn't ever forget that experience; it was like they had branded him with a hot iron. And that's not all. He was obsessed with the issue of torture. He cut out everything he found in the press about it. News, interviews, articles about the prosecution of military figures. He spent a good part of his money buying newspapers and magazines."

"If that's the case, doesn't it seem strange to you that he'd just throw everything away one day?"

"Two months before he died, he told me that he was in treatment with a psychologist, so when he cleaned his room I thought it must be part of the therapy. A way of distancing himself from his obsession."

"Psychologist?"

"I just told you he wasn't able to get over the experience of being detained."

"Do you remember the psychologist's name?"

"I have it noted down in a book I keep on the nightstand. Give me a few seconds to look for it."

I took advantage of the pause to light a cigarette and pet Simenon's head. He seemed to be following the conversation closely. I said to him,

"Haven't you ever asked yourself what your life would be like if you had a master who came home every day and the riskiest thing he did was cross the street?"

"Don't screw with me, Heredia. You know I'm used to your foolishness."

On the phone, I heard the sound of steps and then the voice of the teacher. "The psychologist's name is Ana Melgoza," she said, and then gave me a phone number.

I felt confused after Virginia Reyes said goodbye. Why would I investigate a life that hadn't meant anything to me a few days ago, that I hadn't even known existed? Curiosity. That sick curiosity that always stuck itself into my business like a scalpel. I had the sensation of not having thrown the dice well, and that the key to the game was somewhere else, not in Germán Reyes's room nor in the words of his sister. I went out to the street and walked to Anselmo's newsstand. My friend was listening to a radio broadcast of a soccer game. His bald head was covered by a corduroy hat, and he was wearing a Universidad de Chile jersey. I sat on the wooden bench at the entrance and lit a cigarette. I could hear the happy sound of *cumbia* music coming from one of the bars down the block. The night was calm, and for a second I imagined myself on a raft, in the middle of the ocean, and not going anywhere.

"Don't you get tired of opening the store every day?" I asked Anselmo, who was straightening a pile of magazines to send back to the distributor.

"It's how I make a living. The alternative would be to sit on the sidewalk, stick out my hand, and be a beggar. Why do you ask? Are you going to offer me some business, or did you win the lottery and want to share the prize?"

"I got a job and I'm finding it hard to get off my ass."

"Who understands you, man? Yesterday you were complaining because you were unemployed, and today you're complaining because you've got work."

"I'm not complaining. I'm just thinking about how my bones crunch every day when I wake up."

"Too much time without work, Heredia. Let the enthusiasm spread through your body, little by little, like a drug," said Anselmo. "When I was a jockey I got to ride Bigfoot, an unbelievable horse . . . tall and strong. The handler told me not to push him in the first few meters, to let him shake off his nerves first. He ran a long distance, but it was a pain in the ass to get him into the rhythm of the race. When he finally did, though, he was a machine. Unstoppable. I won two Classics with that horse, always coming from behind and taking the race like a great champion."

"I like sitting by your newsstand and watching life pass by."

"Patience, man. To make it to retirement, you've got to have a lot of patience. You'll be feeding pigeons in the Plaza de Armas soon enough. For now, try to do your work as best you can. What's the new case?"

"A guy who was killed outside his work."

"Any witnesses?"

"Just one that I plan to interrogate."

"Take it easy, man. Let's smoke a couple of cigarettes and then you can go sleep. What do you say?"

"Not a bad idea, Anselmo. I've heard worse ones."

Just as I was setting foot in my office, I heard the annoying sound of the phone. I picked it up and heard Marcos Campbell's gruff voice.

"This is the fifth time I've called in a half hour. Where the hell have you been, Heredia?"

"Making sure the stars were still where they belonged."

"Since when do you drink wine with stars on the label?" he asked, and without waiting for an answer, fired away: "Ginelli was a doctor with the air force, and after the coup d'état he was accused of torturing prisoners at the base at El Bosque. It looks like he was in charge of keeping the prisoners alive so they could be shocked and tortured. He was even accused of torturing some of his fellow airmen. He came out spic-and-span, but a number of people swore they saw him in torture sessions."

"Do you know where I can find him?"

"Probably in the cemetery. He died last year."

"I would have preferred to look him in the eye."

"Sorry to be the bearer of bad news."

"It's just one door closing."

4

Death silences everything. The victims and the guilty are covered by the same earth and swept away by the same rain that washes the tombstones until nothing is left. Had something united Ginelli and Germán Reyes in life? Time passed and erased the signs of the scheming coup, the echo of screams, the cruelty of the executioner, the complicity of the judges, the twisted ink of the papers. The dead are forgotten, their memory crushed by the passing years and words half-spoken. And the pain? The fear? The humiliation? What good was the truth if it didn't bring back the dead or take away the nightmares of the survivors? In silence, and with no other witness besides Simenon, I remembered Campbell's words and asked myself about the meaning of the flyer on which Ginelli's name had been printed. I had a hunch that there was a message embedded in that scrap of paper, but not in the simple way I had imagined it. Time disfigures words and actions. I promised myself to remember that, and not having anything more to feed my thoughts, I sought out the complicity of the bed and the hope that in closing my eyes I could forget the heavy loneliness of the apartment.

Simenon caressed my cheek with one of his paws, and as I opened my eyes, I saw his fat haunches on top of my chest. I looked into his eyes, rubbed his chin, and heard him purr.

"Looks like the beginning of a good day," I murmured. "The sun is still where it belongs, there's no bill collector in sight, and I have work to do. What more could I ask for?"

"My breakfast and the steak that you promised me two weeks ago."

"Be patient. I'm waiting to meet a rich heiress."

"I've been patient since the first day I came into this apartment."

"Skinny and hungry. I gave you a can of mackerel and some water. What are you complaining about?"

Simenon followed me to the kitchen. I got a carton of milk out of the refrigerator and emptied its contents into two teacups. I took a box of crackers from the cabinet and put a couple on the ground next to Simenon, who chewed them enthusiastically and looked at me with renewed expectation. Two more crackers fell between his feet.

"Everything OK, Mr. Heredia? Your health? The cat?" asked the doorman when he saw me come out of the elevator and walk toward the building's entrance.

"All good, Feliz Domingo."

"Félix with an *x*. Don't forget."

"Xylophone, Xerox, I haven't forgotten."

"Have a good day, Mr. Heredia."

"The same to you, Feliz Domingo," I responded, trying to remember the address of the León Lumberyard, which I had found in the telephone book.

The lumberyard took up a whole block, and its interior was a bright maze of aisles and shelves on which were stacked diverse types and sizes of wood and metal, gallons of paint and varnish, tools, nails, screws, and an infinity of appliances, lamps, and home furniture. From the entrance, a mixture of smells circulated: wood, rubber, and metal. My nose wrinkled as I came in the door, and without stopping to look at the sales on hammers and pliers that an attractive brunette was promoting, I kept walking toward the window beneath an enormous sign that said **INFORMATION**. I got in a line with three other people. Behind the window was a rat-faced man who quickly answered customers' questions. He seemed to know everything, from how much coverage one could get from a gallon of synthetic latex to the chemical composition of silicone. When it was my turn, I asked for Darío Carvilio. The talking rat opened his eyes, and for a second I thought he might send me somewhere else with my question.

"Carvilio, Carvilio, Darío Carvilio," he said aloud while thinking of his answer. "He works security. Unless something is going on or he's on vacation, he should be between aisles twenty-five and thirty."

I walked around those aisles for ten minutes, and just when I was ready to go back to the information window, I spotted a guard standing at the end of aisle twenty-eight. He was a tall, robust man with a prominent nose. As I walked toward him, I wondered whether he actually watched the customers or was really a sleepwalker whom nobody dared to wake.

"Darío Carvilio?" I asked when I had reached his side.

The guard looked me up and down and then pointed at the lanyard hanging from his neck. I read the name on the badge and confirmed that I was in the right place with the right person.

"My name is Heredia, and I would like to talk to you about Germán Reyes," I said. "They told me that you saw the robbery that took his life."

"Another cop?" he asked testily. "The day of the murder I talked to a bunch of detectives."

"I'm sure, but none of them had the doubts that I'm trying to clear up."

"What kind of doubts? I don't have anything to add to my statement."

"I don't think that Germán Reyes's death was the result of a normal robbery."

"What makes you think that your colleagues were wrong?"

"I don't work with the police. I'm a private detective, and I'm working for Mrs. Virginia Reyes, the sister of the victim."

"What if I don't want to talk to you?" Carvilio said. He was watching a customer rummage through a drawer full of pliers and screwdrivers.

"I can go to some friends at the police and have them come back to ask you. Don't make things hard on yourself, Carvilio. I just need a few minutes of your time. If I'm not mistaken, you and Germán Reyes were friends."

Carvilio didn't appear to have heard my words. He was giving his full attention to the customer checking out the drawer, a thin young man with a sickly look to him.

"Do you know that guy?" I asked.

"Pedrito, a habitual thief. He comes in, takes a few trips around the aisles, and then leaves with something hidden beneath his clothes."

"Why don't you stop him?"

"He got out of jail six months ago. He's got AIDS and he's dying," said Carvilio and, as if remembering that he was a security guard, looked at his identification badge and added, "Two or three fewer pliers isn't going to bankrupt the lumberyard."

"I like your philosophy, friend."

"I'm not your friend, and you don't have the look of someone who's friends with cops. I used to be a cop, and I just need one look to know what a person's about."

"A cop?"

"For ten years. When they told me I would be transferred to Calama, I decided to look for another job. Before that, I had been sent to cities like Los Ángeles and Rancagua. I was sick of being transferred and wanted to live in Santiago. I was born here and want to retire here, if it's not too much to ask."

"If that's the case, you're in a good position to help me. Listen to what I have to say, think about your friend Germán, and then decide if you want to answer or not."

"The bosses don't like it when people talk at work. My shift finishes in an hour. Wait for me in the bar across the street. It's nothing fancy, but we can talk easier there."

I got the impression that the place had been furnished with the mismatched leftovers of other bars with more pretensions. None of the tables matched, and the seats, which were loose and falling apart, seemed to bear the scars of a marauding horde of vandals. But none of that seemed to matter to the patrons or the waiters, who ran from table to table like medics aiding the fallen on a battlefield.

Carvilio arrived when he'd said he would. He was carrying a canvas bag. Without his guard's uniform, he seemed younger and thinner. He waved at the bartender, and after spotting me, he sauntered over.

"I see you haven't lost any time," he said, nodding at the large bottle of beer on the table.

"I ordered a beer for the wait. It's not great, but at least it's cold."

"I used to come to this place with Germán. At the end of the month when we got our paychecks." After taking a seat, he called over one of the waiters and asked for a draft beer with orange soda.

"What was he like?" I asked. "His sister gave the impression that he was a quiet guy and kept to himself."

"He wasn't very sociable, but once you got to know him, he would talk for a long time. He worked as a cashier, and the bosses trusted him. He was interested in the fact that I had been a cop. Sometimes he would ask me about my old job and about police involvement in what he called the 'repressive activities' of the dictatorship."

"And what did you have to say about that?"

"I just listened to him. I became a cop when the country had already gone back to being a democracy. The crimes they committed before that belonged to a history I had no part in. I liked police work, but I ended up retiring for the reasons I told you before."

"You didn't think anything about him asking those questions?"

"In the beginning it seemed inappropriate, but after a while I understood why he was interested."

"Why was he?"

"One time he hinted that he'd had some problems during the dictatorship. He was never very explicit about it, and I didn't want to dig around in the past. You have to be sensitive with pain like that."

"Did he mention that someone had been following him recently?"

"Following him? Who?"

"That's what I'm trying to figure out. Germán told his sister about it."

"He should have told me that was happening," said Carvilio. "I could have helped him figure out if he was really being followed or if it was just his imagination."

"You witnessed Germán's murder," I said, steering the conversation toward what interested me.

"I was on duty at the front door of the lumberyard. The men arrived half an hour before the store closed for the day, in a red extended-cab pickup. They were wearing dark pants and leather jackets. The first time I saw them, they didn't really grab my attention. I thought they were two customers waiting for a delivery or something. I had to go inside the lumberyard. When I got back, they were still in the same spot. That's when I started looking at them closer. The guys were older, maybe in their sixties. One was thin and bald, and the other was short and stocky, with what they usually call 'distinguished' gray hair. I forgot about them when Germán came out. He told me he was going to visit his girlfriend, and we said goodbye."

"That's it?"

"I watched him leave the lumberyard and cross the street. The two men got out of the truck and started walking in his direction. I'd be lying if I told you I had a premonition or anything like that. Everything happened really fast. The men took out their pistols when they were less than six feet from Germán. The guy with the gray hair was the first one to fire. Two shots. Germán fell to the ground, and then the bald one fired his gun. Another two shots. I came out of the lumberyard and ran over to where my friend was. There wasn't anything I could do. I only had a flashlight and cuffs. The killers got into the truck and took off before anyone could stop them. I wanted to get the plate number, but it was covered in mud. Germán died in my arms."

"I've heard that the killers didn't rob him."

"They were only worried about their bullets hitting the target."

"Do you think they might have gotten spooked when you came out of the lumberyard?"

"That was the police's theory."

I finished my beer and Carvilio did the same with his.

"Doesn't that seem a bit too convenient to you?" I asked Carvilio.

"It seems like the theory of someone who isn't thinking about investigating too much," the guard responded. "Why would they want to rob Germán? Why would they go through the trouble of waiting for him to come out of the lumberyard? For the peanuts he was being paid?"

"Did Germán ever mention anything to you about having debts?"

"No, but I wouldn't be surprised if he had some. Most of the people who work in that place are up to their necks in bank loans and store credit-card debt."

"I was thinking more about gambling debts or drug use."

"I can tell you never knew him," Carvilio said. "Germán was a healthy guy."

"Would you recognize the killers if you saw them?" I asked.

"Sure. I feel like I can still see them clearly. Two geezers dressed like young tough guys."

"The problem is figuring out where to find them. Maybe someone else saw them. Maybe you could ask around to some of the people you work with. If I do it, they're not as likely to talk," I said, fishing in my jacket for one of my rumpled business cards.

"Heredia and Associates," the lumberyard guard read aloud. "Do you work with other people?"

"A lazy cat and Anselmo, a newsstand owner who keeps me informed about neighborhood gossip. Anselmo's cell number is on the back of the card. If you can't get ahold of me in my office and want to leave a message, use that number."

Later, heading toward the door of the bar, I felt the weight of someone staring at me. I looked behind me and saw a tall man sitting by the bar; he seemed interested in what Carvilio and I were doing.

"Do you know the fat guy over on the far-left side of the bar?" I asked Carvilio.

The guard took a hard look and nodded.

"His name is Atilio Montegón. He's been working at the lumberyard for three months. He's some sort of a consultant for the administrative boss. No one really knows what he does. I'm not surprised to see him here. He drinks quite a lot—he's probably looking for someone to get drunk with."

5

"It's not raining, but it's dripping. Every minute I spend on it, this Germán Reyes case gets more unsettling," I said to Griseta, after trying the vodka tonic that Marcelo, one of the waiters at the City, had made for me.

We had gone to the bar after seeing a movie where Clint Eastwood played a trainer working with a girl who was trying to become a professional boxer. The bar was quiet as usual; we were sharing the room with another couple that was having an animated conversation in the corner, away from the door and the prying eyes of the waiter.

"Is this investigation going to go anywhere?" Griseta asked as she opened her daily planner. "The only things you have are the testimony of the guard and Virginia's doubts. Maybe I was getting ahead of myself by bringing her to your office the other night."

"I'll ask a few more questions," I said, not wanting to talk about it anymore. I asked Griseta if she still wanted to come to my apartment.

"I'm traveling to La Serena tomorrow and I have to be at the airport first thing. It's a one- or two-day trip at the most."

"You should tell them that you need a bodyguard or that they need to quit sending you from one end of the country to another, like some kind of flight attendant. In the last three months you've been in five different cities."

Griseta moved her face close to mine and kissed me. "You did better with loneliness before we got back together."

"Even stray cats want to be petted every now and then."

"You're not a cat, and you don't need to be petted. You to yours and me to mine. It sounds like a tongue twister, but that's our agreement."

I left Griseta inside a taxi and saw her moving away from the eastern side of the city. The night was warm, and I could see light blooming from the restaurants near Portal Fernández Concha as they waited on their last customers. On the benches in the Plaza de Armas there were a few couples and a scattering of single men looking to procure company for the evening. I walked around the plaza and then pointed myself toward Calle Puente. I stopped in front of a lit-up display window, and while I lit a cigarette, I read the sign promoting the benefits of a new cell-phone model. After a bit I lost interest in the ad and instinctively looked behind me. A man whose eyes were hidden beneath the bill of a fedora seemed interested in what I was doing. I didn't let on that I'd noticed, but instead continued studying the items on display in the window, and then started walking again. The man did the same. I deduced that he was waiting for the best moment to formally introduce his fists to my body. My two options were to confront him or flee like a rat. The size of the stranger made me go for option two. I wasn't in the mood for an unfair fight, and instead took advantage of my knowledge of the neighborhood's alleys and backstreets. Five minutes later, I checked behind me and saw that no one was trailing my shadow. I breathed a sigh of relief. For a second I asked myself if the man had been real or if he was just in my imagination.

Simenon jumped onto my desk and offered his hairy belly so I could give him his daily dose of love.

"You haven't been doing so well with the ladies on the roof?" I asked him.

"The girls are fast and I'm starting to lack energy. I guess it's time to start living on memories and realize that fourteen cat years are like seventy-five human years. You should buy me vitamins or tonic."

"Isn't a nice piece of steak every week enough?"

"My teeth, Heredia. The problem is my teeth."

"Damn, Simenon! It's time for us to go to bed. I've had a rough day—I even thought somebody was following me."

"As far as I know, you don't owe anyone money."

"The rent and the bills are paid. I must be one of the only Chileans who doesn't use credit cards, doesn't get bank loans, and doesn't owe money to department stores. Am I going nuts?"

"Without debt you're a nobody these days, Heredia. If I were you, I'd be worried."

The medical center was as busy as a Sunday market. The patients—or clients, depending on which side of the counter one was on—formed huge lines, waiting for treatment or lab results. Nurses came in and out of doors that concealed instruments that looked designed specifically to torment the ill, though every now and then one of the white uniforms revealed hints of a body underneath that was well suited to the application of intensive care. A television in the waiting room blared with the sounds of a morning program on which a veterinarian gave pet-care tips.

I asked a guard dressed in blue where I might find Benilde Roos. The man listened to me with an annoyed expression. When I casually mentioned that it was related to a police matter, he began to pay more attention and disappeared behind a door that led to the interior of the center. After a few minutes, he came back and said the nurse would be able to talk with me during her lunch break. I thanked him, checked my watch, and sat down in the waiting area with all the joy of a kid waiting to be called into the dentist's office.

Benilde Roos was a pale, thin woman. She must have been close to forty years old and wore frameless glasses. Her black hair was covered with a nurse's cap. She had a timid smile, behind which, I thought, she hid a strong personality. She invited me to accompany her to the center's cafeteria, and after telling me vaguely about the work she did there, she listened to me attentively while drinking a pineapple juice.

"Germán is dead, and your investigation is not going to change that," she said after I explained why I was there. "The years we dated, our plans to get married, our future together, all that came to an end when he was murdered."

"I respect your feelings, but I'm just trying to do my job," I said, not letting myself get caught up by the fury and sadness behind her words.

"What is Virginia up to? Maybe she feels bad for how she treated Germán."

"What do you mean?"

"Germán lost his job after the military coup. Virginia and her husband turned their backs on him. They both supported the military, and at that time they thought his firing was justified. You must remember all the lies they concocted back then to confuse people. That there was terrorism, that there was a 'Plan Z,' that there were Cuban weapons streaming into the country, that there was gold coming from Moscow. Virginia and her husband were just two of so many people who closed their eyes to what was happening. They even handed over their wedding rings when the military called on everyone to collaborate in what they called 'the reconstruction of the country.' Later on, when the crimes were too obvious, she changed her opinion and her husband had to eat his words. I'm not really sure why, but what I do know is that they offered to let Germán live with them. He accepted the offer so he could save money. But they didn't get along. He and Virginia only spoke to each other when they had to, and he never said a word to his brother-in-law. So I don't understand why she contacted you." Benilde looked around as if trying to find a door that would help her escape her memories.

"How was your relationship with Germán?" I asked.

"What does that matter to your investigation? Or am I on your list of suspects?"

"I just want to have a better idea about Germán's life."

"He was a quiet man, and I felt safe with him. We met each other here. I had to take some blood samples from him, and as much as it sounds like something out of a romance novel, it was love at first sight—or first prick, as he liked to say. We got along well, but that doesn't mean we didn't have our differences and our fights, like any other couple."

"Did he tell you that he thought he was being followed?"

"Where would you get that idea?"

"Germán told his sister that, and she told me."

"It seems hard to believe. Who would follow him?"

"Who and why—that's the problem. I don't know what the motive would be," I said, and after a pause to look around me, I asked, "Did he have any debts?"

"None. Not even a small debt with a department store or a neighborhood grocery. Germán was good with his money, and he knew how to live off his salary from the lumberyard."

"Was he involved with any political party?"

"He wasn't interested, and I'd prefer not to repeat what he used to say about the parties and some of their leaders."

"So what can you tell me about his past? I know that he was detained by the security forces back in the 1970s. What can you tell me about that?"

"They had him in Villa Grimaldi, and as you can imagine, they treated him brutally. Fortunately, unlike some of his friends, he managed to get out alive. He never talked much about his suffering. But just mentioning Villa Grimaldi was enough to make him fall apart."

"Was that why he was being treated by the psychologist?"

"How do you know about that?" she asked defensively.

"A good part of my job consists of asking questions. What can you tell me about the psychologist?"

"She works in this medical center, and she treated Germán in her private practice," said the nurse and, after checking her watch, added, "Like I already told you, I don't think your investigation is going to be of any use, Mr. Heredia."

"Virginia Reyes doesn't feel that way."

"Frankly, I don't care how she feels. She should have worried about her brother when it meant something," said Benilde, and suddenly raising her voice, asserted, "Now, if you don't have any more questions, I should get back to work."

"Did Germán have any friends that he got together with frequently?"

"On Fridays he had a beer after work with one of his coworkers, and two times a week he went to the Cultural Center of the Americas."

"What did he do there?"

"I guess there were a lot of lawyers, professors, and university students there. Germán never finished a degree, but he spent a good bit of his time studying history. I got the impression that he attended talks and lectures."

"You never went with him?"

"Just once, for a book talk."

"Do you know who he got together with at the center?"

"The only person he used to mention was Dionisio Terán, the director."

"I'm starting to sense that even though you and Germán got along well, there were some mysteries between you."

"Germán had parts of his life that he didn't let me into. His past was one of them. At first it made me uncomfortable, but then I learned to accept him as he was."

Before leaving the medical center, I called the office of the psychologist, Ana Melgoza, and made an appointment for the end of the afternoon. On my way back to my office, I thought about how Germán Reyes, like most people, had worn many different masks during his life, and how only the sum of them would permit me to draw his portrait with even half certainty. Then I stopped thinking about him and paid attention to driving my Chevy Nova through a route full of potholes on the way back home.

Simenon wasn't in the office. I figured he must be visiting the neighborhood or on the roof of the Fleahouse bar, jealously watching the clients come and go. I made myself a tuna sandwich and washed it down with the last can of beer in my refrigerator. All that was left was a jar of fig marmalade and an apple. After that I read part of a chapter of *The Moonstone*, by Wilkie Collins, and listened to some Joaquín Sabina songs. I had my music, my books, and a case to work on while the hands moved around the clock on my office wall.

I arrived at the psychologist's waiting room five minutes before the appointment. A pleasant receptionist told me to go into the office: a large, well-lit room with a desk and two seats that faced each other. Ana Melgoza was a tall, attractive brunette. Her black eyes contrasted with her pale, almost vampiric skin, and I could see lines of accumulated tiredness drawn on her face. She pointed toward one of the two empty seats, and for a few seconds we observed each other with evident curiosity.

"First time I've ever been face-to-face with a private detective," she said. "Until I got your call, I was convinced that people like you didn't really exist."

"We exist in novels, and sometimes we stick our noses into the real world, and vice versa. But don't be afraid. When I work I don't bite. I save biting for more intimate occasions."

Ana Melgoza smiled and took a pack of cigarettes from one of the drawers of her desk.

"Do you mind if I smoke?" she asked.

"It's your office, your tobacco, your lungs. It doesn't bother me, but I am a bit worried about a psychologist who can't control her own vices. I'm sure some people come to see you to overcome their addictions."

"I know I'm not a good example for my patients, but I don't do it during therapy."

"You don't have to apologize. Politicians and businessmen are usually much worse examples."

"You have a sharp tongue," Ana Melgoza said, after using her lighter. "Your call piqued my curiosity. Your work must be interesting."

"And pretty similar to yours. Ask, listen, and draw conclusions. Sometimes I also manage to put someone behind bars."

"You must have a lot of clients."

"Fewer than you, for sure. Depression, anxiety, and other problems are in style these days. We private detectives provide a luxury service."

"We could share experiences, Mr. Heredia."

"I see you're still thinking about the idea of biting," I said, smiling.

"I was thinking about the business of asking and listening," said the psychologist as a sensual wisp of smoke escaped her mouth. "What would you like to know about Germán?"

"I know he was your patient. Maybe you could help me understand more about his personality and what was worrying him."

"He was my patient for two years, Mr. Heredia."

"His girlfriend and sister talked about weeks."

"I'm not surprised. Recognizing that he needed professional help was one of the most difficult barriers for him to break through. He didn't want anyone to know that he was coming to my office. As part of his therapy I pushed him to tell the people he was closest to. Family members, his girlfriend, friends. The worst part is that he was getting close to overcoming his fear."

"Fear?"

"It sounds strange, but he was afraid of people finding out that he had been tortured. He had been detained at Villa Grimaldi. More than thirty years later, he was still afraid of telling people his story. He felt guilty, almost as if instead of having been the victim, he had been the victimizer. We had to work really hard to get him to give his testimony to the governmental commission that was collecting information on the torture of political prisoners. It was called the Valech Commission."

"I listen to the news on the radio, and sometimes I even read the newspapers."

"It was difficult for him to accept my professional help. In the beginning, he would come regularly for a while and then not show up for a few weeks. It wasn't very long ago that he accepted the need for systematic treatment." The psychologist took another drag from her cigarette and added, "Getting up the courage to tell his sister and girlfriend that he was coming here was an important step, but it came late. The next one was limiting his obsession with the torturers. A good part of our sessions were about them and the things they did, and not only what they did to him. He was obsessed with compiling information about torture. This worried me, because obsessions can become destructive, and in Germán's case, it kept him from putting distance between himself and the past, and making new connections that would allow him to live a happier life."

"I heard about the information he compiled, and I also heard that he threw it all into the garbage before he was killed. Did you tell him to do that?"

"We talked about it, but I didn't give him any explicit instructions. It would have meant making a decision for him that he had to make for himself."

"Did he mention that he thought he was being followed?"

"What are you talking about, Mr. Heredia?" the psychologist asked, her uneasiness seeming to exceed professional interest.

"People who trail other people. Did he have paranoid delusions or anything like that?"

"He used to remember having being followed after being detained. Men in sunglasses, blonde women."

"Did he talk about it as if it were in the past?"

"Always in the form of memories," said Ana Melgoza as she played around with her pack of cigarettes.

"Did Germán talk about the Cultural Center of the Americas?"

"Once. After an appointment, I gave him a ride to a building close to the Plaza Brasil. He told me it was the office of a cultural center."

"Perhaps you could take me there too."

"I'm not going to that part of the city today, Mr. Heredia."

"Not even out of curiosity?"

"Curiosity about what?" asked the psychologist, smiling.

"About the Cultural Center. What else?"

"I'm tired, and my husband and two kids are waiting for me at home."

The psychologist's perfume stayed with me until I got to the underground garage where I had left the Chevy Nova. The garage was dark and bore the stench of burnt rubber. I started up the car, and as I began to accelerate I saw the lights of a Jeep turn on behind me. I drove out the exit, and after I'd gone five blocks, the vehicle was still right behind me. I decided that I had better figure out if I was being followed or if my imagination was getting the best of me. I waited for the next corner and turned right sharply without signaling. The Jeep kept going. I took a breath of relief and lit a cigarette, remembering my conversation with Ana Melgoza. Fear? Most people are full of fear. Of the past, of unemployment, of being assaulted on the street, of being robbed, of going to jail for not paying debts, of the boss who watches the time clock. Fear festering under the skin of a country that hides its truths beneath a layer of consensual lies.

When I walked into my apartment, Simenon was in front of the small television that Anselmo had bought a couple of days ago and brought up to my office to try out. On the screen was a Formula One race, and Simenon moved his head from one side to the other, following the passing cars.

"What are you doing glued to that screen?" I asked him, picking him up and petting his soft white back.

"Let the cat have some fun, man," I heard Anselmo shout from the kitchen. "I'm making some food for all three of us. Poor man's steak. Meat, eggs, onion, and a bunch of french fries. What do you say?"

"Anything worth eating is full of cholesterol," I said, and walking into the kitchen with Simenon in my arms, I asked, "What are we celebrating?"

"A good tip on the fourth race today."

"I don't remember you telling me about that."

"I played a couple thousand pesos in your name. The winnings are in the top drawer of your desk."

"I don't know what I'd do without you, Anselmo."

"Save your tears for some other time. Open that bottle on top of the TV and serve us some wine. I bought a nice one."

I obeyed my friend, and just when I was about to lift the first glass of wine to my lips, the telephone rang. I yanked up the receiver and heard the voice of Carvilio, the lumberyard guard.

"Heredia?" he asked in a low voice.

"What's new, Carvilio?"

"I asked the questions you wanted me to and didn't get any positive results. Nobody saw anything."

"Maybe tomorrow it'll go better."

"I've been thinking about what we talked about and I want to find the killers."

"We both want the same thing, then," I said, not wishing to drag out the conversation.

"Are you busy? I wanted to tell you a couple of things."

"I'm looking at something hot," I responded, watching Anselmo struggle to hold three plates in his arms.

"Don't worry about it, Heredia. I'll call back."

6

Virginia Reyes was in the garden, with her knees on the ground and her hands on the roots of a plant that she was trying to move. The smell of humid earth floated through the air, mixed with the perfume of a jasmine plant that crawled along the heavy brick wall surrounding the space. When I'd arrived, one of Virginia's daughters had opened the door and, without being very interested in why I was visiting her mother, led me through the tiled hallway toward the interior courtyard. The sun fell upon the trees, creating a play of shadows that moved from one corner to the other of the lush garden. I took a deep breath as I walked toward Virginia.

"Did you come to give me a progress report?" she asked when she saw me at her side.

I offered her my hands to pull herself up to her feet. I saw her smile for an instant as she went toward a bench in the shade of a tree.

"Did you find out anything about the killers?" she asked once she was comfortable on the bench.

"I'm still trying to understand who your brother was. I get the impression that once I discover the different facets of his personality, I'll be able to figure out who killed him."

"I don't understand what you're trying to say to me, Mr. Heredia."

"Your brother's killing might have been motivated by something that he did or quit doing. A motive that allows us to discard the theory that his murder was just the product of a botched robbery by a couple of incompetent criminals."

"It seems like we are right back where we started when we first met," she said with some disenchantment, and then commented, "Griseta told me that you were usually efficient."

"Your brother lied to you," I said, ignoring the woman's words. "He had been working with his psychologist for the last two years. He didn't want anyone to know."

"I should be surprised by what you're saying, but I'm not. Like I told you the last time we talked, I sometimes think I never knew my brother."

"A lot of the time we don't know what's happening with the people closest to us," I said, and after lighting a cigarette, I added, "I also heard that you turned your back on him after the military coup."

"Who said that? Benilde?"

"Is it true or not?"

Virginia Reyes took a handkerchief out of her apron pocket and wiped the sweat from her cheeks.

"It was during the first year of the dictatorship. My husband and I were against Allende's Popular Unity coalition, and when they fired Germán we thought he had only suffered a good scare and then life would go back to normal. We were wrong, but we couldn't recognize it at the time. My husband never got bent out of shape about the crimes that were committed back then, and at that time there were a lot of things going on that people didn't know about. You should remember—"

"I remember that the truth was in the air, within reach of everyone," I said, interrupting the teacher. "I don't believe the hypocrites who say they were misinformed or living in a bubble that kept them from seeing what was happening. That excuse smells rotten. But I'm not here to argue with you about it. Just tell me what made you change your mind."

"After my husband died, I had the opportunity to talk with Germán in a way we never had before. One night we were watching a news story about a commission that was compiling reports on the people tortured during the Pinochet government. I remember telling him that it sounded horrible and I couldn't imagine how anyone who had lived through that could keep going. 'Do you want me to tell you?' he asked. 'I'm one of the survivors who gave testimony before that commission,' he said. Then he told me every detail of the suffering he went through. Because of that conversation, when they killed him, I thought that I couldn't turn my back on him a second time. But I didn't know what to do until I talked to Griseta and she told me about you. I know it's not worth much, but it's a debt I owe him. Every time I remember his words, I get chills."

"Did he ever talk to you about his activities in the Cultural Center of the Americas?" I asked, trying to get her to focus on less painful memories.

"No. One time he came home with a man who he said was the director of that place. A nice young man, but poorly dressed. I remember he knew a lot about plants and trees. We talked for a long time here in the garden," responded Virginia Reyes, looking around.

I walked toward Marcos Campbell's office. My journalist friend was still trying to keep his police-and-crime magazine, *The Bloody Print*, going. He didn't lack topics to write about, but he suffered the trials of Job attempting to sell ads to finance the magazine's operations. He had trouble getting more than a dozen small ads from auto-parts stores, "motels for fleeting lovebirds" (as Edwards Bello used to call them), pastry shops, and the *cafés con piernas*—"coffee with legs," where drinks are served by waitresses in high heels and miniskirts—that were close to his office on Diez de Julio. His dream was to land ads from public services, but they preferred to finance newspapers from the big publishing conglomerates, thus minimizing the acid that they soaked their pens in.

It had been some time since I had used the long staircase that ended at Campbell's office, and as I came in I was surprised by the changes in the office since my last visit. His desk was surrounded by stones of different sizes and colors. On the walls, where before there had been posters of beautiful movie stars, there were now posters of rocks and more rocks. The journalist was standing next to one of the windows that looked out on the street, his thoughts apparently lost in the horizon.

"Who were you hoping would come in here? The muses or King Midas?" I asked him loudly.

Campbell jumped a bit and spun around, meeting me with a half-hearted smile. His wavy hair was still full and black. Only his gray beard and thick glasses gave away the cost of a life filled with an endless stream of urgent keyboard strokes and ashtrays full of butts. We had met at the university at the end of the seventies, at an event sponsored by a number of departments.

"I need both the muses and Midas. The girls to write the articles I'm supposed to have ready between now and Sunday, and the king to pay the printing bill."

"Money and words. You've got the same problems you always have."

"That's why I've surrounded myself with natural energy," said Campbell, pointing at the stones.

"What the hell's gotten into you, Campbell?"

"If you surround yourself with the power of nature, your energies multiply," he responded. Seeing the incredulity on my face, he added, "I suppose you don't give a shit about the stones and you came to see me because you've got some problem. Am I right?"

"I need one of your computers, and I need you to help me download information from the internet about the results from the National Commission on Political Imprisonment and Torture. I want to read some of the supporting documents in the commission's report and check whether a certain person appears on the list of the recognized victims."

"I'm going to make your life easier, Heredia," said Campbell as he pulled a thick, oversized blue book out of one of his drawers. "In there you'll find the conclusions that the commission arrived at, as well as the list of the victims of imprisonment and torture."

"On paper, like in the times of Gutenberg?"

"Take the whole thing. The sooner you get out of my sight, the sooner I'll be able to get my work done."

"Your hospitality stinks, Campbell. I thought you'd at least buy me a drink."

"Some other day, Heredia. I have to finish my articles."

"They're right when they say you can't always get what you want."

"If you want a good place to read and have a drink, head to the bar across the street."

I followed Campbell's recommendation and arrived at a bar so miserable that the only customer was staring at the walls with the glassy eyes of a drunk about to wreck his ship for the day. I had a seat at a table away from the door, ordered a beer, and opened the book with the blue cover. Horror ran between the words of the text that described human beings torn apart for no reason other than hate. I stopped on a page that reproduced a fragment of testimony of one of the prisoners:

> They put cotton balls on both of my eyes, a piece of duct tape on top of that, and then tied a black hood around my neck. They tied my feet and hands tightly, and then they dunked me in a barrel that was full of urine, excrement, and seawater. They pushed me down until I couldn't hold my breath anymore and my lungs

> were burning, and then they repeated it again and again, as they punched me and asked me questions. They called it the submarine.

And on the following page, the words of a woman were printed with the indelible ink of dread:

> They took me into another room where they made me take off all my clothes. After that they tied my wrists to my ankles, immobilizing me. Then they put a bar between my ankles and wrists, and suspended me on supports. In this position they pounded my ears with cupped hands and applied an electric current to my temples, my eyes, my vagina, my rectum, and my breasts.

I put aside the testimonies and focused on the appendices, where I found the list of victims. I moved through the names, listed in alphabetical order, until I arrived at Germán Reyes. Why did he take so long to tell people about his ordeal? Had he told someone who was invested in keeping the story a secret? I didn't have answers, but I guessed that, as on other occasions in recent years, the truth was fighting to emerge from the past.

"Our objective is to keep the memories of what we lived and dreamed alive," said Dionisio Terán, moving closer to a desk stacked high with magazines and multicolored papers that seemed to be the axis around which the Cultural Center of the Americas moved. It wasn't difficult to find the place, steps from the Plaza Brasil, on the third floor of an old house whose aging structure stood between two big new apartment buildings. I went up a staircase that had two landings and arrived at a room that looked like the chaotic workshop of a painter with a fat brush. The walls, high and unpainted, were covered with banners bearing slogans invoking justice. On the floor, there was a confused collection of brushes, scraps of canvas, wrinkled paper, and abandoned flyers.

Terán was somewhere in his forties. He had a shiny bald dome and a black mustache on his thin face, from which jutted an uncommonly large nose. Nearby, two kids were drawing letters on an enormous white canvas. Terán moved closer to me. I explained the reason for my invasion of his space, and the mere mention of Reyes made his distrust fade immediately.

"The idea of a street robbery seemed convincing," he said once I had finished my story. "But hearing you talk about it, I'm beginning to have my doubts. What can I help you with, Heredia?"

"Germán came to this office every week," I said, looking at my surroundings. "I'm interested in knowing what he did here."

"Have you heard of a *funa*?" asked Terán, and without waiting for my answer, he said, "It's an activity designed to expose criminals. What we do is uncover the identity of the torturers who live with impunity. If we can't achieve justice through the courts and tribunals, we expose them publicly. We're nonviolent. We use performance art to denounce criminals and generate awareness. Nowadays, there are a number of groups like ours. The majority of them are made up of torture victims and the families of the detained and disappeared, or the survivors of the executed. The first funa that our group performed was in 1999—it was designed to expose Werner Ginelli, a doctor who helped torture detained persons in the first years of the dictatorship.

"Germán was one of the founding members of the group," Terán continued. "I met him during a funa we had both been invited to by a mutual friend. After a few months, we decided to create our own group. Germán had the idea of not limiting our funas to the best-known victimizers, but instead to focus on those who lived in anonymity and who had never been mentioned in court cases or the press. His main work was compiling the information we needed to locate the torturers. He also helped create an archive for visitors to the cultural center. He always said that discontent and rebellion have to be fed with ideas."

"That's why he kept an archive of news clippings with information about the oppressors."

"Funas aren't done without evidence. We take care to vet the intelligence we obtain. We examine the cases that are stuck in the courts, whether from judicial negligence or because there aren't enough details to try the cases. It's not easy. Some accuse us of looking for revenge, and there are plenty of politicians who say our actions endanger the fragile democracy that we live in. The truth is that we only want justice."

"It would seem that not many people knew about Germán's activities. Even his sister and his girlfriend didn't know about these investigations," I said, lighting a cigarette.

"He watched his back. We never talked about it, but I get the impression that he never lost his fear of being tortured. That's why he worked in a supporting role. He studied the cases and tracked down possible targets. He hardly ever participated in street protests. He hated the commotion just as much as the anonymous letters we received—which we figured came from ex-military men worried about what we were digging up. Those guys are afraid of being discovered. Some of them get together in retired-military clubs that reek of old fascism and neo-Nazism."

"Did he tell you he was being followed?"

"He told me, but I didn't really pay much attention. Germán used to see stains where there were only shadows. A few times, we established security for him because of his paranoia, but we decided that he didn't have anything to fear. Sometimes his imagination got the best of him."

"So you don't think someone was actually following him?"

"I blamed his fear, but after what you've told me, I don't know what to think," said Terán, looking toward the door as though an undesirable stranger had just arrived.

"What's up?"

"Your questions about Germán made me remember what happened to Julio Suazo, a friend of mine who was hit by a car eight months ago. It was a hit-and-run. Some of the witnesses identified the model of the car and took down the plate number, and with that information they figured out that the vehicle belonged to a retired army sergeant. A lawyer from our group pressed charges, but he wasn't able to get an investigation started."

"What's the lawyer's name?"

"Francisco Cotapos. He's a legal consultant for our group and is one of those who keeps working to put the guilty in jail."

"Where can I find him?"

"He called yesterday. He said he would be away from Santiago for a few days, but that he would come back to take part in the activity we have planned for this weekend. Do you want to come with us? You could see our work and talk with Cotapos."

"I prefer not to interfere with your meetings. Give me his number."

"It's not a meeting. It's a funa. Do you want to participate?"

I spotted the Writer as soon as I came through the revolving door of the bar. He was sitting in a corner, with a cigarette between his lips and a glass of wine within reach. He seemed to be concentrating on filling a blue notebook with his sloppy handwriting. I stopped in front of his table and, without him noticing, watched him for a second. He looked tired and his stubble was at least a few days old. His eyes, hidden behind frameless glasses, closely followed the text he was writing. I sat down across from him. He took a few seconds to come back from the world in which his thoughts and his ink were wandering.

"Are you writing or adding up bills?" I asked.

"I'm writing what might be the beginning of another novel," he responded after setting his pen down on the table.

"Don't you get bored with writing? Haven't you thought about changing settings or characters?"

"What for, if I've found a character that I identify with? I've spent a lot of years writing about your pained existence, and it's still entertaining me. I haven't forgotten that the first chapters of the first novel were written in a boardinghouse in Buenos Aires on Pasaje San Lorenzo, where I ended up after winning a literary competition."

"Just the same, your persistence is remarkable. One of these days we'll have to switch roles. You investigate and I'll write."

"Heredia is sick and can't get out of bed. A client has come to see him, and he calls the Writer and asks him to take the case so that he doesn't lose it. It's a simple matter, but the Writer turns it into a snafu and takes too long to solve it. It's then that he figures out that fiction is one thing, and reality is another. What do you think?"

"With a bit of elbow grease it could work."

The Writer put out his cigarette in the glass ashtray in front of him and called the waiter over.

"What are you going to drink?" the Writer asked me.

"The usual."

"Vodka tonic with two ice cubes and a lot of hurry. I know you as if I gave birth to you," he said, and after asking the waiter for the drink, inquired, "Are you still looking for work, or are you wrapped up in some new mess?"

"Investigating the death of a guy who got shot leaving work," I said, and told him about the case.

"He was killed by a jealous husband," stated the Writer after I had finished my story.

"Reyes had a girlfriend and was as faithful as a caged canary."

"Drug trafficking? Bootlegged cigarettes?"

"Could be one or both at the same time."

"I have a feeling that's not what you think. Let the cat out of the bag, Heredia."

"Reyes was on the heels of ex–security forces agents. Guys with murky pasts who had avoided even a brush with justice."

"A few of those guys are in jail and the rest are going to die in their beds. If I were you, I'd look into the drug angle. The guys who worked as torturers are well hidden today. They live like any Tom, Dick, or Harry, and I don't think they're up for murder. The quieter they are, the less likely it is that they'll go to jail. They know that once the big fish were put away, they left the minnows alone. Trust me, look into the drugs and don't forget about the butler."

"It's been a long time since the butler did it in anyone's detective novel. You must know that better than I do."

"Just checking to see if you were paying attention."

"Talking with you doesn't help me much with my investigations."

"On the other hand, it helps me prime my imagination."

"We'd better hurry up with these drinks. It wouldn't surprise me if closing time came and they kicked us right out the door. At our age, getting our ass kicked hurts more than it did when we were twenty."

"Finally, something we can agree on."

"Do you think so?"

"Yes, and I also just came up with a new idea to solve your case. There must have been a robbery in the lumberyard that Reyes discovered, and he was going to blow the whistle."

"Not bad, Writer. You surprise me. I'm going to contemplate that possibility."

I said goodbye to the Writer a little after ten that night. I saw him moving into the crowd of people shuffling toward their homes, and I imagined he had gone back to thinking about the novel he'd been beginning when I interrupted him. In one way or another, both of us were investigators. I did it to discover those responsible for some crime or offense, and he did it to explain the world in which he lived.

When I could no longer see him, I retraced my steps in the direction of Calle Aillavilú. In front of Anselmo's newsstand, I heard the screech of a car braking violently. I looked behind me and saw Desiderio Hernández get out of a Mazda driven by a man whose face I couldn't see. My neighbor passed by me without saying hello and walked toward the elevator.

"Good manners aren't his forte," I commented to Feliz Domingo, who had watched Hernández's brusque steps.

"I shouldn't say it, but I agree with you, Mr. Heredia."

"I'm glad we agree on that, Feliz."

"Félix, with an *x*," said the doorman, and after that, moving toward the mailboxes behind the reception desk, he took out a sheet of yellow paper and, passing it to me, said, "A gentleman came to see you, and since you weren't here, he left you a note."

I took the sheet and read the message that Carvilio had written on it: I found a neighbor who saw the murder. She doesn't want to get into any trouble, but I'm sure I can convince her to talk.

A lot of trouble for so little, I thought as I put the note into my jacket.

"Good news?" asked Feliz Domingo.

"Nothing that's going to keep me from sleeping tonight. A warm shower, a good novel, and bed."

"I forgot to tell you that . . ."

"Tomorrow, Feliz. Tomorrow."

"Félix, with an *x*. Remember."

"My memory is a disaster, Feliz," I said as I moved toward the elevator door.

The doorman shook his head and returned to his seat behind the reception desk.

◆ ◆ ◆

The penetrating smell of humid books hit me as soon as I walked into my apartment. For a second I managed to think about the shower that I wanted to take before sleeping, but something in the look that Simenon gave me made me fear that the night had some surprises in store for me. I looked around and didn't see anything out of place. As I crossed the threshold to the bedroom, I had the impression of traveling ten years backward in time. Griseta lay on the bed, barely lit by the moonlight coming through the window. Her skin had a glow that contrasted with the white bedsheet. Attempting not to make noise, I took off my jacket and tossed it on the floor, then did the same with the rest of my clothes until I was nude. I moved to Griseta's side, and the contact with her skin chased away all the ghosts of my tiredness. I kissed her softly on the back and waited for her to surface from her dreams.

"Where were you?" she asked after a bit, sleepy.

"Why didn't you tell me you were coming tonight?" I asked her.

"I got in from La Serena and wanted to surprise you," she responded, turning onto her side to look at me.

I searched for her lips and she let me kiss her. Her breasts pressed against my chest and we kissed again. I heard Simenon's steps as he left the room. Griseta was in my arms, and it didn't matter to me if the whole world outside the bed that held us came crashing down. I stroked her hair and kept kissing her until morning.

7

I let two days go by without giving much thought to Germán Reyes. Griseta didn't have to go back to work until the next week, and since we had time, we spent the first day walking around Parque Forestal and went into the Museo de Bellas Artes to see the permanent collection of Chilean painters. We spent the second day exploring bookstores and holed up in a movie theater watching an old Ettore Scola film that we both liked, *We All Loved Each Other So Much*. At night, lulled by Mahler, we made love with the patient rhythm of those who know the hidden secrets and desires of their partner. Morning found us in bed, and only a long shared shower made us close the parentheses and come back to reality.

"Pleasant time burns faster than tinder," I said to Simenon, looking out the window as we watched Griseta walking away.

"Don't be dramatic. Tomorrow or the day after you'll have her in your arms again," Simenon replied, putting great effort into licking his right paw. "Separations and reunions have their charm."

"I would have liked it if the parentheses hadn't closed so soon. Griseta's trips are longer and farther away every time. I'm afraid she'll move away for good someday."

"You get more sentimental every year, Heredia."

"Is that such a bad thing? Since when did you turn into such a stone-hearted cat?"

"Don't forget that I was born in an alley. Five siblings and a mother who gave us just enough to get on our feet and start walking."

"Your childhood was sadder than *Oliver Twist*."

"Don't laugh. Yours wasn't that great either."

"Maybe that's why we understand each other so well."

Simenon finished cleaning himself and, in a few leaps, landed beside the pistol that was sitting on the desk.

"I know I've got work to do. I don't need you to order me around," I said.

"Someone has to worry about the future of Heredia and Associates."

I went to a bar across from Plaza Ñuñoa, where a waiter danced to the infectious rhythm of tropical music while he prepared mixed drinks. I drank a glass of wine and read a newspaper that someone had left on the table. The breasts of a bleached-blonde vampire occupied a good part of the front page. The blonde had won a beauty contest, and it didn't take a psychic to know that the judges hadn't gotten much further than observing her voluminous cleavage. The inside pages didn't get much better. I found four police briefs that discussed an equal number of robberies in wealthy homes, and a story on the exchange of blows between candidates sharpening their teeth for the next parliamentary election. It was a jumble of phrases that ping-ponged from one side to the other. I left the paper on the bar and concentrated on my wine. When I looked at the clock on the wall across the room, I realized that I had just enough time to finish my drink and arrive at my appointment on time.

In the plaza, I found about thirty people carrying picket signs and chanting various slogans demanding justice. Among them, I spied a few young people with painted faces blowing plastic trumpets, as though they were in the middle of a carnival. In one of the corners of the plaza, a detachment of police fought against their natural desire to arrest the protesters.

Terán recognized me as soon as he saw me. He was accompanied by a short, fat, redheaded man who looked at me attentively when I approached the leader of the funa.

"I owe you an apology. I didn't think you would come," said Terán and, turning to the redhead, said, "Cotapos, this is the detective I told you about."

I extended my hand to the lawyer, and he nodded slightly. I felt as if he was observing me with the attention of an entomologist, and I resisted the temptation to react until Terán invited us to join the protesters, who had begun to occupy the street.

"Is this your first time participating in a funa?" asked the lawyer.

"Yeah, and I'm sure that makes me suspicious," I said with a touch of aggressiveness in my voice.

The protesters walked in silence until a collective shout shattered the calm of the morning: "Where there is no justice, there are funas!" Some of the people on the sidewalks stopped to look at the column and then continued on, propelled by fear or apathy. The slogan burst out again, this time accompanied by the noise of the trumpets.

"I met Reyes during the organization of an activity like this one," said the lawyer and, raising his voice, asked, "Is it true that you have some doubts about the cause of his death?"

"Unfortunately, all I have is doubts. That's why it would be better for you to stop glaring at me and tell me what you know about the death of Julio Suazo."

"Terán told you about Suazo?" asked Cotapos with a hint of a smile. The column stopped in front of a building with pretty vines creeping up its balconies. Terán took the megaphone passed to him by a blonde girl and quickly gave a speech, saying that the building was administered by Danilo del Monte, a former army officer responsible for torturing political prisoners in the National Stadium. While he spoke, a couple of protesters handed out pamphlets to neighbors who had stopped to see what was going on. Others stuck up posters on trees, while the rest shouted the name of the perpetrator. The protest was brief, and after it had finished another shout could be heard: "Alert! Alert, neighbor! There is a murderer working next to your house!" The protesters took to the street again, handing out pamphlets to the people they passed on their way back to the plaza.

"What do you achieve with all the noise?" I asked Cotapos.

"We open a small door to the truth."

"Do you think most people care about the truth?"

"Just because a lot of people are tricked or confused is no reason to forget about justice and respect for human rights. Even if we were the only two interested, I would keep going."

"Have you found a clue that will help you find the killers?" the lawyer asked later, while we were drinking the coffee that Terán had begged off, saying he had to attend a debriefing session for the funa that had just happened.

"I've got a hunch that it wasn't a normal robbery. The killers waited for Reyes and then they acted in a cold, calculated way. I've thought about the possibility of something shady or illegal going on inside the lumberyard. Reyes was aware of the money going in and out. Maybe he found a scam, and this was not to the liking of the ones involved."

"Your hunches make sense. The only thing I can add is that the police closed the case pretty quickly, without showing any desire to investigate more."

"Maybe there wasn't any evidence to point toward something other than a robbery."

"Just the same, you think there might be another explanation."

"Right now, it's only a shot in the dark," I said, and after drinking my coffee, added, "It's time for us to talk about Julio Suazo."

"Suazo was another member of the group. He was hit by a car outside the high school where he worked as a doorman. A witness caught the plate number, and it turned out that the vehicle belonged to a retired member of the military. I won't go into details, because I understand that Terán already talked to you about it. What's for sure is that despite the information delivered to the court, the judge closed the case almost immediately."

"Suazo and Reyes both belonged to Terán's group. Apart from that, is there any connection between them?"

"Up until now I hadn't thought about it," murmured the lawyer. He lit a cigarette and said, "Both of them appear in the report of the National Commission on Political Imprisonment and Torture."

"That doesn't help much," I said, and after a pause, I added, "Terán told me that you take cases on human-rights violations."

"I handle the cases in which we've been able to identify the guilty, and I ask the courts to undertake appropriate investigations. It is then up to them to interrogate military members and other people who are in a position to provide information. It's too slow for my taste, though."

"Were Reyes and Suazo involved in any of those cases?"

"I don't remember. I coordinate a team of lawyers, so I'm not caught up on all the details of every case. Generally, I attend to the cases that are being argued before the courts. My colleagues work on the preliminary stages. That mostly involves investigating the backgrounds of the victims and the perpetrators."

"I'm interested in whether Suazo and Reyes are mentioned in any of these cases," I said, trying to get the lawyer to offer to provide me that information.

"What are you thinking, Heredia?"

"Suppose both were witnesses in the same case and that the accused, to avoid being exposed, decided to get rid of them."

"You're weaving a fine thread, but I wouldn't be surprised if you're going down the right path. Despite what they say in the press and the official statements, impunity still reigns. And not just that. The few military personnel who've been convicted were sent to prisons with pools, tennis courts, cable television, and other privileges that your run-of-the-mill criminal doesn't get."

"Can you check on what I just mentioned?"

"It might take a few days."

I lit a cigarette and looked out the windows of the café. People walked down the street, far removed from the uncertainties that swirled around our table.

"Did Suazo have relatives?" I asked.

"His daughter survived him. His wife died of cancer three years ago. Yolanda, the daughter, works in a tailor's shop."

"I'd like to talk with her."

"I'll give you her phone number and try to call her to let her know you'll be in touch. She's a timid, skittish woman."

"That would help a lot," I said, and after a few seconds, I added, "It looks like your apprehensions about me have disappeared."

"My work doesn't allow me to trust people. But don't worry, you passed the test a while ago." Cotapos looked at his watch. "I've got to go. My wife and I have tickets to a tango show at the Teatro Oriente. I'll talk with Yolanda tonight, and on Monday I'll ask my colleagues to check whether Reyes and Suazo were witnesses in the same case."

Memory, inexhaustible memory, kept working, crouching in the corners of the city. Life continued on its course, the newspapers wrote with fresh ink about the present, and the young people looked at the past as if it were a dried-up moth. But then there were Terán and Cotapos, who persisted in trying to bore through the stone of forgetfulness. My work was similar to theirs. I delved into the memory of people or the city, which I walked through like a stray cat. Sometimes I got lucky, and other times I ended up with my tail between my legs. People remembered the good times and hid away pain and fear in order to survive, holding on to the illusion of a better future. However—and I had experience with this—sometimes it was impossible to run from your memories, and there was no option but to grit your teeth until the memory stopped working on you and you could once again lift your head and look forward.

I arrived at the Calle Aillavilú as Anselmo was lowering the metal curtain of his newsstand so he could take a break from work to get some lunch. Hunger was scraping my guts, and after remembering that I could only hope for a hard crust of bread and some eggs in my apartment, I decided to go with him.

"I haven't even seen your shadow lately, man. You must have a good case to work on. How's that business with the cashier going?"

"For the moment, he's still a dead man trying to see the faces of his murderers."

"You're speaking in code, man."

"I guess I'm saying that I'm more or less in the same place I started out in."

"Or in other words, you've just been farting around."

I smiled and followed Anselmo toward the Touring. The restaurant was jammed with customers, and at one of the tables I spotted Desiderio Hernández. My neighbor looked worried and stared at his plate of food without moving. It seemed like someone could blow a trumpet by his ear and he'd stay absorbed in his thoughts.

"Do you know that guy?" asked Anselmo.

"His apartment is on the same floor as mine."

"He came to the neighborhood five months ago, and he's a bit of a grouch."

"Seems like a lonely guy."

Anselmo made a gesture that indicated he wasn't interested, and immediately called over a waiter and asked for the daily special.

"I have a tip for the races this afternoon," he said after the waiter had served us two overflowing plates of pasta. "Chico Paredes. He's a horse that's making a comeback, and at the corral they think he's a sure thing. He'll probably pay well."

"I hope you're not wrong," I replied, looking at Hernández, who still sat without trying his food.

"You look worried. What's up?"

"I would like to find a clue that can help me solve the case that I'm working on."

"Be patient, man. The rabbit always jumps out when you aren't looking for it. By the way, have you talked with Micaela?"

"Not that I remember. I would need the memory of an elephant to keep track of the names of all the girls who've passed through your life."

"She's been working in one of the stores around the corner for years, and I never noticed her. Yesterday I did, and we had our first date."

"You never learn, Anselmo. You'll walk into hell with three chicks hanging from your neck."

"Some people look for the pot of gold at the end of the rainbow, and I look for the girl of my dreams."

"Up until now you've only managed to find the women of your worst nightmares."

"Give or take a few, I can't complain. Besides, who can take away food I've already eaten and songs I've already danced to?"

I said goodbye to Anselmo, and instead of going up to the apartment, I walked to where my car was parked. I waited for the motor to start, lit a cigarette, and pushed softly on the gas pedal. The vehicle roared like a tiger awakened from a nap. It bucked a few times and slid onto the asphalt with the grace of a two-hundred-pound ballerina.

I wanted to talk with Carvilio and find out whether he had gotten anywhere with his investigation. I didn't have much luck. When I got to the lumberyard, the guard by the door told me Carvilio had finished his shift and was on his way home. Noting my disappointment, the man asked if it was an urgent matter. He seemed like a curious type, maybe even a gossip. I talked with him about Reyes's death, and the guard instinctively moved his right hand toward the billy club on his belt.

"That wasn't the first time they tried to rob the lumberyard," he said.

"What makes you think it was an attempted robbery?"

"What other motive could there be?"

"Were you here when the shooting happened?"

"No. It was my day off."

"There are some who think that the killers were trying to silence Reyes. That there was internal theft he was going to blow the whistle on."

"The lumberyard is managed by one of the owner's sons, and I assure you that the guy is like a rock when it comes to the books. He doesn't miss a single cent."

"Someone might be stealing merchandise."

"Nothing and nobody comes in or gets out of here unnoticed. The employees have to pass through a checkpoint. You can't even take a miserable little screw without them knowing. And you, why are you so interested in this? Are you a cop?"

"You've got a good eye, my friend," I told him.

The guard smiled, satisfied by the compliment. "I thought the police had finished with their investigation."

"Sometimes there are crumbs that the greedy mice miss," I said, and to discourage any further questions, I began to move toward the exit.

Leaving the lumberyard, I looked back toward where the guard was and saw the consultant, Atilio Montegón, approach him. I went out to the street, heading for the spot where Germán Reyes had been killed, and for an instant I tried to imagine his last minutes.

8

I called Griseta at work and wasn't able to reach her. She was out of the office at a meeting, and her secretary couldn't tell me what time she'd return. I looked at my watch and calculated that she wouldn't be back in the office until the next day. The information that I had on Germán Reyes bounced around in my head, and nothing felt like a concrete motive for his murder. After walking down Paseo Ahumada, watching the people and the street vendors, I went into Café Haiti, one of the more respectable *cafés con piernas*. The customers were squeezed into tables, and I had to wait a few minutes to get a coffee with cream. From a distance, close to the entrance of the café, I recognized some of the regulars. The retired professor who only read novels about pirates; the short, crazy guy who made passionate speeches against dress straps. There was the strange guy who made a real effort to care for his hair but had a mustache that made him look like Hitler; two or three former soccer stars; and a fat man who looked like Orson Welles. Existence was made up of routines. If I went into the café at the same time on any day of the week, I would see almost the same people, with their typical masks and costumes, performing the role that had been assigned to them in the great theater of life.

I remembered the testimonies compiled in the book that Campbell had given me and asked myself if any of the people around me had bothered to read it, or if it was no more than passing news to them, like soccer scores or the weather report. The horrors of the past were a devalued currency, and after some well-rehearsed public statements by politicians and political prisoners, the report had gone to the junk drawer. Everyone else—those who drank a coffee every morning, paid their bills, and put in their hours at the office—followed a rhythm set by the media. They preferred to talk about the latest episode from the red carpet and not to recall where they had been or what they'd been doing when the doors of the clandestine jails shut at night, or when the kid from the corner was forced into a car that took him to a street with no exit. Guilt, forgetfulness, fear, complicity, indifference. Horror turned into a few ambiguous sentences in the history books.

I drank my coffee and walked around town until I found myself in the heart of the night. I recognized my face in a shop-window mirror, and I asked myself what the point of my work was. I had a long list of solved cases, and even if they hadn't given me a swollen checking account, they permitted me to feel the satisfaction of a job well done.

I sat on a bench in the Calle Estado and breathed the nighttime air of the city that I loved. I thought of a Piazzolla melody and a Wim Wenders movie in which Dashiell Hammett wrote on his typewriter lit by a bare lightbulb. I watched people walking by, and I told myself that every person contained within themselves the promise of a story worth telling. An old man came up beside me to ask for a few coins to pay for the flophouse where he tossed his bones each night. I dug around in my jacket and passed him a wrinkled two-thousand-peso bill. He observed me, surprised, and once he was convinced that the bill was as real as the moon that shined on us, he continued walking south. I followed him and didn't stop until I had arrived at my office. There, Simenon crept between my legs. I picked him up and moved closer to the window that looked out over the Mapocho River. For a moment, I thought of the old guy and imagined him shuffling along with the fleeting happiness of having a roof to sleep under that night.

"It's closing time for this bar," I said to Simenon, feeling tiredness shut my eyes with its customary insolence.

The cat yawned, indifferent to my worries.

"Which side of the bed do you want?"

"Doesn't matter to me," responded Simenon.

An hour later, I woke to someone knocking on my office door. I put on the robe that an Argentine boxer I had met in Punta Arenas had given me years ago, and I shuffled to the door, half-asleep. When I opened the door, I was greeted by the phantasmal face of Detective Bernales. I hadn't seen him for two years. He had gotten old. He was beginning to go bald, and at first glance he looked like he had gained twenty pounds. One glimpse of his forced smile told me that nothing good had compelled him to visit me in the middle of the night. We weren't friends, but we had shared a few investigations in the past that had helped him advance his career.

"That police salary isn't good enough to afford a watch?" I asked.

"Your office still smells like a sewer."

"I'm sure it does. I've let in a lot of unexpected visitors."

"You're still the same smartass."

"The last time we saw each other, your ass was expanding in an office."

"I got bored with paperwork and asked for a transfer to Homicide."

"Homicide?"

"Death is a booming business."

"I'm guessing you're not here to philosophize about death," I said, lighting a cigarette, which made me cough.

"Carvilio. Does that name mean anything to you?"

"Should it?"

"Your business card was in the deceased's jacket. I thought about leaving it there for my men, but I remembered the favors I owe you and

I decided to help you avoid a rough time. I respect you, even if you are a bit of an asshole."

"Carvilio is dead?"

"As dead as anybody who falls from a twenty-story building. Why did he have your card on him?"

"I met him while I was investigating the possible murder of someone he worked with. I gave him my card so he could call me if he found out anything interesting."

"Your story is too simple, Heredia. Try to remember the details."

"Germán Reyes," I offered, and I didn't stop talking until I had brought Bernales up to speed on what had happened to the lumberyard cashier. I also mentioned the doubts I had about Virginia Reyes and my meetings with Terán.

Bernales took a few steps around the desk and stopped in front of the window. He took a piece of gum out of his jacket, unwrapped it, and put it in his mouth.

"Have you been able to find out anything about the killers?" he asked.

"I have two possible motives, but neither one convinces me."

"Was Carvilio helpful?"

"He asked a few questions in the neighborhood around the lumberyard, but he didn't turn up much."

"Too bad, Heredia."

"And now he's dead. Murder, accident, or suicide?"

"The circumstances appear to point toward an accident," he said. "He lived in one of those new buildings with a pool on the roof. Carvilio liked to go for a swim after work. He went up to the pool and swam for half an hour. It sounds like when he got out of the water he went over by the railing, lost his balance, and fell. There aren't any witnesses, or if there are, they're afraid to talk and get mixed up in this mess."

"First Reyes and now Carvilio. Too many dead people in too little time. I'd like to be sure that the guard died accidentally. If I don't, I'm going to think that someone decided to make him fly. I'll swing by the building."

"Don't stick your nose into my work, Heredia."

"A couple of glances and a few questions."

"I don't gain anything by telling you not to," said Bernales, his words accompanied by a nervous smile. "Promise me that you'll keep me in the loop, whatever you find out."

"Count on it," I affirmed and, nodding at the hallway that led to the bedroom, grumbled, "If you don't have any more questions, I'd like to go back to bed."

"I envy you," replied Bernales as he walked toward the door. "I have to drive through half of Santiago to get to my house."

"Everybody's got their own issues. In my case, I'm probably not going to close my eyes for the rest of the night."

"One last thing, Heredia. Do you remember my colleague Doris Fabra?"

"She isn't easy to forget. A while ago we investigated the death of a government employee together. What happened to her?"

"Last week I traveled to Temuco and had some meetings with her. She said to say hi. It seems like you two used to be very friendly."

9

The building where Carvilio had lived was next to Parque de Los Reyes, in a wooded sector with recently paved streets. It was one of those places where tall buildings were multiplying and banners announced the real-estate developments that were transforming the face of the city. I pressed the intercom button for Carvilio's apartment, and after a few seconds I heard the trembling voice of a woman who said she was his widow, Pamela Vega. I told her I was with the police and explained the reason for my visit. The woman listened in silence and, after a pause, opened the electric gate.

Pamela was a slim, short woman. Her long dark hair fell down onto her shoulders, and her eyes were filled with tears.

"You were lucky to find me," she said after offering me a cup of tea, which I turned down. "I came home to rest a bit. My children stayed with their father's body in the parish."

"I knew your husband, and I'm truly sorry about what happened."

"It's so absurd. He used the pool almost every day. I don't know what he was thinking when he got close to the edge of the building. My husband was careful with anything that could cause an accident. The faucets, the pilot light of the water heater, his car. He even closed off the balcony of the apartment."

"Forgive the questions, but I just want to clear a few things up," I interrupted. "Were you and your husband getting along? Were you having any financial problems?"

"We never argued except over small household things. And as far as money goes, between his job and mine we had enough to make ends meet. We were always thrifty. We bought this apartment with our savings and an inheritance that I got from an aunt."

"Did he ever get depressed? Did he drink? Do drugs?"

"If you're thinking that my husband committed suicide, you're very wrong. He would have never done that, and he didn't use drugs or liquor."

"Pardon me again, but it doesn't make sense to me that your husband suffered an accident," I said. I stood and moved toward the door of the apartment, adding, "Maybe your husband had an enemy—someone who would have wanted to hurt him."

"Are you implying that my husband was murdered?" Pamela asked, tilting her head as if to say that my question was absurd, out of place.

"My work makes it necessary to think about all the possible causes for the death of your husband."

"Impossible. That's impossible. No one would murder my husband, not even in my worst nightmares."

"It was probably an accident like you say, ma'am. I hope my questions didn't make things more difficult for you."

"I should go back to the church," said Pamela, concluding our conversation.

"Thank you for your time, ma'am. If it's possible and doesn't make you uncomfortable, I would like to take a look at the roof of the building."

"I'll call the doorman and ask him to let you come up."

The doorman, a scrawny type with baggy eyes, didn't make the slightest effort to move from his seat behind the reception desk. He simply looked me up and down and then pointed toward the elevator bank across the lobby.

The pool was in the middle of a tiled terrace. To one side was a sort of pergola that protected bathers from the sun, and behind that a canvas sunshade above a wooden table, and beyond it a gigantic grill for cookouts. Access to the edges of the terrace was limited by a high railing that could be crossed through a latched door. On the horizon were empty space and the roofs of the neighborhood houses far below. The sun fell hard on the pool, and for an instant I felt the urge to take off my clothes and dive in. Everything was clean and well ordered. I opened the door of the railing and passed into the prohibited territory. From the edge of the terrace, I looked down at the street and felt vertigo tickling my stomach. All it would take was one step to follow Carvilio's path. The void began to attract me, and my legs grew stiff.

"Be careful!" I heard someone behind me shout.

I stepped back and saw a young man carrying a bag of potting soil and some gardening tools.

"You shouldn't be on that part of the terrace," he warned as he moved toward one of the planters that surrounded the pool.

I crossed back to the other side of the rail and approached the gardener.

"I'm with the police. I was having a look at the site of the accident you probably heard about."

"No one in the building is talking about anything else."

"Did you know Mr. Carvilio?"

"I usually saw him when he came up to swim."

"Did you see him yesterday?"

"We bumped into each other on the elevator. He was coming up, and I was going to look for some copperwood plants that I had in the garden on the ground floor. We said hello and that was about it. It took about thirty minutes to get the plants ready, and when I was about to come up again, I heard the doorman shouting."

"You didn't see anyone strange when you were coming down in the elevator?"

"Nobody."

"Could someone have gone up without you noticing?"

The gardener looked at me closely but remained silent.

"Everything you say will just be between us," I said to quiet his sudden mistrust.

"The doorman is a bit careless. He usually lets salesmen and other strangers in without bothering to ask them which apartment they're going to. Sometimes he slips down to the basement to grab a few drinks and leaves the door open. The building super has reprimanded him a bunch of times, but the guy must be bulletproof. I don't know how they haven't fired him. There must be hundreds of people out there who would be better doormen."

"So you're saying that some stranger could have come in without anyone seeing him."

"Correct. And don't forget that there are two elevators."

"After he fell, did you go back up?"

"The police wouldn't let me into the pool area. They asked me questions and then told me to go back downstairs."

"What do you think about what happened?"

"A real shame. What else?"

"Did you ever see Carvilio outside of the railing?"

"Never."

"I'm surprised that it's so easy to open the gate."

"Three weeks ago the lock was broken. The super was supposed to buy another one but he hasn't done it yet."

"Bad luck for Carvilio."

"That's life. When it's your turn, it's your turn," the gardener philosophized. Looking up at the sun, he added, "If you don't have any more questions, I'm going to get back to work."

I took advantage of my trip past the reception desk to ask the doorman where he had been in the minutes before Carvilio's fall. The guy turned white for a few seconds and then replied, rudely, that he had been in the basement cleaning the room that held the garbage containers. Perhaps it was true, or maybe it was a lie to hide a trip to his secret bottle, but for my purposes it didn't matter. The doorman had abandoned his post.

I left the entrance and crossed the street. For a few minutes, I observed the building and had the impression of standing in front of an antediluvian beast that might move any minute. I dug around in my jacket for my pack of cigarettes and found out it was empty. There was no kiosk or shop in sight. I swore silently until I spotted, by the entrance of a parking lot across the street, a man seated beside a cardboard box on which he exhibited an assortment of candies, cookies, and chips. I approached his improvised counter. He was old and thin. He wore a dirty jacket that hung loosely on his shoulders and black pants as wrinkled as the skin on his face.

"Do you have any cigarettes?" I asked him.

"Belmont or Derby?" he asked in a gravelly voice. "I sell them loose."

"Derby."

"One hundred pesos," he said, fishing a cigarette out of the pack he had on display.

I looked for a coin in my jacket and passed it to him.

"How's business?" I asked him as I lit the cigarette.

"With what I sell, plus the change they give me for taking care of the cars, I've got enough to eat and pay my rent. In the morning, the students come by, and in the afternoons, the construction workers from the neighborhood."

"Are you here every day?"

"Morning and afternoon."

"So you heard about what happened yesterday in that building?"

"I heard about it and I saw it."

"What did you see, exactly?" I asked urgently.

"Why are you interested?" he probed, suspicious.

"I'm a journalist and I'm writing an article about the accident."

"If you're going to make money with what you write, it's only fair that I should get a bit, wouldn't you say?"

I took a two-thousand-peso bill out of my jacket and passed it to him.

"Try again, bub. Doesn't the paper pay you better than that?"

I put two more bills into the hands of the man, who put them in his pants pocket.

"Write whatever you want, but don't mention me."

"I assure you I won't write even half a line about you."

"It all happened so fast. The guy moved to the edge of the building and came down face-first. I didn't even hear him scream—and he just missed a truck I'd been cleaning by a few feet."

"That's it? You didn't see anyone else on the terrace?"

"Nobody. But now that you mention it, I looked toward the entrance and I thought I saw a guy running out."

"Are you sure? Could you see him well?"

"I've got good eyes, but not good enough to see him clearly. The only thing I can tell you is that the guy had white hair."

"Gray?"

"Albino. Like cotton balls."

"It could have been one of the other residents."

"I know everyone in that building, and there isn't anyone with hair like that."

"Did you see him after that?"

"How could I? The ruckus started and the street filled with people. Curiosity seekers, neighbors, cops. I have no idea where on earth all those people came from."

"Did you talk to the cops?"

"What was I supposed to talk to them about?"

"The man with the white hair."

"Not even if I had a screw loose. I don't want to get involved, and who would pay attention to me anyhow?"

"I'm listening to you."

"You're different. You want to write about what happened. You probably work for one of those tabloids with the naked girls on the front page."

"Do you think the guy with the white hair might have pushed the victim?"

"The only things I think about are the things I have to sell and the cars I have to take care of."

"Did you know the dead man?"

"I saw him come by sometimes. We never said a word to each other."

"What did the neighbors say about him?"

"That he was a good man and that he worked in the lumberyard."

"And about his death?"

"Some say he must have been going after a towel, others think it was just carelessness, and even more think he meant to jump."

"And what do you think?"

"I don't think anything. I just think about my sales—"

"You already said that," I interrupted.

"Then we have nothing more to talk about," said the man, taking a few steps away.

"Sell me two Derbies for the walk."

"Go ahead and grab them. They're on the house."

"Thanks."

"Don't thank me. I'm helping you fuck up your lungs."

"A guy with white hair. What do you think?" I asked Simenon, who was spreading out on top of the desk blotter.

"The doorman probably did it."

"The building where Carvilio lived had a doorman and a gardener. Neither one has white hair."

"And the building super?"

"I don't know if he has white hair. I didn't see him."

"In any case, I wouldn't forget about the doorman."

"Over the years you've gotten as stubborn as a mule!"

"I call it wisdom."

I thought about saying something else, but the ring of the telephone made me change my mind. I picked up the receiver and recognized Bernales's voice.

"Do you have something to tell me?" he said.

"Nothing."

"Don't try to fool me. I went to Carvilio's visiting hours and his wife told me you had been in her apartment pretending to be a cop. You'll never change, Heredia."

I asked myself if I should lie to Bernales, and decided not to. When I told him about the man with the white hair, I had the impression of a jolt on the other end of the line, as if someone had gotten an electric shock.

"How did we miss those details?" he asked, angry with himself.

"Maybe because you've got a steady paycheck or you're trying to close the case quickly to bump up your statistics."

"Where did you hear about the white-haired man?" asked Bernales, ignoring my commentary.

"I promised to mention the miracle, not the saint."

"I think this stuff about the white hair is something you just invented. Tell me the truth. What did you find out when you went through the building?"

"I tell you the truth and you don't believe me. Did you sit so long at that desk that your brains got soft?"

"What did you find out?"

"The doorman pushed Carvilio."

"Bullshit. Don't try to screw me on this, Heredia."

"Simenon doesn't trust the doorman."

"Your cat?"

"Cats tend to have good intuition about these things."

"Don't fuck with me, Heredia. What did you find out in the building?"

"White hair. White like the baking powder that your wife uses to bake the cakes that make you so fat."

Bernales left me with the phone in my hand.

"I try to tell the truth, and the bastard doesn't believe me."

"There's nothing worse than a bad reputation, Heredia."

"Leave the ethics classes for some other time, you pain-in-the-ass cat."

I took advantage of having the phone in my hand to call Griseta and ask her if we'd see each other that night. I was out of luck. She was tired, and the next day she had to turn in an interminable report for her work as a counseling psychologist. She told me that she loved me, and I had to be happy with a kiss that slowly limped its way through the telephone line.

After we said goodbye, I left my office to get a steak sandwich. In the hall, I crossed paths with Desiderio Hernández. He moved past me with his head down and didn't respond to my greeting. I got into the elevator quickly and forgot about my neighbor's melancholy. I was hungry and had a lonely night ahead.

10

The next morning, I awoke to the destruction Simenon caused as he tried to hunt a gigantic moth. The cat ran back and forth, bumping into the bed, and every now and then, when the moth rested in a corner, he looked at it with the expression of a bloodthirsty tiger. I decided to go help. I grabbed the shirt hanging from the headboard and unloaded on the moth.

It wasn't fair to the moth, but it broke my heart to see a fat, old cat jumping around like a teenager.

Simenon saw the stunned moth fall to the ground and ran over to buffet it with his claws. He delivered a severe look for about three seconds, and then proceeded to devour his prey with enthusiasm.

"There's nothing like fresh food. Or am I wrong, Simenon?"

I put on my pants and looked at the clock on the nightstand. It had just turned seven, but from the window the sky looked gray and unwashed.

"I'm glad you've learned not to talk with your mouth full," I said to Simenon, who was still busy with his snack.

I went to the kitchen and made some coffee. I fried the remaining egg from the refrigerator and toasted what was left of a roll that looked like it had been found in a sarcophagus. Then I tuned in to the news and, disinterested, considered my breakfast.

"I should have eaten the moth," I said, observing the sad appearance of my fried egg.

I tried the coffee, and the flavor reminded me of the cough syrup they made me take in the orphanage where I spent most of my childhood.

"In an impressive victory, Magallanes defeated San Antonio Unido four to zero at the Santa Laura Stadium," I heard the radio announcer say.

"That's some good news to start the day with," I said aloud.

"Are you planning on spending all day contemplating that egg?" Simenon had climbed onto the desk and was getting dangerously close to my breakfast.

"No. I should make a phone call and a visit that I have planned."

"Carvilio's widow?"

"Suazo's daughter."

"Don't you think you've got a few too many dead people in your life?"

I agreed to stop in and see Yolanda Suazo at work, and from there we'd go someplace where she could talk about her father. The lawyer, Cotapos, had filled her in on my case, which helped her overcome her distrust of strangers. Yolanda worked in a dark shopping center in the interior of a building off Avenida Providencia, where frame shops, photo labs, print shops, bookkeepers, and tailors still survived. Yolanda worked at a tailor's. She was forty-five, of medium stature, with sunken shoulders. Her hair seemed faded, and her eyes disappeared behind the thick glasses perched on her nose. She worked in a small space barely large enough for the two sewing machines and the table covered with pants and dresses waiting to be hemmed. She had a joyless smile that only managed to escape her halfway when I walked in.

"What are you afraid of?" I asked her, noticing that she was staring at the two people standing in a neighboring tailoring business across the hallway.

"Mrs. Pérez, my boss. She doesn't like us to waste time talking."

"These old shopping centers stopped making money centuries ago."

"She doesn't like to hear me talk about my father, either. She was against the Allende government and thinks his supporters deserved what they got after the coup. She even told me, not long ago, that she thought the stories of the detained and disappeared were invented by the Communists to smear the military." Yolanda Suazo finished sewing a button on the jacket in her lap and added, "I asked for the afternoon off. Wait for me at the entrance to the mall."

"These right-wing dinosaurs and mummies aren't just creatures from the past," I said. "They stay quiet and keep yearning after the general who allowed them to mistreat the poor 'scumbags.'"

"Why did you want me to come in my car?" I asked her when we met up again later. "Where do you want to talk?"

"A place that I think is appropriate for talking about my father and my brothers."

"Why so much mystery, Yolanda?"

"I spent a good part of my childhood hiding my family history. I couldn't talk about what my father and I went through or share what we discussed in family conversations. My mother was suspicious of people she didn't know and never let me bring friends home. One time, in school, the history teacher asked if anyone had a parent who had been a supporter of the Popular Unity party. I raised my hand, and the teacher marked my forehead with chalk and forced me to spend the whole morning in a corner of the classroom. I know things have changed, but I still can't stop being afraid. I'm the daughter of a pariah, and I still feel the teacher's mark on my forehead."

"Now I understand."

"Have you been to Villa Grimaldi?" she asked without acknowledging my comment.

We arrived in front of a thick wooden gate bordered by adobe walls painted red. Close to the large gate was a smaller one where one could enter a large fenced park containing buildings and trees. We walked toward the house that served as a reception area. Yolanda told me to wait a moment while she went inside and talked to a man in a yellow shirt. While I waited, I grabbed a pamphlet that someone had left on the ground by the entrance. I opened it and read a random paragraph:

> From 1862, the Peñalolén estate belonged to the family of Don José Arrieta, and was used for cultural events, such as concerts and literary readings. During the 1940s the portion that comprises Villa Grimaldi Park was sold to Don Emilio Vasallo, who transformed the estate house into a restaurant and a center for political, intellectual, and artistic meetings. In the last part of 1973, Mr. Vasallo was forced to hand the property over to the Directorate of National Intelligence (DINA), which began to use the space as a clandestine detention, torture, and extermination center beginning in December of that same year. Historians estimate that some 4,500 people were detained and tortured here. Official information contains a list of 226 people either killed or disappeared from Villa Grimaldi.

I stopped reading. The silence of the place was overwhelming. A light chill ran up my spine, and for a second I thought I could hear someone screaming from a corner of the park. I took a few steps and more decisively moved away from the house and toward a diorama of what had been one of the principal torture centers during the military dictatorship. The hanging tower; the parking lot where prisoners were run over; the tiny cells for holding prisoners between interrogation sessions; the giant *ombú* tree that must have witnessed so much pain and death; and the pool where the stubborn who tried to remain silent were submerged. *The horror, the indelible horror,* I said to myself as I approached the stone wall on which the names of the dead had been engraved.

"Two of my uncles are on this list," said Yolanda, behind me. "Both were killed here. We have never been able to find their remains. My father was luckier, but he lived with survivor's guilt and constant fear."

"How did he manage to get out of here alive?"

"Some of the other prisoners recognized him, and one of them, who managed to get out a few days after my father was kidnapped, gave my father's name to a religious organization that made his detention public and presented a writ of protection to the courts."

"Did your father ever mention the names of his torturers? Or those responsible for the deaths of his brothers?"

"He never wanted to talk about it until recently, when he and Cotapos presented charges to the tribunals. I think he had recognized and located one of those responsible. Before he died, my father was preparing the document that was to be used as his official testimony."

"Where is that document now?"

"I don't think he ever finished it, so it should be among his personal effects. I haven't wanted to go through them, even though it has been a while. I just put them in boxes and left them in the storage room."

"I think the time has come to open those boxes."

"Why are you interested?"

"As I explained a while back, I'm looking for the men who killed a friend of your father's."

"You think my father's death wasn't accidental?"

"Right now I'm just looking for a starting point."

"If you think it's important, I'll check the boxes." Yolanda walked toward the ombú, whose roots were exposed in the sun.

I followed her beneath the tree and offered her a cigarette, which she held between her trembling fingers. I lit it and she sat on the roots of the tree, which were just as thick as its branches.

"I come here every now and then. I don't know if it's good for me, but the truth is that it doesn't really matter. As long as I'm still around, the history of my uncles and my father has some meaning. I don't know what will happen after I'm gone. I don't feel very optimistic about the future. Time swallows everything, and they, like so many others, will be forgotten. They'll just be names engraved in stone."

11

I left Yolanda Suazo in front of the Salvador metro station and kept driving through Providencia, in the direction of Parque Forestal. The afternoon was warm, and for a moment I felt the temptation to park the car and take a walk along the park's paths, which would be covered in gravel and dry leaves. The park brought back memories of my university years. A time of long hair, a love that I thought would be eternal, and a rebelliousness that could have cost me my life.

After waiting ten minutes for a space to free up, I parked on the Calle Aillavilú and went toward my apartment. In the entrance, I met Feliz Domingo, who was putting great effort into waxing the floor. He stopped working when he saw me arrive and moved quickly toward the pigeonholes where the mail was kept. He gave me a few envelopes, and I noted a certain disapproval on his face when he saw me put them straight into my jacket without the least bit of interest in their contents.

"Maybe they contain important news," he said.

"Don't worry, Feliz Domingo. My nose is rarely wrong, and I can smell that these envelopes don't have anything but ads in them. And as long as no thieves have been in my office while I was gone, I already have everything I need."

"Don Anselmo came to see you two or three times. He said to tell you to pass by the newsstand. It sounds like he has an important message."

"He probably has a good tip for the races on Sunday."

"You like to bet on horses?" asked Feliz Domingo with a tone of reproach in his voice.

"I like to bet, and I like the spectacle of the beasts running. Nothing compares with the uncontrollable dance of nerves when you see a photo finish that is decided by a margin as thin as a hair in your nose. I like watching the rainbow of jerseys and hearing the shouts of the bettors in the galleries. It's more than a sport; it's a lesson on life. Hope is consumed in a few seconds, and win or lose, the bettor knows that happiness and frustration are fleeting. Once the race is finished, another is immediately born, and with it another opportunity for triumph."

"I'm sorry to tell you that I don't share your feelings. Ever since I was a kid, my mother taught me that horse races are a vice that one should stay away from."

"Hell, Feliz Domingo, you can't be serious."

"You shouldn't blaspheme, Mr. Heredia. And remember that my name is spelled with an *x*."

"They say that every man carries his cross."

"What does that mean, sir?"

"That I'd better go see my friend."

Anselmo was reading a science magazine. He looked like he was concentrating, and as soon as I stuck my head through the window of the newsstand, he stopped reading and greeted me with his usual enthusiasm.

"I never stop being surprised, man," he said. "Did you know that the planet is heating up? It absorbs more solar energy than what is reflected back into space, and the height of the oceans has increased by three to four centimeters per decade. Doesn't that make you nervous?"

"About as nervous as the suicidal tendencies of cockroaches."

"We'll end up with water up to our necks."

"Don't we already have water up to our necks? Stress, debt, low salaries, unemployment, and a few other plagues. Isn't that enough?"

"Don't make fun of me. I'm talking about the water that will flood the earth."

"When that happens, we'll have turned into a little pile of dust and bones a long time ago."

"You don't think about the future, man."

"I don't do anything but worry about what lies ahead. Speaking of the future, do we have a good horse for the races next Saturday?"

"A few, but that's not what I wanted to talk to you about."

"Are you still stuck on this thing about global warming?"

"I wanted to know if you gave anyone my cell-phone number."

"I did, but I doubt that person is in any condition to call you." I brought Anselmo up to speed on Carvilio's death.

"That's rough, man. It looks like the departed tried to communicate with you before playing human kite."

"What are you talking about, Anselmo?"

"Look at it yourself." He took out his phone and showed me its screen. "The stiff sent you a text message."

Montegón, detec, buln, Peña, I read on the cell-phone screen.

"I don't understand. Is it some kind of code?" I said.

"I'm guessing that the deceased was in a bit of a hurry when he wrote this message."

"In a hurry?"

"Either he was in a rush to throw himself over the edge, or someone was chasing him."

"Your imagination is getting away from you, Anselmo."

"Write down the message and think about it a bit. I'm not a fortune-teller or a detective, but I'm guessing that the dead guy tried to tell you something before going to the park for quiet people."

I pulled my notebook from my jacket pocket and took Anselmo's advice.

"What does that paper say?" asked Simenon, who had jumped onto my legs a moment before.

"*Montegón* evidently refers to the administrative supervisor of the lumberyard. *Peña*, assuming it's a complete word, must be someone's last name. *Detec* and *buln* are cut-off words or abbreviations that don't mean anything to me right now."

I grabbed the dictionary from my desk and looked for words that started with *detec*. There weren't many. Detection, detect, detective, detector. Was it a key? An abbreviation? As for *buln*, there were no words beginning with those letters. Another abbreviation, or a half-written name?

"Damn, Simenon. I've never been good at solving puzzles."

"Why fret so much about it? Talk with Montegón and ask him what the words mean."

"I'm not going to confront Montegón and ask him if he killed Carvilio. Even the most ferocious tiger circles before pouncing on its prey."

The ring of the telephone separated me from my thoughts. Simenon jumped from my legs and went toward the corner where his water and food bowls were. I picked up the phone and heard the voice of Terán, from the cultural center.

"Are you still interested in the investigation that Germán was undertaking?" he asked. "Do you remember how I told you he was documenting the backgrounds of victimizers who might be the subject of funas?"

"Did you find some information?"

"I remembered that lately he'd been obsessed with investigating a guy named Javier Toro Palacios."

"Who's that?"

"One of the bosses at Villa Grimaldi. As he was putting together the testimonies of political prisoners who'd been there, Germán realized that Toro was one of the officers who interrogated him while he was detained."

"Do you have any idea where I can find Toro?"

"That's a problem Germán wasn't able to solve. Someone told him that Toro had gone to Brazil, but he wasn't ever able to prove it. He asked for help from the Brazilian police and they couldn't give him any information. He checked with a human-rights organization in São Paulo, and they told him that there was no record of a Javier Toro traveling through or staying in Brazil."

"He might have faked leaving Chile."

"Reyes talked with a fellow Villa Grimaldi survivor who said he had recognized Toro at a bank when he went to apply for a loan. It looked like he was the chief of security there. Reyes went to check the information and was informed that nobody with the last name of Toro was employed by the bank."

"Maybe the person who thought he'd seen him was wrong."

"Reyes staked out the bank and never saw anyone leave or enter who matched Toro's description. He kept investigating, and as far as I know, he never found any new clues about Toro's location."

"The door closes on us again."

"The truth is that I wasn't sure if it would be a clue or not. I just remembered about Toro and thought I would share it with you."

"I'm glad you did. You never know which will be the piece that completes the puzzle."

Terán made small talk with me and then said goodbye. Out the window of my office I saw Anselmo putting away his newspapers to wrap up the day's work. I thought about opening the window and shouting a joke at him, but at that very moment a car stopped in front of the newsstand and the blonde who lived on the fifth floor got out. She was dedicated to the profession of consoling souls in pain. The woman asked Feliz Domingo, who was beside the building entrance, a question and then kept moving. The vehicle that had dropped her off continued down the street and rapidly disappeared from view. Anselmo put the padlock on the metallic curtain of his kiosk and walked toward the Touring bar with a tired gait. The rest of the neighborhood continued its habitual rhythm. Only a few drunks who'd stepped out of the Fleahouse disturbed the calm of the afternoon.

I went back to my seat and took out a novel by Bill Pronzini, featuring the detective Nameless. I wanted to forget the investigation and escape for a few hours into the rabbit hole of a good story that would make me forget the reality that was pulsating just a few steps outside my office door.

12

I walked down one of the aisles of the lumberyard and stopped to listen to a painter promoting the benefits of a synthetic oil paint to a group of about twenty customers, who were listening without understanding a word of the technical details he was describing. I wasn't sure what I was looking for, but I kept walking through the aisles, imagining what could be done with the near-infinite variety of screws, bolts, and nuts displayed on the shelves.

Half an hour later, when I was ready to leave, I saw the guard I had talked with on my last visit. He wore a bored expression and was leaning against a pile of tires, watching the customers in the tool section. I came up beside him. As soon as he recognized me, he gave me an effusive handshake.

"I suppose you're aware of what happened to Carvilio," he said, continuing to watch the customers. "When we heard, nobody could believe something that messed up was true."

"It wasn't easy for me either," I said in a low voice.

"Were the two of you friends?"

"Lifelong," I lied.

The guard drew an expression of sadness on his face and shook his head vigorously as if exorcising a demon.

"Carvilio and I were good friends," he said. "Sometimes we would get together for beers, and on the last Independence Day I invited him to my house. He came with his wife and we had a great time. He was an affectionate guy, and everyone here at the lumberyard liked him."

"If you don't mind, I'd like to ask you a few questions about Carvilio, and about the lumberyard."

"Shoot," replied the guard good-naturedly. "What would you like to know?"

"Does anyone named Peña work here in the lumberyard?"

"I don't know any guards by that last name, and I don't know any of the other employees' names."

"What is your boss, Montegón, like?"

The guard's expression changed from sad to questioning. "You're not here to buy anything, are you?"

"Can I trust you?" I asked with a hint of complicity behind my words.

"It depends on what for. I don't want to get in any trouble."

"I'm investigating possible embezzlement in the lumberyard."

"Do you suspect anyone in particular?"

"Each and every employee," I responded, and before giving him a chance to comment, I asked, "What's your opinion of Montegón?"

"I don't really have an opinion. I haven't been here very long, and I haven't had anything to do with him."

"Carvilio told me Montegón watched the employees pretty closely, and that he even visited the neighborhood bars to figure out who has a few drinks after work."

"That seems like an exaggeration to me. Montegón likes to tip a few back," said the guard, keeping his eye on a customer who had decided to buy an electric drill.

"I'll keep that in mind," I said, and then asked if he had seen a man with white hair hanging around the lumberyard.

"Gray hair?"

"White hair, albino."

"Not that I remember. Hundreds of customers come in and out of here all day long."

"*Detec*, *buln*. Do those names, abbreviations, or codes mean anything to you?"

"This is the first time I've heard those words."

"It's possible that they're part of some kind of security code."

"I doubt it. Where did you get those names?"

"I can't tell you. It's confidential."

"I understand," responded the guard with a downcast look. "I shouldn't know more than I need to."

"Cobbler, stick to your last."

"Are you going to speak with Montegón?"

"At some point."

"Do you think he might be mixed up in something illegal?"

"No," I lied.

I saw a blond man waving his hand to get the guard's attention. The man was wearing a clean white coat and gave the impression of having some authority at the lumberyard.

"It looks like he's calling you over," I said to the guard.

"Larenas, the accounting supervisor. He probably needs me to watch the office for a money drop. I should go. But if I can help with anything, don't hesitate to stop by."

"There is one thing you can help me with right now."

"What's that?"

"Keep your mouth shut and don't tell anybody about our conversation."

Had I made a mistake in trusting the guard? I asked myself that as I saw him move away with the supervisor. It was probably fine—the guard seemed convinced that I was a policeman prepared to split him wide open if he broke his vow of silence. I had to hope that he'd keep quiet until I could come back with something more than doubts and a vague interest in bolts and nails.

I looked for the exit, and as I arrived at the main door, I saw Montegón in the company of a man who wouldn't look out of place as the center on a basketball team. I tried to leave without him spotting me, but failed. He saw me when I crossed the doorway, and I didn't need to look back to know that he was scrutinizing my every step. The time still wasn't right to confront him face-to-face. I needed information, or at least a theory, with some proof, of his role in these unsolved riddles.

After Simenon and I shared some steaks from the butcher shop on the corner of the Calles San Pablo and Puente, I picked up the phone and called Griseta. She had just gotten out of a meeting in which they had approved her report about the education levels and employment rates of indigenous residents of southern Santiago. When this didn't generate an exclamation of astonishment on my part, she asked how my investigation was going and then invited me to dinner that night at a restaurant in the Bellavista neighborhood. We agreed on a time, and I told her I missed her.

"You'd better get used to me not being around," she said. "My next project will have me spending a few weeks in Chiloé."

"So tonight's invitation is like the Last Supper?"

"I'm going to leave for a while. I'm not going to crucify you."

"Don't worry. I remember our deal perfectly. Each to his or her own, and the no-man's-land a space for luck and tenderness."

"Are you complaining?"

"No. It's just that lately I'm more interested in tenderness than luck."

"If you keep going down that path, one day you might want a change of jobs."

"That's rough. A while ago I read a philosopher who said people should love the little skills that one learns along the way."

"You're incorrigible."

"Do I need to be corrected?"

"I put up with you the way you are, Heredia. But don't abuse it."

I said goodbye to Griseta, took out a Juan Gelman book that I kept in the desk drawer, and read a poem where he talked about his son, who had been killed during the Argentine dictatorship of Videla. The horror that emerged from the pen of the poet reminded me that every one of my steps was associated with a past that had divided my life in two: the age of illusion, and a time of disgust from which I could not escape. Just as I couldn't toss my skin into the hamper with the dirty clothes, I could not stop believing in the inexhaustible hope that pushed me to the window every morning to make sure the sun was still in its place.

I read Gelman's poems until it was time to meet Griseta. A breeze was blowing when I left the office. As I was crossing the Mapocho River, I heard the sound of the water as it pushed its usual load of garbage and debris. I leaned on one of the railings and lit a cigarette. The lights on the horizon seemed to indicate that life was following its course in spite of the pain, and I had to rescue whatever was worthwhile. When the tobacco ashes had become part of the current, I stopped thinking about the river and sped up until I reached the Calle Antonia López de Bello. The darkness beat its wings upon the poorly lit sidewalks. The stores that animated the neighborhood by day had their metallic curtains shut, and along the length of the street some cardboard collectors appraised their trash. A few dogs sniffed the garbage for leftovers, and it didn't seem like there was much for them or the bum who followed in their steps, ready to fight over the scraps of a banquet that he would never be invited to. I felt a chill and thought I heard the echo of footsteps behind me. I stopped, looked around, but didn't see anyone. I thought about the pistol that I had left on my desk beside the dog-eared Juan Gelman book. I kept going, and soon afterward heard the sound of steps again. This time I waited a few seconds before looking back, and as I did, I saw the shadow of a man with a hat hiding in a doorway. I walked toward him, but when I got to the doorway I found only a black cat who observed me distastefully before running off to some other dark corner of the neighborhood. I took a quick look around and didn't move until, minutes later, three girls passed by me. They were outlandishly dressed in platform boots, wool jackets, and muslin skirts. I watched them until they were far away and then thought again about my date with Griseta.

"Half an hour late and with anxiety painted on your face," she said as I took a seat at the table where she was drinking a mojito in an attractive blue glass.

"A problem with phantom shadows," I responded as I raised my hand to get the waiter's attention. "But for now the only thing I'm worried about is catching up with you. You're one drink ahead."

"What phantom shadows are you referring to?"

"I thought someone was following me in the street. It must have been my mind playing tricks on me."

"You always exaggerate, Heredia. If I didn't know you, I'd be worried about everything you do."

"Don't let down your guard, Griseta. One of these days I'll surprise you."

"I've had a long day and I need some food that speaks to my heart," she said as I reached for the menu.

"Dinner by candlelight. What a nice way to begin the evening."

"The Last Supper. Isn't that what you called it this afternoon?"

Griseta left after breakfast. From the balcony of my apartment, I saw her leave the building and walk down the Calle Aillavilú in the direction of Cal y Canto metro station. It was a foggy morning, ideal for staying inside with a good book or an old Robert Mitchum movie, or even Cantinflas.

"I like gray days like this," I said to Simenon while I tuned the radio. "I feel like on these days the authentic face of the city shows itself, and it gives me a certain tranquility, like looking through a photo album or hiding a bar of chocolate beneath the pillow."

"I prefer sunny days," said Simenon as he yawned with enthusiasm. "Sun and a good nap on the balcony."

"You've been making a real effort to contradict me lately."

"What are you talking about, Heredia?"

I ignored the cat's question and turned to a book by John Berger that Griseta had left on my desk with the recommendation that I read it as soon as possible. It was a volume of short stories; one was about a farmer who found consolation for his loneliness by playing the accordion to his cows as they lay in the stable.

I wrapped myself up in reading and didn't stop until after noon, when Yolanda Suazo came into my office. Her trepidation was the same as the first time we met, and from the look on her face it was clear that she had come to tell me something important.

"You should clean up your office and get some plants," she said.

"Someday I'm going to make a compilation of all the improvements suggested by people who come to my office for the first time."

"Sorry. I didn't want to bother you, Mr. Heredia. I came to tell you that I found the document that my father was writing for Cotapos. It wasn't easy. I had to search through a bunch of folders."

"What does it say?" I shot back, impatient.

"It's hard to believe that the life of a man could be reduced to three boxes and a few plastic bags," replied Yolanda, unaffected by my eagerness.

"The notes?" I insisted.

"My father had horrible handwriting. I took it upon myself to transcribe the papers that I found." She handed me a brown envelope that contained ten pages of manuscripts and another four typed pages.

"What does the text say?" I asked, and without waiting for the answer, I started to read.

> I decided to go back to work after the military coup. I went to the public office where I worked in an administrative position, and I only had to eat lunch one time in the break room to understand that nothing would be the same as it had been before. I got into contact with some friends who had survived the detentions, and they made me understand that my name must be on the list of the union leaders who had supported Allende, and that sooner or later the new authorities would find me. I didn't listen to them, and during the next days I kept working at my desk as usual. Some of my coworkers had been in favor of military intervention, and I began to think that their hate had been satisfied. For five months nothing special happened and I began to believe that my name being on the list of undesirables had been bad information. As with so many other things in my life, I was wrong. The detention occurred on a Thursday. How could I forget the day? I was getting ready to cross Avenida Providencia when I heard someone say my name. He was a tall, blond man wearing a brown leather jacket and dark glasses that covered his eyes. He said my name again and when he came to my side, close enough for me to smell his breath, he told me to follow him and not try to escape, as there were three men behind us with guns pointed at me. I

remembered what I had been told about the detentions of other comrades, and was sure that I had fallen into a pit that I would never leave. I've always thought that I should have run at that moment, but I didn't. I obeyed and they made me walk toward a white car that was parked on the side of the street. Inside the car was another man with sunglasses who worked as a driver, and out of nowhere two more appeared and ordered me to get in the backseat, one on either side of me. The tall, blond man sat in the front passenger seat. They made me put my head down, and the car began moving toward the western part of the city. In Plaza Italia it turned toward the edge of Parque Forestal and stopped one block before the Museo de Bellas Artes. At that moment, they permitted me to raise my head, and I could look around for a second. One of the men put packing tape over my eyelids and then covered my eyes with sunglasses. The car began to move again and after half an hour stopped on top of unpaved ground, judging by the sound that the vehicle made when it braked. One of the men got out of the car and opened a gate. After that he returned to my side and the vehicle began to move again. I feared the worst, but for a number of hours nothing I was expecting happened. Once I was out of the car, I was handcuffed and taken to a room that reeked of cat urine. There I was alone with my fear and my memories. I can tell you that what they say about people's lives flashing before them in dire situations is true. From the neighboring room, I could hear the sound of a television. I listened hard and realized it was a variety show that I used to watch with my children. For a second I remembered their laughter. After

> that I began to feel the loneliness again. No one had observed my abduction. None of my coworkers knew where I was. Only the jaws were real, and I was the only one who knew I was between them. I shook my head and managed to make the sunglasses fall to the floor. The packing tape had come a little bit loose and I could see the fragile ray of light that entered through one of the edges of the door.

I stopped reading Suazo's notes, guessing that the rest of his memories would be made up of the most brutal part of his kidnapping.

"It was hard for me to accept that my father was the person who narrates these pages," said Yolanda. "I knew what he had been through, but never in so much detail."

"It must not be easy to be confronted with his memories."

"I remembered him a lot while I typed up the notes. I could almost see him underneath the trellis in our house. He spent hours and hours there in silence, with his head down, probably waiting for them to come and take him away again. As a little girl, whenever I came up beside him, he never said anything. He only ran his hand over my hair and smiled."

"I'm sure he wanted to avoid having the family share his pain."

"Do you think these notes will help you in your work?" Yolanda asked.

"To answer that question, I have to finish reading them."

Yolanda gave me a brief smile and turned around and walked toward the door.

I thought about starting to read again, but I didn't. I needed the air of the street and a momentary break from Julio Suazo's memories. I put the notes in my jacket and left the office. On the corner of Bandera and

Catedral, I stopped to observe a shady-looking guy who was passing out flyers for a nearby strip club. Close to him, dressed in a tight T-shirt that drew attention to her body, a young brunette announced the advantages of a telephone call center. At the side of the cathedral, a number of Peruvians were having an animated discussion about the cuisine of the country they had left behind. There wasn't anything new in the neighborhood, or at least I didn't manage to see it. At the same time, my thoughts returned time after time to Suazo's writing, reminding me that, despite appearances, the past was still alive. No one talked about it much, but all you had to do was dig into people's stories to see traces of it.

I finished my walk at a soda shop, where I ordered a coffee and a pastry, which was dry and looked like it had spent several lonely days inside the glass case. I lit a cigarette and continued reading. The horror Suazo described was what one would imagine, and among multiple beatings, I found two paragraphs that caught my attention.

> The first night they locked me in a room where I could barely move, and the next morning I was put in another where there were four or five other prisoners. Since I refused to answer the questions they asked me, I was moved to a place called the Tower, an isolation cell where the prisoners were hung by their arms for hours at a time. The whole time I was detained, I asked myself many times who my torturers were. I was never able to see their faces, and as far as their names go, I only heard two nicknames: Crazy Horse and King Midas. Later, when I got out of Villa Grimaldi, a comrade told me that the second of those nicknames had been given to an officer named Javier Toro. I have never been able to confirm this information, and even though I usually read news related to the military, I have never read nor heard any new mention of that name.

The second paragraph was shorter.

> With the passing of time, I understood that the physical torment was not the only suffering, nor was it the end of the indignities. The worst came afterward. The worst was the fear that I continued to live with. Fear of being captured again. Fear of telling people that I had been detained. Fear of people not believing me, of their cruel comments, and of the rejection I received from some people when I talked about my experience.

I put away the notes, said goodbye to the pastry that was still uneaten on the table, and thought about the next piece that I would move on my chessboard of ghosts.

13

From a distance and among the shadows, the lumberyard looked like a strange, sleeping animal. It was my fourth night of staking it out. I didn't know for sure what I might find, but rolling around in my head was the idea that something might happen there during the night.

I had slept until the beginning of the afternoon, and after eating Peruvian fish stew in a local restaurant, I had gone to my office and waited for night to come, reading whatever my disorderly library put into my hands. I reread three chapters of *A Shadow You Soon Will Be*, a novel that Osvaldo Soriano had signed for me after a conference put on by the Society of Chilean Writers. I also reread part of a story by Philip K. Dick, "The Minority Report," whose opening pages hit a little too close to home, as a character suddenly discovers that he is getting fat, bald, and old. The "old" part fit me like a ring on a finger, but my hair was still there and the extra pounds had been coming off after the caress of a street knife had forced me to spend some time in bed.

I recognized that I liked spending the night in the shadows, listening to the strange noises and every now and then taking a sip of whiskey from my trusty flask, a gift from a poet. The flask bore a dent, a souvenir from the stabbing that a thug had tried to deliver as I chased him around the neighborhood of the Central Market, but it was still useful for carrying a few drops of alcohol.

The instant I emptied the flask, I looked toward the lumberyard and saw the fleeting image of a man with a hat crossing in front of the entrance. I remembered what had happened before my date with Griseta and instinctively moved my hand toward the pocket where I kept my Beretta. The man advanced slowly and paused in front of a kiosk that looked abandoned. I wanted to light a cigarette, but I stopped myself. The stranger didn't move from that spot. Five minutes went by and impatience began pulling on my ears, pushing me to leave my hiding spot and find out who the man was. But I didn't move until a while later, when the calm of the street was interrupted by the heavy noise of a truck passing by. I thought the vehicle would stop in front of the lumberyard, but I was wrong. The truck went by, and when I saw it submerged in the shadows, I noticed that the stranger had abandoned the protection of the kiosk and had begun to walk. I tracked his steps, and in a short time we had left behind the dark street and turned onto a well-lit avenue. I recognized him from a distance, but didn't dare to murmur his name. I followed him up to a dive bar that still had its doors open, waiting for the most vulgar drunks of the night. I went in and surveyed the tables. The man with the hat was sitting at a small table in the corner. The waiter served him wine as the radio played the wretched sounds of a bolero. The man looked toward where I was standing, and I thought I could see an ironic smile on his face. I stopped thinking about it and advanced to meet him.

"It's about time we had a conversation," I told him, sitting down at his table.

Montegón observed me without surprise and took a sip of wine. "Yes. It is time for us to see each other face-to-face, Heredia."

"How do you know my name?"

"When I run into someone two times in a row, I want to know who he is. First I saw you at the lumberyard, and then I saw you in the bar with the dead man, Carvilio."

"And after that you decided to follow me around Bellavista."

"Pure chance. I happened to be over there, I recognized you, and decided to figure out what you do with your free time. Your girlfriend is a beautiful woman. You're lucky, Heredia."

"I'm warning you that she can't be part of any game you're playing."

"It wasn't a threat. I was trying to be polite," Montegón replied with a smile. He called over the waiter to put a glass by my side.

"Why were you watching the lumberyard?" I asked. "What are you looking for?"

"The same questions as you, Heredia. The problem is who answers them first."

"We have two options. One is to keep thumping away at each other until one of us decides to talk. The other is to converse like reasonable people."

"I'm more interested in talking, as long as we commit to honesty. I suggest we put our cards on the table. No tricks or kicking each other below the table."

"Agreed. The only problem is knowing who will talk first," I said, attentive to his movements.

Montegón took a coin out of his jacket and showed me both sides.

"Tails," I said.

He tossed the coin softly into the air and let it fall onto the tablecloth.

"You lost," he said when the coin had stopped moving. "You get to start."

I looked around as if waiting for someone to tell me that I was embarking on a game that I wouldn't do well at.

"I'm looking for the killers of Germán Reyes, the lumberyard cashier. Someone asked me for help and I couldn't avoid the request."

"That was a shame, but what makes you think his death was a murder and not the result of a failed robbery?"

"Call it my nose, a hunch, or the bad habit of looking beneath the water."

"Three good ways to waste time," said Montegón, and after drinking more wine, he asked, "What did you hope to find across from the lumberyard?"

"A lucky break."

"Did Carvilio talk to you about the robberies at the lumberyard?"

"No."

"You're lying. Do you think I'm going to believe that you were whistling at the moon?"

"OK. Carvilio mentioned the matter of the robberies. I wanted to know if it was true and if it was related to Germán Reyes's death."

"Now you're being honest, Heredia. You win a glass of wine."

"Thank you, but after a certain time of night I only drink alone or with friends."

"You're missing out."

"What makes you think I'm telling the truth?"

"I've been in the business for twenty years. I can recognize when someone's lying or trying to sell me a pig in a poke."

"What business are you referring to?"

"The same as yours, but with better luck."

"What do you know about my luck?"

"What they say in your neighborhood."

"Carvilio said you were an administrator at the lumberyard."

"That's what I've led the employees to believe."

"And what's the truth?"

"They hired me to investigate the lumberyard from inside."

"The robberies?"

"No. That came up by chance. The owners of the lumberyard are worried about a union that's being organized. They want to figure out who the leaders are and what they want."

"A paid rat. That's a despicable job."

"I prefer to call it industrial espionage."

"No wonder you hang out in the same bars as the employees. I don't envy your work."

"Nor I yours."

"I thought it would be more difficult to talk to you," I said, touching the butt of my pistol beneath my jacket.

"I'm not interested in knocking heads. I want us to form a partnership. You know the expression: One hand washes the other and they both . . ."

"How does that help me?"

"I probably know some things that you don't."

"That could be. As a matter of fact, I do have one doubt that you might be able to help me clear up. Before he died, Carvilio sent a text message to a friend. In one part it said *Montegón, detec.* Maybe you silenced him so you could keep working undercover."

"You surprise me, Heredia. I didn't know Carvilio was onto me. Did the message say anything else?"

"Why would I tell you?"

"To follow the right lead. I know the people who work at the lumberyard, and that can help us solve the case."

"That's not a good-enough reason."

"I've already told you that I don't like my job. You can trust me, Heredia," he added, looking me in the eye.

I decided to take a risk and put a piece on the table.

"*Buln. Peña.* Do those words mean anything to you?"

"I don't know what *Peña* is. *Buln* could be part of the last name of the finance manager of the lumberyard, Fernando Bulnes. I met him in a meeting when I started the job. He's one of the oldest bosses, and the owners trust him."

"A finance manager must be aware of the inventory on hand. He could also falsify the numbers."

"You think quickly, Heredia."

"Do you know anything else about Bulnes?"

"Nothing else."

"Are you sure?"

"We're supposed to be operating on trust. If I knew anything else, I'd tell you."

"I haven't said anything about trust. I don't want to be part of your investigation or responsible for what happens to the employees that you turn in."

"If you don't want to make a deal with me, why did you come to my table?"

"Sometimes you have to get your feet wet to cross a river."

"Some philosophy, Heredia. What do you say? Can we work together?"

"The only thing we have in common is our profession. That doesn't say much. Despite what they say, not all cats are black at night."

"Don't look down on my help," said Montegón, his tone softening. "Will you share the information you get from here on out?"

"Everything in its time and place."

"The guys who told me about you were right," said Montegón, laughing so hard his fat cheeks quivered.

"What did they say about me?"

"That you're a fucking asshole. What else?" Montegón pointed at the bottle of wine and said, "Help me empty that. No commitment. Just the fleeting complicity of two guys who meet in the middle of the night. What do you say, Heredia? A few glasses might make you change your mind."

14

I shared the bottle with Montegón, and we agreed to meet the next day in front of the lumberyard. I said goodbye without accepting his offer of another glass of wine.

I stopped to observe the moon's reflection. *Life keeps going,* I thought, *and I don't have anything but my memories. What* was *always seems more real than the future, and on the street I'm nothing more than an attentive set of eyes, the lookout who forgets his name as he looks into unknown faces. An anonymous traveler who wants to travel in peace, even though sometimes hate fills his pockets and makes his hands turn to fists.*

Could I trust Montegón? Should I accept his help? The questions hit me as I began to walk, and I couldn't find an answer that wasn't a transitory puff of intuition. I would accept his company and let him act, without failing to watch his movements closely and weigh the meaning of his words. I continued on my walk, when suddenly the name of a strip club on a poster stuck to a wall made me remember Humberto Balseiro, an acquaintance I hadn't seen for a few months. I checked my watch and decided to try my luck. Balseiro was a printer who was detained after the military coup and accused of reproducing pamphlets and printing a union magazine. He had spent a few weeks in Villa Grimaldi, and even though he had gotten out, he was never the same again. Something inside of him had broken as he fought to survive the electric shocks and the immersions in drums of water and shit.

Was he dominated by fear or by regret? I never got an answer from him. I visited him every once in a while in the afternoons, and we passed the time talking about anything that didn't touch on his past.

He worked as a doorman at the Red Diamond, a dump where the strippers landed after moving down through all the circles of hell. At the doorway of the club I ran into a muscle-bound type who had the dual role of doorman and bouncer. He was dressed in black and wore a shirt that was stamped with a Chinese dragon. He recognized me and with a slight nod of the head made me understand that I had sufficient credit to walk in the door.

"How is business tonight?" I asked him.

"There's never any lack of drunks and horny guys."

"I'm here to see Balseiro."

"He got here an hour ago," grumbled the doorman. "But there is better company in there than that nutjob. Yesterday a couple of Dominicans worth taking a look at started working."

"I'm sure you'd like to take your work home with you."

"All the time, brother. But the girls know that doormen don't have a lot of money in their pockets."

"You could always find another way to attract them."

"You think I'm going to seduce these chicks with my soulful eyes? Cash, brother. That's what they want."

"Just like everyone else in the world. Today, happiness is measured in bundles of bills. If you don't have it, you have to put up with watching the party from a distance. You know what I'm saying?"

"You and Balseiro are messed up in the head."

I went into the club and gave my eyes a few seconds to get used to the darkness. The place wasn't very impressive. Lights, a stage where an attractive brunette danced, customers, and a dozen women on a mission of conquest. I spotted Balseiro beside the bar at the edge of the room.

His hands were crossed over his gut, and his eyes seemed locked on a faraway horizon. He gave the impression of being as old as the world itself. His hair was thin, and he had grown a beard that didn't hide the wrinkles that plowed his face. I came up to him and said hello with a soft clap on his back.

"Out drinking or looking for a soft leg to warm up the night?" he asked.

"Neither one. I came to talk to you."

"It's been a few months since the last time I saw you. Don't worry, though. Everything is the same in my life and in this den of sin. I don't know why, but I'm still stubborn enough to survive. I sleep in the morning, after noon I walk around the neighborhood, and later I come in here."

"Don't you get sick of seeing so much fresh meat around you?"

"Fresh meat?" he asked as he waved at the closest women. "You should see them in the daylight."

"Can I buy you a drink?"

"You'd be better off spending your money on the girls."

"I want to talk to you, Balseiro."

"From your tone, I'm guessing you're not here to talk about soccer or horseracing. What's up? Do you need a bit of blow?"

"You know I'm not interested in blow. Just booze and women, and only up to a certain limit."

"You've never had limits in women or drinks. But let's stop beating around the bush. What do you want to talk about?"

"Villa Grimaldi."

"I talked to you about that place once and you promised we'd never bring it up again."

"Does it hurt that much to even mention it?"

"Sometimes I think it would have been better to die on the electrified bed frame. No memories, no nightmares, no regrets. You're into horses—you know what they do with horses that break their legs."

"Javier Toro. Does that name mean anything to you?"

"Don't make me remember."

"It's just a name."

"Not for me, Heredia. You can't imagine what it was like being there."

"So you're saying that you know the name Toro?"

"Nobody who was there could forget that name."

"What do you know about him?"

"It was a fake name, like all the ones they used."

"Fake?"

"That's what the detainees said. But it doesn't matter, because after the kidnapping I never tried to find out anything about those pricks."

"Did you ever see him while you were there?"

"No."

"Did you see any of the others?"

"Shadows, yelling, punches. Don't make me remember," muttered Balseiro, and he added, "You were going to buy me a drink."

Balseiro called over the bartender and asked for two *piscolas*. He waited for his drink to be made, and as soon as he had it in his hand, he gulped it down.

"Too bad it's not good for much," he said, observing the liquor left in the bottom of the glass. "It puts you to sleep, but it doesn't kill you."

"I'm sorry to insist so much."

"Why are you interested in Toro?"

"I heard his name while I was investigating the death of someone else who was in Villa Grimaldi. I thought you might be able to give me information that could help me find him."

"What's so special about this dead guy?"

"I think they killed him for digging around in the past."

Balseiro emptied the contents of his glass and looked back toward where the bartender had been.

"Can I have another one?"

I signaled the bartender and he gave Balseiro another dose of alcohol.

"What's the point of investigating?" he asked. "A lot of time has passed since then."

"I don't like it when killers are free to roam the streets."

"You must have a lot of work, Heredia. Murderers and their accomplices don't just walk the streets. They also smile in the press and pretend to be respectable."

"Right now, I'm only worried about one particular killer, and I believe you might be able to help me find him."

"You shouldn't swallow everything I tell you hook, line, and sinker."

"Why?"

"Without getting into it too much, I lied to you a while ago, Heredia."

"Do you know who Toro is?"

"No, but during one of the torture sessions I managed to see the face of one of the men who was with him. I never forgot it, and years ago, maybe twenty years ago, I saw him again. I was working in a cabaret close to the Salvador metro station, and he came in with a couple of guys who looked like government workers. I paid one of the dancers to get his name. Guillermo Zuñeda."

"Then what did you do?"

"The girl found out that he worked at a minor job in the military government. I found his office in one of the ministries, and for a long time I thought about confronting him. But I never did it, and months later I lost his trail. Whenever I asked about him, they told me he had changed jobs and they didn't have any more information."

"That's it?"

"A year ago I found him again. He was sitting on a bench in the Plaza de Armas and didn't look good. He looked old and abandoned. When he got up, I followed him. He walked around the Calle 21 de Mayo for a while and went into a strip club on Calle San Antonio."

"What happened there?"

"Once again, I didn't do anything. I think I followed him out of curiosity. Or maybe since I saw he was in such bad shape, I figured life had given him what he deserved."

"I don't understand you, Balseiro."

"The damage is done, Heredia. I could have killed him, but nothing would have gone back to the way it was before. I just watched him mess around with the ladies and drink until he stumbled out."

"I honestly don't understand you," I repeated. "It seems like you feel guilty for having survived."

"I survived because others didn't. I couldn't stand the pain and I gave up my friends. That's something that there's no cure for, Heredia. We have one life, and mine's fucked. There's nothing that will let me change my luck. The only thing I'm interested in is that the nights go quickly, that the customers and the girls leave, and that I can close the doors and lie down to sleep among the leftovers of a party that I don't have any connection to. You can stay here with me if you want, but don't ask me any more questions."

15

I said goodbye to Balseiro as the first rays of sun were filtering through the crack under the cabaret door. Neither one of us had much left to say. We hugged each other for a few seconds and then I hit the street.

I stopped at a corner to watch the laborers and office workers as they headed, without enthusiasm, toward eight or ten hours in an office or a factory. *Life as constant repetition,* I thought as I looked for a cigarette in my jacket. I only found useless betting slips from horses that had given out in the middle of the track. I threw them on the ground and kept walking until I got to a café that was receiving its first customers of the morning. I resisted the temptation to go in and order a coffee with milk. I wanted to get to my apartment and bury my nose in a pillow. I wanted to sleep and wake up on an island where no one was contaminated by the plague of ambition. When I arrived at the Calle Aillavilú, I ran into Anselmo. I helped him hang the newspapers and magazines on his newsstand, and having run out of energy to go up to my apartment, I sat down and asked him for a smoke.

"You look like a zombie out of a horror movie," he said.

"I'm tired and I've got a lot of booze in me."

"You're too old to be out all night. I'm telling you for your own good, man."

"You've told me a bunch of times, and my body reminds me all the time too."

"Go sleep and forget about work for a few hours."

"Do you ever feel like life doesn't have any meaning?" I asked suddenly. "That it doesn't matter whether we're here or not?"

"That's not a question to be asking at six in the morning. What's up with you?"

"I was thinking about a friend I just said goodbye to."

"You know I'm an optimist twenty-four hours a day."

"You're right. It's not something to talk about at six in the morning." As I was getting onto my feet, I asked, "Have you ever heard anyone talk about a guy named Guillermo Zuñeda? They told me he hangs around the neighborhood strip clubs and cabarets."

"First time I've ever heard that name."

"If I don't come back out before six in the evening, come to my apartment and wake me up. I've got to study the shadows tonight."

It was twenty minutes before seven at night when Simenon jumped onto my chest. I brushed him off, got up, and headed to the bathroom. The mirror showed me the bags beneath my eyes, the thick stubble of my beard, and the ghastly expression that was supposed to be a smile. I turned on the faucet and drank a bit of water. I cursed the acid that splashed around in my stomach and quieted it with another sip. Simenon jumped up to the sink and licked the stream of water with enthusiasm. I took the shaving brush, covered my face with soap, and applied the blade to my cheeks. Then I took a cold shower and put on the last clean shirt hanging in my closet.

"Heredia comes back to life," I said to Simenon, who was looking at me from the corner, as serious as a plaster cat. "Does that sound like a good title for a movie?"

"It sucks," he responded, and without giving me a chance to answer, asked, "Do you have any intention of making food?"

"I don't lack intentions, but I doubt we have anything to throw in the pan," I responded as I walked toward the kitchen.

In the cupboard, next to a bag of salt, I discovered a can of tuna and two tea bags. I opened the can and slid its contents onto a plate. Simenon balanced himself over the fish and in no time had finished his lunch.

"Satisfied?" I asked.

Simenon licked his whiskers and gave me a friendly look.

I checked my watch and decided it was time to leave. I took my jacket and opened the door. The hallway that led to the elevator was dark, and from one of the apartments I could hear the noise of a TV sports program. Life remained intact. I touched the Beretta asleep in the right-hand pocket of my jacket and pressed the elevator button.

I didn't see any sign of life at the lumberyard, other than a yellowish light in the guard shack beside the main entrance. I leaned on a tree trunk that hid me and lit a cigarette with the secret hope of finishing the night with something besides cold in my bones. The moon drawn on the sky looked like a huge Ping-Pong ball that was just out of reach, and every once in a while, some clouds covered its face and then continued on their way, indifferent to the suffering of us mortals.

"Someone with your experience should know better than to smoke during a nighttime stakeout," I heard a voice say. Startled, I stuck my right hand into the pocket where I carried the Beretta. But I didn't do anything, because as I was grabbing for the pistol, I saw the face of Atilio Montegón emerge from the shadows.

"If I had wanted it that way, you would be a lump at the foot of that tree," he said.

"I've learned my lesson, trust me."

"Good for you. You won't always have a friend watching your back."

"Who said we're friends? We'll help each other while we're investigating what's going on in there."

"Yeah. We talked about that yesterday. Maybe if I explained a bit more . . ."

"Save it for someone who cares," I said, and then, to change the subject, I added, "It looks like we're in for another all-nighter."

"Be patient," said Montegón as he pulled a flask of *pisco* out of his jacket. "Want to make the wait a bit easier?"

"I'll pass for now."

"Your answer doesn't fit with the image I have of you."

"It's not hard to get a bad reputation."

"You're missing out, Heredia," said Montegón, lifting the flask to his lips.

"Why are you watching the lumberyard at night? Don't tell me it's because you're worried the workers are forming a union."

"They've told me that the guard is a union member and that his comrades show up at the lumberyard at night."

"Secret meetings? Nighttime unions? Someone is messing with you, Montegón."

"Don't tell me how to do my job," growled the detective, obviously bothered by the comment. "I have just as much, if not more, experience than you."

"You're right. I'm forgetting about the conditions of your filthy job."

"I'm going to pretend that I didn't hear you," replied Montegón before seeking the warm breath of the flask.

After that we were silent for a while, until we saw a truck appear and stop in front of the lumberyard. The headlights of the vehicle blinked, and almost immediately the guard opened the door to allow the truck to enter.

"It looks like luck's on our side tonight," said Montegón.

"If I were you, I'd wait a bit before getting too happy."

The truck drove away from the lumberyard, and for the next half hour I followed it while keeping an eye on Montegón's vehicle in the rearview mirror of my Chevy. The detective drove a red Jeep covered in dents. The truck stopped beside a shack on Calle Franklin. It parked beside a chestnut tree with meager branches, and the men immediately got to work unloading boxes from the rear. Once they had finished, one of them climbed back in the truck, and the others went into the house.

"What do we do?" asked Montegón, who had gotten into the Chevy a few minutes before.

"You don't need to use the plural. This stopped being your business a while ago. Or did you think that the thieves might be forming a union?"

"You're in no position to refuse my help, Heredia. There were three guys in the truck, and if we add the others that are probably in the house, the math doesn't work out in your favor."

"If you want to help, get back in your Jeep and follow the truck."

"You're not thinking about going into the house and confronting them, are you?"

"The days when I would walk into anyplace with my pistol drawn are over. I'm a lazy, patient cat now."

"Even if you catch them sleeping, there will always be more of them."

"The truck is leaving. You've got just enough time to get to your car."

Montegón waved his hand in resignation and climbed out of the Chevy. I saw him get in his Jeep and drive toward the shadow of the truck. *In situations like this it would be useful to have a cell phone,* I said to myself, looking in the rearview mirror. *Also a machine gun, and a tank, or a half dozen men to help.* I found a public telephone, dialed Bernales's number, and found him in his office, just about to begin the night shift. I told him about the robbery at the lumberyard, and when I had finished, I noted increasing enthusiasm in his voice.

16

"Tools, plumbing supplies, paint, glue, screws, and other things that are easy to sell in flea markets or on the street. The robbery you discovered last night wasn't the first in that lumberyard," said Bernales while he dumped sugar into the coffee that he had asked for to drive away the tiredness.

We were in a cafeteria near the headquarters of the Investigative Police, and I could still hear the sirens, shouting, and gunshots that broke out a few minutes after my phone call. Bernales was tired but satisfied with the results of the investigation.

"I owe you one," he said. "We still haven't gotten them to confess, but one of them, Cabrales, has told us enough that we have a general idea of how the gang worked. He's fifteen, and he has already been to juvenile prison. The leader's name is Gabriel Peña, and his rap sheet lists arrests for burglaries and pimping."

"Is the guard with them?" I asked, remembering the text message from Carvilio.

"We don't know yet. He says he cooperated with them under threat, but I'd be willing to bet he's lying."

"How did they get all the merchandise out without anyone noticing it was gone?"

"They had Bulnes, the head of the finance department, working with them. I ordered them to arrest him in his house, and they should be bringing him in right about now. Cabrales says that Bulnes altered the inventory records and made sure the products were replaced quickly."

"Now Carvilio's message makes sense. Discovering the thieves cost him his life."

"None of the guys we arrested can be linked to his death, and I doubt they'll confess to it unless they have a good reason. It's one thing to go to the slammer for robbery, and entirely another to be convicted of murder."

"You need someone to talk to them a bit more tenderly."

"If you think you're going to get to talk to the prisoners, forget it."

"You just told me you owed me a big favor."

"I can't let you talk to the prisoners."

"If we're lucky, they'll talk after they've spent some time in a jail cell. But I was already thinking about something else, Bernales. Can you look for information on a guy named Guillermo Zuñeda?"

"Who is he?"

"Check your files and see if you find an answer to that question."

I said goodbye to Bernales and drove back to my apartment. The streets were clogged with cars and buses that dashed from one lane to the other like frightened rabbits during a night hunt. I didn't have much hope that Montegón would turn anything up. The matter of what was really going on at the lumberyard seemed to have arrived at its natural conclusion, unless Bernales's interrogations found some kind of connection to the killing of Carvilio. But I didn't have any illusions. The discovery of the robberies and my question about Zuñeda were the final casts of a fisherman who tosses his bait in without hopes of catching anything but an inedible goatfish. I was tired. Sleep was closing my eyes, and I had to admit that Anselmo was right when he said I was too old for all-nighters. Unfortunately, my romance with the pillow lasted less time than the sigh of an old maid. As soon as I had put my head down, I heard the insistent ringing of the telephone.

I wavered between closing my eyes or answering the phone, and in the end curiosity won out against exhaustion. I picked up the phone, and Griseta's voice greeted me.

"Is something wrong? I called you a bunch of times last night," she asked after saying hello. Before I could answer, she proceeded to tell me that she was about to get on a bus that would take her to Dalcahue, in the remote south.

"I was staking out a lumberyard," I told her, and after I had finished recounting the details of capturing the thieves, I added, "Thank you for calling. I needed to hear a familiar voice."

"Are things that bad?"

"I feel like I'm running around in circles."

"This isn't the first time you've said that. Be patient. Tomorrow's another day."

"Don't worry. I'll call my patience dealer. Meanwhile, buy me a bag of those crunchy *chonchina* donuts from the market in Dalcahue and save your best kisses for when you get back. I miss you."

"I miss you too, Heredia. Be patient."

"Lately, you've been asking for a lot of patience."

"What else do you want me to say?"

"That you're going to forget about Dalcahue and get on the first plane to Santiago."

"I have to finish this job."

"I know. I was daydreaming for a few seconds."

"Bye, Heredia."

"Farewell, my lovely," I replied, remembering the title of the Raymond Chandler novel I had read while I worked as a hotel guard and spent a good part of most nights reading novels given to me by the retired cop I worked with.

Three hours later, I woke to a knock on the door of my apartment. I threw on some clothes in a bad mood and pulled on my shoes with the intention of putting them into the ass of whoever had dared to interrupt my dreams at a time when even the most enthusiastic hookers in the neighborhood were sound asleep. I opened the door, and as if it were the beginning of a horrible nightmare, I found myself face-to-face with Montegón's haggard mug.

"What are you doing here at this hour?" I asked him, trying to lean away from his wine-fouled breath.

"I came to tell you that I followed the guy in the truck and managed to have a few words with him," responded Montegón as he entered the apartment. "His name is Belfor Méndez and it wasn't hard to get him to sing."

Montegón moved toward the seat in front of my desk and let himself fall into it with all the grace of a sack of potatoes.

"You got something to drink?" he asked, gazing around the office. "I need a little something to keep me afloat."

I got the emergency bottle from the desk and served him two fingers of whiskey in a paper cup that Anselmo had left a few days ago. The whiskey had been between the Petit Larousse that ruled the chaos of the desk and an overgrown cactus, a gift from a client for services I didn't even remember providing.

"You're not going to join me?" he inquired once he had the cup in his hand.

"I never drink before breakfast," I responded, and after updating him on Bernales's intervention, I asked him to continue his report on Méndez.

"He worked for a while in the lumberyard, before they caught him taking merchandise. Sometime after that, one of his old bosses called him. Méndez thought they were giving him another chance, but the boss suggested that he get in touch with Gabriel Peña. That's how he started participating in the robberies, and until today he was happy to be a part of such an enthusiastic team of entrepreneurs. They had been stealing for more than a year and never saw their business threatened. In his confession, he mentioned Bulnes, who he knew was a big shot inside the lumberyard."

"That matches the story that Peña told the cops. The case will probably be closed when Bulnes takes responsibility. Nobody knows who they're working for, Montegón. None of us found the answers we were seeking, and the cops will be the only ones who benefit from our work."

"I wouldn't be so sure about that, Heredia. I asked Méndez about Carvilio. At first he denied knowing him, but after a few light touches he admitted he had heard of him. A few days ago, Peña told him that the big boss was upset about all the questions that Carvilio was asking in the lumberyard."

"Upset enough to order someone to shut him up?"

"I asked Méndez the same thing, but he couldn't really give me an answer. If you want, we can go talk with him. He's a little rat who likes to sing."

"What did you do to him?"

"I have him put away for safekeeping. Gagged and tied up tighter than a mummy in a pyramid."

"It would have been better to give him to the police."

"First I wanted to know what had happened to you during your visit to Ali Baba's lair."

"I suppose you're still entertaining ideas about the union?"

"Don't remind me. I'm afraid I'll be out of a job soon."

"Who hired you to investigate the lumberyard?"

"Solares, the CEO."

"At least you can tell him about catching the thieves."

"And after that, I'll be on the street," said Montegón.

"There will always be ways to fill the time."

"Do you need a partner?"

"I appreciate your help, but I don't think I could ever associate myself with someone like you."

"Do you think you're better than me?"

"No, but it's evident that we walk different paths."

"There's space in your office for another desk," said the detective. Standing, he asked, "Have you read all the books on your shelves, or are they just there for decoration?"

"I've read the majority of them."

"Why do you read so much?"

"To live, to dream, to know what kind of world I'm standing in."

"My father never let me have much contact with books," said Montegón, heading toward the door. "Even now, he says that an excess of books and jerking off softens the brain. What do you think?"

"There are those who think that such noble occupations strengthen the imagination."

"I'll tell my father that the next time I see him."

17

Despite my doubts and the extra pounds he carried on his back, my bet on Fontanero was a good one. Before coming around the last turn, the horse was in fourth, and as he entered the homestretch he pulled ahead to easily beat his rivals. It had been the last race of the program, and at that point in the day the air in the building was a thick mass of sweat, cigarette smoke, and alcoholic vapor. The bettors around me were like characters in a daily tragedy. Tired, poorly dressed, and with the unmistakable stigma of failure in their eyes. Mixed among them were the waifs selling cigarettes and the old harlots trying to flatter and flirt with the few winners.

Anselmo was beside me, his gaze fixed on the screen where Fontanero's victory was being replayed. I showed him my tickets with the delight of a young kid who'd just kissed a woman for the first time, and the newsstand owner gave me a disparaging grimace, as if winning a bet that increased my money by a factor of fifteen was something that could be done any day.

"What's up, Anselmo? Did you play the horse I told you to?"

"Sorry. I didn't even bet on him to place. Your hunches are about as trustworthy as a politician's smile."

"And what about friendship?"

"Friendship is one thing and betting is another, man."

"So now what?" I asked.

"The laws of betting have no gray areas. He who wins buys the bottle."

"You're getting too sly for your own good!"

"Is it my fault that you never thread the needle? Is it my fault that your hunches always come together late in the afternoon?"

"It's not the money we didn't win that hurts as much as the lack of confidence."

"Enough drama, man. Shakespeare wrote the only ones worth reading."

"Promise me that you'll bet on my next hunch."

"I promise," muttered Anselmo without much conviction.

We left the building and went to the Central bar, where a dozen patrons were lined up two deep watching a soccer game. We drank the first glass in honor of Fontanero, and to accompany the next one we ordered some steak sandwiches that brought our souls back to our bodies. Later, when some of the Universidad de Chile fans celebrated a Marcelo Salas goal, I paid the bill and we left to walk around the neighborhood with the lazy steps of retired men. Paseo Puente put on its usual noisy show of singers and street vendors. A woman with long braids read tarot cards, and two boys dressed up like cowboys sang a *ranchera* beneath the attentive gaze of a rather unsavory man who must have been their father. We grabbed one last drink at the Marco Polo before we separated in front of the central post office. I watched the newsstand owner head down the Calle Catedral, and I lit a cigarette that accompanied me until I arrived at the doorway of my building. Feliz Domingo saw me come in and made a point of passing me the three letters that were sleeping in my pigeonhole.

"I hope they contain good news, Mr. Heredia," said the doorman without taking his eyes off the envelopes.

"I don't have that much hope. I'll be happy if they're not late bills."

"Today I had to work the night shift," noted Feliz Domingo sadly. "I prefer to be here in the morning or the afternoon. The neighborhood is dangerous at night."

"Not any more than going into a bank during daylight."

"The things you say, Mr. Heredia."

"You've never been tempted to peek into any of the cabarets in the neighborhood?"

"Never! You shouldn't open the doors of sin."

"What monastery did they educate you in, Feliz Domingo?"

"Don't blaspheme, Mr. Heredia."

"Did anyone come to see me?" I asked, to change the subject.

"Nobody. But you're starting to sound like your neighbor Mr. Hernández. Every time he comes in he asks the same question."

"And why is that special?"

"I get the impression that you're both afraid of finding an unpleasant surprise."

"Since when do you spend time looking beneath the surface?"

"Don't get mad, Mr. Heredia. It's just an observation."

"I'm not mad, Feliz Domingo. But be careful about sniffing around more than you should. There are people who don't take it so well."

I opened one of the windows of my apartment and observed the nighttime city that, in the light of the moon, had the apparent calm of a lake. The sneaky old lady didn't fool me, though. I knew about the misery and the secrets crouching in the corners, the pain nesting beneath the bridges, the humidity of the tenements, the drunk resignation of those who slept on the sidewalks, the sadness of the streetwalkers by the gates, and the cry of the brat who panhandled on the last bus to nowhere. I knew the city and I could move through her however I wanted, with no limits besides tiredness or the desire to stop for a drink. I looked toward the horizon and asked myself if the killers I was seeking were in some corner of that dark mass. Maybe I should have rubbed a rabbit's foot or asked a fashionable saint for help. My work over the last few days had the scent of a fiasco, with no hint of a sudden change in fortune. I threw my misgivings out the window, and accompanied by the quiet steps of Simenon, I went to the bedroom. I got into bed, turned on the radio, and closed my eyes.

Next morning, I woke to the sound of the weather forecast. I shut off the radio, and as I was getting into the shower, I heard the maddening clang of the telephone. I shut off the water and ran naked into the office, where Simenon was sleeping on top of a pile of racing programs. I picked up the phone; it was Cotapos, the lawyer. He had the information that I had sought from his collaborators. I agreed to pass by his office before noon and we hung up. I went back to the bathroom and immersed myself in the water again. For an instant I had the sensation of running on the bank of a river.

Cotapos's office was small and dark. Its only window looked out on an interior patio surrounded by gray buildings. On the walls hung three reproductions of Goya paintings and two university diplomas that indicated specializations in penal and labor law.

"How's the investigation coming along?" he asked, pointing toward a seat beside his desk.

"I haven't found anything important. Questions, inconclusive answers, thefts of merchandise, suspects that last as long as a cascade of bubbles."

"Don't get too down, because I have some news that should bring back your optimism. Searching for a link between Reyes and Suazo brought us something concrete. My colleagues looked through the cases that we're preparing, and in one of them, both men are mentioned as witnesses."

"What's the story?" I asked, interested.

"It's a lawsuit against Braulio Serrano, who was identified as a torturer at Villa Grimaldi. Does that name mean anything to you?"

"First time I've heard it. Who is he? Where can I find him?"

"In 1973 he was a lieutenant in the army. His name is mentioned in a number of cases, and it's known that in addition to his stint at Villa Grimaldi, he was assigned to the Cuatro Álamos prisoner camp. At the beginning of the 1980s he was placed in a regiment in the north of the country and came back to Santiago in March 1985. The next month he died in a car accident."

"Sounds like he's a road that leads to nowhere," I interrupted the lawyer.

"Hold your judgment for a bit, Heredia." He closed the folder on his desk. "In the lawsuit against Serrano there are two others accused. Toro Palacios and someone named Fullerton. What's more, there are witnesses able to corroborate that those mentioned belonged to the detachment at Villa Grimaldi and that they participated in criminal actions. The three officers in the case are named Víctor Moltisanti, Vicente Tapia, and Danilo Uribe. All three of them are retired military officers and were agents of DINA and CNI, the intelligence agencies at the time."

"Except for Toro, this is the first time I've heard those names."

"The names of intelligence officers were always protected, and many of the guards used false names. However, to build a better case and solicit concrete action from the tribunal, we gave the court information on where to find the officers. We know where to find Moltisanti, Tapia, and Uribe, and I think one of them might be able to locate Toro."

"Can I have access to that information?"

"It was hard for us to get it, but as of three months ago the subjects were located at the addresses indicated in the brief. The army never wanted to cooperate, but we have the help of a functionary in the Ministry of Defense who allowed us to access classified information.

After that we looked for the officers who were still alive and, in the cases of Uribe and Tapia, found them through their places of work."

"I see that you've gone to great pains."

"It hasn't been an easy or a pleasant job. We've fought against lies and the desire of the victimizers to remain anonymous."

"What's the status of the case that Reyes and Suazo are mentioned in?"

"Stalled without the possibility of being reopened. Before Reyes's death, I was hopeful that he would be able to give us the proof we needed to have them arrested. Germán had compiled quite a lot of information about the officers. The last time I talked with him, he assured me that he was on the verge of confirming a few key pieces of information. Unfortunately, I never found out what they were."

"He was investigating Toro Palacios."

"I know that, but I don't know what he was able to find out. Toro is an enigma. He is mentioned in a number of survivors' testimonies, but we've never been able to track him down."

"Apart from you and Terán, did anyone else know about Reyes's work?"

"Not that I know of. Germán was very private with his investigations."

"I feel like I have good cards in my hands, but I don't know how to play them."

"We're interested in finding Toro. I think it is possible that the ex-soldiers I mentioned before know where to find him."

"What makes you think they'll cooperate? They're not lowlife thugs that can just be smacked against a wall. I also assume that they won't want to see themselves involved in something that reminds them of their past."

"You don't lose anything by trying."

"My neck and my head."

"I doubt that bothers you, Heredia. I had you checked out and I know you're a hard nut to crack. You accepted the investigation of

Reyes's death, knocked on Terán's door, and then asked me to check the files that I keep in my office. All of that shows me that you know how to do your job."

"If I end up with a bullet in my brain, don't forget to bring flowers to my grave."

"Are you scared?"

"Sufficiently scared to keep my eyes open and my back against a wall. But what really worries me is that I don't run as fast as I did thirty years ago, when I set up my office and a calendar that seemed like it had an infinite number of pages in it."

18

Despite the public rites and the well-intended declarations, the past kept emerging through fissures in a society accustomed to appearances, elaborate decoration, and shady deals in back rooms. Cotapos's brief was on the table. I reread the names in it and then picked up the phone. Bernales was still in his office, revising the reports of the detectives working under him. I asked him about Bulnes, and he told me that the executive had still not confessed to his role in the robberies at the León Lumberyard.

"It won't be long before the other shoe drops," he sighed. "His accomplices' confessions don't leave him much room to maneuver. In the meantime, we're still looking for the driver of the truck that was used in the robbery."

"You still haven't found him?" I asked, remembering my conversation with Montegón.

"He either ran away from Santiago or got swallowed by the earth."

For an instant I thought about mentioning Montegón, but I decided to omit his name until I talked with him again.

"Did you find any information on Zuñeda?" I asked.

"I've been too busy, Heredia. I'm not complaining, but sometimes I'd like to be in your shoes and not have to answer to a boss."

"It's an unlucky day for you, then, Bernales. I want to add a few more names to my request: Vicente Tapia, Danilo Uribe, and Víctor Moltisanti."

"Who are they?"

"Former military intelligence."

"We don't have any information on that in my unit. I'd have to ask my colleagues in the Human Rights and Special Investigations Department."

"You can try. There's nothing to lose by asking, Bernales."

"Only that they tell me to go to hell or complain to my superiors that I'm asking for information that's above my pay grade."

For a few minutes, I tried to convince him to help me out, but when I sensed that the wall wasn't getting any softer, I said goodbye without so much as a *talk to you later*.

I picked up Cotapos's brief from my desk, but dropped it in front of Simenon with a bit of irritation after trying to read it for a few minutes. The cat sniffed the paper and, without showing much interest in its content, brushed it to the side.

"You should be in the street, tracking down these names," he said as his eyes followed a fly orbiting above my head.

"I don't want to deal with more questions today."

"What do you want? Do you think these guys are going to knock on your door or move into the building so you don't have to bust your ass?"

"Sure, genius. Which of the three names should we start with?"

"Vicente Tapia, the real-estate broker. Maybe he'll offer you an apartment where the water faucets work."

"Any reason for starting with Tapia?"

"The real-estate business is probably doing well, and I doubt he wants you to throw a wrench in it. That could help to put some pressure on him."

"Good idea. Sometimes you manage to do justice to your reputation as a smart feline."

"If you would listen to me once in a while you'd have fewer problems."

Cotapos's brief indicated that Vicente Tapia was the owner of a property brokerage located on Calle Suecia. I drove there, and after ascending fifteen floors in a mirror-lined elevator, I found myself in front of a secretary who wasted no time informing me that Tapia was out of the office supervising sales of recently built townhomes in Peñalolén. Arriving at the new address took an hour of driving through traffic lights in disrepair and detours for construction on the highway that circled the city, which would soon require a toll for entry. Everything had become a business opportunity, thanks to the geniuses who imposed free-market principles on our economy—highways, cemeteries, hospitals, the use of plazas, the light of the moon, and the healthy ocean air. *One day they'll charge me to pass through the door of the office where I live,* I thought as I stomped on the accelerator, transforming my discontent into velocity.

The development was on the brink of a desolate hillside. The townhouses were big, surrounded by grass and rosebushes, hydrangeas, and geraniums, my favorite flower. The homes were attractive, but it only took a glance at the price to know that I could never even afford one of the roof tiles. I parked beside the sales office. As soon as I walked in, I was confronted by a redhead with the most beautiful blue eyes I had seen in years. Warm blue eyes that gazed at me from behind a desk full of catalogs and brochures. I asked for Tapia, and she told me that he was showing a house to two clients.

"Will he be long?" I inquired.

"That depends on the clients' interest," responded the redhead. After evaluating the wrinkles in my shirt with a certain distaste, she asked if I was looking for work.

"No. I have a bit of business to discuss with him," I answered.

"If you'd like a price, you can talk with me."

"Do I look like I can buy one of these houses? I know appearances can sometimes be deceiving, but it's difficult to fake the size of the wallet."

"In that case, there's not much I can do for you."

"Can you tell me where to find Mr. Tapia?"

"House H. Take the main road into the development and drive toward the twin palms. Turn right and keep going until you get to the gated house. You should see Mr. Tapia's green truck parked in front of it."

"Thank you. If I were twenty years younger, I'd ask you out to dinner."

"There are women who like older men."

"Are you saying I've got a chance?"

"None. I'm not one of them."

According to the information in Cotapos's brief, Vicente Tapia was sixty-one years old, with a good amount of those years spent in the army. He started as a cadet and was then moved around until his early retirement in 1990. His tour through the military intelligence services was registered between 1974 and 1982. After that he had been sent to Ecuador as a military attaché, and upon returning to Chile four years later, he was placed in the enlisted men's academy as an instructor. With his background in mind, I moved toward my encounter with the ex-soldier. The front door to house H was unlocked, and I only needed to push on it lightly to enter a room that was big enough to accommodate four Ping-Pong tables. In the rear of the space was a window that looked out on the mountains. I took a few steps, appreciating the finish of the floor, and went toward the door that opened to the kitchen. I heard voices coming from another part of the house, and upon returning to the front room I saw a couple, followed by a tall, thin man whose gray hair was cut severely.

"Take a walk around the house and we'll talk," the tall man told me with studied friendliness.

I went over to the window and from there observed the couple. The woman was blonde, about thirty years old, and a bit fleshy. Her husband looked older. He was dark and short, and his potbelly pushed out from under the belt that was trying to squeeze it in. The man wanted to ask questions, but the woman drowned him out with hers. Tapia responded patiently, giving precise details about the features of the house. I tried to imagine the real-estate broker wearing a military uniform and couldn't quite do it. Fifteen minutes later, I saw him watch the couple as they walked away from the house and climbed into a car parked in front of his green truck.

"Sale didn't go through?" I asked, moving a few steps away from the window.

"They'll be back. The woman loves the house, and that matters more than the husband's doubts. I've been in this business a long time and I know how people think," replied Tapia. He came to my side and asked, "So are you interested in the house too? We've got two that are the same style and size."

"I like the house, but I'd have to live twice to buy it."

"We've got other developments with more economical townhomes," added Tapia, heading toward the door. "The manager in the sales office can give you more information and answer any questions you might have."

"I don't want a house, Mr. Tapia. I'm looking for Toro and Fullerton, your old brothers in arms."

Tapia's look transformed into a stiletto that could puncture the walls around us, and I realized pretty quickly that if the soldier decided to resort to violence, I didn't have much chance of coming out alive.

"If you don't know the way, I'll call my guards and they'll take you to the exit," said Tapia, opening the door and looking outside.

"Save your threats. I only want to talk to you."

"I don't know the people you mentioned," he breathed, not quite recovering the pleasant tone he had used with the couple.

"Think about the clients your office will lose if it's covered with signs denouncing your time at Villa Grimaldi. Or what your contractors will say when they know the crimes that you are implicated in."

"Who are you to threaten me?"

"Someone who's playing with a few aces up his sleeve."

"Who are you?" Tapia asked again, this time with a tone of authority.

"My name is Heredia, and I'm a detective interested in your memories."

"Police?"

"I work for myself," I answered while Tapia was taking a cell phone out of his jacket. "And leave your guards alone. You can't beat me and make me disappear like in the old days. I have friends who know where I am and who I'm with."

"I will tell you very clearly and briefly. I worked in intelligence, but I never had anything to do with torture," said Tapia.

"Your name appears in the testimony of many prisoners who were in Villa Grimaldi."

"My hands are clean."

"No one who has been in hell can say they don't know about fire."

"My work consisted of analyzing information related to the unions and professional associations. I read the information given to me by operative units and prepared reports that were put into the hands of my superiors."

"You were never bothered by how they got the information?"

"We were at war. We had to obey orders and do our jobs."

"I've listened to that speech a lot of times and it always has the same nauseating sound of cowardice. Toro and Fullerton. I want to know about them. The rest, as far as I'm concerned, is between you and your conscience."

Tapia closed the door of the house and took a few steps into the room. I lit a cigarette and let him meditate for a few seconds. Maybe he had told the truth, maybe not, but the past clearly made him uncomfortable. I moved close to the window and looked at the clouds that covered part of the mountains. The snow kept coming down near the peaks, and for a moment I saw myself lost in the cold, waiting for the sun to melt the ice and show the path that led back to the city.

"Our work was compartmentalized," I heard Tapia say. "Each unit did its job and knew nothing of what the others were doing. Each group was assigned an objective. The political parties, the unions, the universities, public service, the church, neighborhood groups, sporting clubs, artists' and writers' societies. All the fronts you can imagine that had any impact on political affairs. Each group had analysts and operatives. Coordinating the groups was the responsibility of our superiors."

"Where are you going with this explanation?" I asked, interrupting the ex-soldier's speech.

"Toro was the boss of a different group than mine. They spoke of him with admiration. He directed an operative group that was credited with eliminating various cells of the Communist Party and the Revolutionary Left Movement. He had another last name, but I never knew what it was. We saw each other a few times after I left the intelligence services, and then I never heard from him again. I imagine he's still alive, but I have no idea where he is."

"And Fullerton?"

"I heard people talk about him, but I never saw him. He must have been an assistant to one of the higher-ranking bosses who sometimes came by the villa. That's all I know. I was a small cog in the machine—I received orders and obeyed them. I know that more than one person was fired from their job or jailed because of me, but I never tortured anybody."

"Maybe you just didn't have the opportunity. Or maybe you couldn't avoid the occasional death, pressuring, or detention. You and the people you worked with were happy with what was going on. You celebrated your crimes and believed you were heroes of a war that only took place in your imaginations."

"Every war leaves victims, among the victors and the defeated. That war belongs to the past. Today, I just want to live in peace. I have a wife, kids, and a good job. I'm not remotely interested in what's going on in the courts, unlike some of my old comrades."

"You're still alive, while many of those you were fighting are dead."

"This conversation is useless. We'll never agree."

"Definitely not. Agreements are almost always used to cover the truth," I said, and as I rubbed out the cigarette on the immaculate floor, I added, "If I discover that you've lied to me, I'm going to disturb the peace you so cherish."

"In that case, unless you decide to buy one of my houses, we aren't likely to see each other again."

On the way back to my office, I realized I should have asked Tapia about the other names in Cotapos's brief. Then I told myself that it would have been a mistake, because if Tapia knew them, he would probably alert them about the private detective out there digging through their past.

An hour later I was back in my territory in downtown Santiago. I left my car in the parking lot and walked to the City with the intention of downing a drink and burning the sour taste of the conversation with Vicente Tapia out of my mouth.

I didn't see anyone familiar in the bar. I asked for the Writer, and one of the waiters told me that he had passed by at noon, accompanied by a poet from Puerto Peregrino who drank beer with enthusiasm. I looked for an unoccupied table, ordered my customary vodka, and for the first time all day long I felt like things around me made sense.

I left the bar when the shadows began their play with the last of the light. The vodka spread through my body, and a certain absurd optimism brought a smile to my lips. I had gotten Tapia to admit to his past and to the existence of Toro and Fullerton. Two phantoms who could be moving around the streets of Santiago, fooling people into believing they were honorable citizens. I let the tired air of the night carry me away and walked toward Paseo Puente until I got to the Calle Aillavilú. I watched a couple of customers stumble out of La Piojera and I kept walking, uninterested in the invitations to enter the cabarets. Anselmo's kiosk was closed and a dog was circling around the outside of it, trying to choose the best side to piss on.

Feliz Domingo stopped me as I was about to get in the elevator. He seemed agitated, and his words took longer than usual to transform themselves into understandable sounds.

"There are situations that I frankly can't accept, Mr. Heredia," he said nervously, like a dry leaf that can feel the wind coming.

"What are you talking about, Feliz?"

"Félix with an *x*," spat back the doorman, and after checking that the knot in his tie was still in place, he said, "It's one of your friends. He came, asked for you, and when I said you weren't here, he insisted on waiting in your office."

"What's so bad about that? My office door is usually open, and so far no thief has shown interest in stealing my books. Which doesn't surprise me—most people value books less than the paper they're printed on. We live in a country where people don't understand what they read and think that Don Quijote is the name of a chain of pizzerias."

"The problem is that I tried to keep your friend out."

"And?"

"He pulled a revolver from his jacket and pointed it at my throat."

"And that probably made you nervous."

"Nervous doesn't describe it. I soiled my underwear."

"So what's the problem? You can change them and begin life again."

"You'll have to forgive me, but I'm going to have to report this to the building administrator."

"That's your thing, Feliz. It's been years since I cared about the administrator."

"Really?" asked the doorman, and after thinking about my answer, added, "If you ask your friend to apologize, I could forget about talking to the administrator."

"That sounds like a deal. But you still haven't told me which friend it was who gave you a hard time."

"His name is Atilio Montegón, and he's been sitting outside your office for more than an hour. He's chain-smoking and drinking from a bottle in his jacket."

"I'll talk with him, Feliz Domingo."

"Thank you, Mr. Heredia. But remember, I'm Félix with an *x*."

"X as in Xammar and Xipe Totec."

"Who are they?" asked the doorman.

"Luis Fabio Xammar, the Peruvian poet who lived during the first half of the last century, and Xipe Totec, the Aztec god of corn, spring, and sacrifice."

Montegón was still sitting by the door. His eyes were closed and the soft snore of an infant bloomed from his chest. An empty bottle of pisco hung from his right hand. I gave him a soft kick in the ass and watched him wake up with alarm, like a rabbit caught by a spotlight in the middle of the night.

"Get up!" I ordered. "I can give you a coffee and a good splash of water to wake you."

"I fell asleep waiting for you," said Montegón as he leaned against the wall and tried to find his feet.

I opened the door and went into my office. The detective followed. I pointed toward a chair, then went to the kitchen and put the teakettle on. Waiting for the water to boil, I heard noise from the bathroom and figured Montegón had decided to take my advice. When I eventually returned to my office, I found him with his hair freshly combed. I put the coffee down beside him and took a seat.

"What did you do with the truck driver?" I asked as I lit a cigarette. "As of this morning, the cops were still looking for him."

"I wanted to talk to you about that," said Montegón. "I freed him, but before I did I decided to have another conversation with him. It was a good decision, because I asked him about Carvilio again, and he said he'd heard that Bulnes wanted to hire some guy named Chito to teach him a lesson."

"What the hell is a Chito?"

"I'm guessing he's one of those guys who would kill his own mother for a few coins. At least, that's the impression the driver got from Bulnes."

"Do you believe him?"

"I know where and how to hit people."

"Where did you let him go?"

"I didn't let him go. I left him tied to a seat and then called the cops. Right about now he should be enjoying their hospitality."

"Did he say where we could find this Chito guy?"

"Bulnes is the only one who can give us that information."

"Unfortunately, the police have him in custody."

"Not anymore, Heredia. They set him free on bond," said Montegón, and after drinking a sip of coffee, he added, "It's good for us that he's cut loose. It means we can talk to him."

"What are you thinking?"

"Paying him a visit. He probably doesn't want to be linked to Carvilio's death."

"I doubt Bulnes is in the mood to receive visitors. He's probably got company already."

"He's got to be alone at some point."

"Why are you so interested in him?" I asked, suspicious.

"Have you forgotten what I told you the other day? I'm trying to show you that I'm more than just a union snoop."

19

I woke up to the singing of the birds that clung to the railing of the tiny balcony in front of my bedroom window. At first I thought it was the tail end of some indecipherable dream, but I listened harder and confirmed that the sound was as real as the glass of water on the nightstand, beside the ceramic ashtray. It was five in the morning, and in an hour most of the trilling would be drowned out by the noises of the neighborhood. Buses, cars, shouts, steps, the city with its entrails open, bleeding out, like an animal left to die by the side of the road. I closed my eyes and remembered that Montegón had slept in the office, under three blankets and the annoyed watch of Simenon, who had not easily accepted the presence of the uninvited guest. I got up and silently went to the corner where Montegón was still out cold. I went back to bed and grabbed a Mankell novel that was waiting its turn to be read. I got wrapped up in it and only put the book down when I heard Montegón moving around the office.

Later, watching him dump five spoons of sugar in his breakfast coffee, I asked him, "What's the plan?"

"Get Bulnes to invite us into his house or wait for him to come out."

"I doubt he'll open his door to us."

"You need more optimism, Heredia. And food in your cupboard."

Our attempts to talk with Bulnes were useless. Neither Montegón pretending to be a journalist, nor I with my fake police credentials, managed to get farther than the iron gate that blocked access to the house. We were equally unsuccessful trying to reach him by phone. The end result was a wasted morning spent watching the corner near his house. He didn't come out, nor did we see anyone enter. Around noon, I told Montegón that it was time to throw in the towel. He continued to watch the place, but I wished him good luck and said goodbye.

I walked to the nearest bus stop and got on a bus that took me to where Danilo Uribe worked. During the trip, I reread Cotapos's brief. The information on Uribe was very similar to that on Vicente Tapia. He was sixty-one years old, had served in the intelligence services between 1975 and 1984, and had retired in 1991 after a posting in the north of the country. He had been married twice and had two children from his first marriage. Since his retirement from the army, he had worked as the chief of security at the Barrio Alto mall.

Wanting to meet with Uribe as soon as possible, I walked quickly through the corridors of the temple of the God of Consumption and resisted being tempted by the songs of the provocatively dressed sirens who continually popped out of the stores and the food court, which stank of fried chicken, hamburgers, and Chinese food. Eventually, like Ulysses nearing the coast of Ithaca, I took a breath of relief as I descended to the basement where the security office was.

A thin guy with a close-shaved mustache and a high-and-tight haircut intercepted me as soon as I entered the office. I gave him my name and asked for Danilo Uribe.

"What do you need him for?" he asked with the arrogance of a soldier.

"I'm with the Investigative Police," I responded, putting my fake police ID an inch from his nose. "I'm trying to catch a group of shoplifters operating in the mall."

The guard opened the door to the interior office, went in, and after a few minutes told me that his boss would receive me. Uribe was a thick man of medium height. A purple stain stood out on his right cheek and extended to the base of his nose. He was dressed in a black suit with a lapel pin from a veterans' group, and he had gold rings on both hands. He observed me with his blue eyes, and I felt like I was in front of a lynx about to tear its prey apart. I resisted his stare and greeted him, trying to make my voice sound sure and convincing.

"Cajales, my assistant, says that you are from the Investigative Police," he said. "Can you show me your credential?"

The question took me by surprise, but I put the ID on Uribe's desk. He took it and studied it for a couple of seconds.

"Your ID is fake and you don't look like a cop," he said, handing it back to me. "Who are you and what do you want?"

"I'm trying to find some friends of yours," I said. "Fullerton and Javier Toro, who you knew at Villa Grimaldi."

"Who are you?" he asked again, standing and taking a menacing step in my direction.

"Someone who has been paid to find your friends."

"What do you want them for?"

"Your friends have some debts to pay with the law."

"You must work for those scumbags who keep making noise about human rights. This isn't the first time I've dealt with these questions. You're wasting your time with me. I don't rat on my own, not like some people have been doing."

"So you're saying you know Fullerton and Toro."

"I didn't say that. Even if I knew them, you can bet I wouldn't tell you."

"In case you haven't heard, the time when people like you could do and undo things has passed," I said, containing my rage.

"Sooner or later they'll ask the soldiers to intervene again. Then we'll finish the work that's still left and repay the people who turned their back on my general."

"Toro was one of those in charge of the operatives at Villa Grimaldi," I said, interrupting the officer. "You were there, so you must know him."

"I don't know who you're talking about," said Uribe in a low voice. He sat on the edge of his desk and added, "I can only tell you that it wasn't easy being part of the brigades that operated in Villa Grimaldi. You had to show that you had the balls to fight against the Communist plague. Our fellow soldiers envied us. We were the ones chosen to confront the enemy on the front lines. I've always been proud of that, and I'm not going to hide it in front of a stranger."

"If you don't want to talk to me, maybe you'd like to talk to the police. Have you heard about the Human Rights and Special Investigations Department of the Investigative Police? I have a friend there who would be very interested in talking to you."

"Don't threaten me!" thundered Uribe, and before I could do anything to stop him, he pressed a button on the side of his desk.

I heard some steps behind me almost immediately and saw Cajales come in accompanied by two angry-faced gorillas.

"Get this intruder out of here and make sure he doesn't want to come back," Uribe ordered them.

Cajales and one of the men grabbed me by the arms, and the third man gave me a hard punch below the belt. The pain made me fall to my knees. I couldn't stop them from dragging me out of the office. I felt a punch to my back and felt myself being pulled through a hallway that eventually emptied into a far corner of the mall parking garage. I tried to resist, but didn't manage to improve my situation. They punched me in the ribs. I fell to the ground, where they kicked me a few times. They lifted me to my feet and made me walk toward the exit. The daylight blinded me and I couldn't see my surroundings. I felt them picking me up and dropping me into a dumpster. The smells of pizza crust and cigarette butts filtered into my nose. I tried to shout but only managed to swallow a bit of garbage. Then I heard the steps of the guards receding. I closed my eyes and tried not to think about the pain.

A few minutes went by before I felt someone tipping the container. I fell to the ground, and when I could open my eyes, I saw a man in blue overalls looking at me with curiosity and compassion.

"Did they catch you stealing?" he asked. I didn't know what to tell him. The man pulled me by the armpits until I was lying beneath the shade of a tree. He took a plastic bottle out of his overalls and had me drink a sip of water that mixed with the blood flowing from my upper lip.

"It doesn't look like you have any broken bones. I've seen others come out worse," he sympathized.

I tipped the bottle back and drank from it until it was empty.

"Can you get onto your feet?" asked the stranger.

"Get me some more water and I'll try," I murmured.

The man disappeared and came back shortly with the bottle filled again. I wet my face and drank another sip of water before I felt like the pieces of my head were returning to their usual places.

"Who are you?" I asked the man.

"I'm in charge of emptying the garbage containers. I saw when they took you out of the building. It's not easy to steal in that mall."

"I'm not a thief. I just went in the wrong office."

"Can I do anything for you?" he inquired without giving much credence to my answer. "I'd like to stay with you a while longer, but my supervisor will start checking to see if I'm working."

"Find me a taxi driver," I answered, the taste of blood in my mouth. "One who drives fast and doesn't ask questions."

"Do you want me to call a doctor?" Anselmo asked for the fifth or sixth time after he had seen me roll out of the taxi and stumble toward the door of my building.

"Just fill the tub up with hot water."

Anselmo followed my instructions, and a few minutes later I dipped my bruised humanity into the water. The heat seemed to make the pain worse for an instant, but it wasn't long before I began to feel its healing caress. I had bruises on my ribs and my back, cuts on both lips, and a persistent pain in my testicles.

"Do you feel better?"

"With a few hours of sleep, I should be back to normal."

"Do you need anything else?"

"I'd feel better with a dose of my favorite medicine."

"I'd have to go to the emergency liquor store."

"What's stopping you?"

Anselmo left the bathroom, and fifteen minutes later he came back with a glass in which he had poured a miserable quantity of Jack Daniel's.

"They only had the miniature bottles," he said, somewhat ashamed.

"Better than nothing, Anselmo. We're getting close to Christmas, and Santa Claus will probably bring me a more reasonably sized bottle."

"Now are you going to tell me what happened?"

"I ran into a guy who doesn't like questions and has a couple of King Kong clones to follow his orders."

"Sounds like the deaf lion that eats the violinist."

"What lion and what violinist?"

"From the joke, man. A violinist goes into the jungle and trains two lions with his melodies. The beasts stop roaring to hear the music, and everything's going fine until a deaf lion comes along and eats the poor fellow."

"That joke is older than black thread, Anselmo."

"I'm just trying to lift your spirits, man."

"My spirits weren't what got hit," I said, and after taking a sip of liquor, I asked, "Do you really want me to tell you what happened at the mall?"

Anselmo helped me to the bedroom and left me to get comfortable on the bed. Before he returned to his kiosk, I asked him to put Mahler's Fourth Symphony on the tape player. Simenon jumped onto the bed, and with him in my arms I let the exhaustion take over. I fell asleep, and in my dream I found myself lost amid stairways and tunnels that didn't go anywhere. It was cold, and the faraway sound of dripping broke the silence. The ringing of a bell woke me up, and I discovered that night had crept into the apartment. The bell rang again before I realized that the noise was coming from the telephone on the nightstand. I picked up the receiver; a voice said my name.

"Griseta?" I asked with a frog in my throat.

"What's going on, Heredia? Are you OK?" She sounded worried.

"I fell asleep. I was tired and lay down for a while."

"Did you have too much to drink?"

"One or two," I answered, determined to not mention my excursion to the mall. "I miss you. I'd like to see you."

"Are you sure you're OK, Heredia? You've only sounded like this a couple of times, and I remember the shape you were in."

"Even the thickest skin gets softer as the years go by."

"Don't lie to me. Something's up with you—"

"How's your work going?" I interrupted.

"Don't change the subject."

"How's your work going?" I insisted, trying to put a bit more energy into my voice.

"I've been in Achao since yesterday. I spent a good part of the day interviewing women from the town. I'm at a motel right now. I'll be here a few nights. I can see the little fishing boats pushing off into the sea. You'd love this place."

"Someday we can go back to Chiloé together. We can go to San José de Tranqui, that little island where years ago I tried to track down that fellow who was running away from that CIA operative, Soul's Eye."

"I keep thinking there's something wrong with you," said Griseta.

"The investigation is still stalled, and I'm beginning to doubt that I'll reach the end of the rainbow."

"That's it?"

"I've also been thinking about the future."

"Since when do you worry about the future?"

"If I'm lucky I'll live twenty more years or so, and I've been asking myself if I can do something else with those years or if I should keep watching the pages on the calendar turn, consumed with enigmas. I'm tired of staring at the stains on my desk as I wait for clients and the clock keeps ticking. I'm tired of so many miserable people. Tired of forcing myself to get my hopes up and dragging my body around, when I'm not as spry as I used to be. There are days when my heart falls to pieces and I can't stand seeing my face in the mirror."

"I think you need a soft touch, or maybe someone to pull you by the ears."

"I miss you. I wish you were here with me."

"That's the second time you've said that in the last few minutes. Why won't you tell me what's going on?"

"Send me a kiss and tell me about what you see through your window."

I rested my head on the pillow and watched Simenon dozing at the foot of the bed for a moment. I tried to get up, but the pain forced me to stay put. I went back to sleep trying to imagine the landscape that Griseta had described to me, and the next morning I woke to Anselmo's voice. It seemed like he must have been there for a while. I moved slowly in the bed, and the pain wasn't as bad as it had been the night before.

"What time is it?" I croaked.

"Time to eat breakfast, have lunch, and get ready for an afternoon snack. It's going to be five o'clock soon. If it weren't for your snoring,

I'd think you belonged in a graveyard. Apart from the pain, it seems like you were running low on sleep."

"You should have woken me up, Anselmo."

"What for? There's no line of clients waiting outside your door."

"I wasn't thinking about new clients."

"Are you thinking about going back to the mall?"

"Not right now. One beating in a week is enough."

"That Bernales cop came to see you a few times. I let him know about your trip to the mall, and he said he would come back to talk to you."

"Did he say what he wanted?"

"No. And I didn't ask. The truth is I didn't talk to him much. You know detectives give me a rash."

"Just like street cops, guards dressed in blue, and any other person who imposes the law through beatings."

"Don't mess around, man," said Anselmo, and after taking a few steps around the room, he added, "I boiled some water for coffee. Do you feel like getting up or should I bring it in here?"

Bernales came into the office as I was pouring my second cup of coffee. He looked tired, and without saying anything he sat down in front of my desk. Anselmo made some faces behind the policeman's back and took advantage of the door being open to duck out of the apartment.

"Anselmo has to take care of his kiosk," I said to Bernales.

"I get the sense that your friend doesn't like me too much."

"That can be fixed with a conversation." I drank some coffee and added, "You were here earlier."

"I came in the morning. And then at noon. What happened at the mall sounds pretty bad, Heredia. Are you going to make a report?"

"If I do, they'll probably accuse me of robbery or something worse."

"I don't agree, but I'm not going to waste time trying to convince you. I came to tell you that I didn't get anywhere with your requests. Tapia, Uribe, and Moltisanti, the ex-soldiers you asked me to check out, none of them are mentioned in the cases that the Human Rights and Special Investigations Department is investigating right now. As far as this Guillermo Zuñeda goes, everything points toward him being in the wind. In the 1970s, under Allende, he was processed for participating in a bombing of high-tension electric towers. Back then he belonged to Patria y Libertad, the ultraright group that worked to destabilize the Popular Unity government through acts of terrorism. His case got swept under the carpet after the military coup. Zuñeda went to law school at the Catholic University, and after 1973 he occupied a number of positions in the Ministry of the Interior. His last public appearance was in the 1990s, when he ran for mayor in a town in the south. He lost the election, and he's never appeared in public again. We only know that in 1996 he taught some classes at a private university."

"Do you know where to find him?"

"They've dug around and can't find him. The earth, as they say, must have swallowed him."

"Have they asked among his family and friends?"

"Yes, but it hasn't been easy. He doesn't seem to have any family, and the two or three friends they've found don't want anything to do with him. They also interviewed a public employee who knew him in the Ministry of the Interior, and he made it clear that Zuñeda was one of the civilians who profited from the military dictatorship. You know what I'm talking about—lawyers who gave legal cover for war crimes, journalists who invented lies, functionaries who lied under oath, pencil pushers who edited speeches, mediocre writers who sang the praises of the military in exchange for a prize or a diplomatic post."

"Thanks for the information, Bernales. At least we know what kind of guy Zuñeda is."

"I still haven't said what I came to tell you. The driver of the truck from the lumberyard robbery showed up. He told us a few things that incriminate Bulnes as the architect of the whole operation. He also told us that the day of the robbery, he was kidnapped by a stranger who kept him prisoner in a warehouse and beat him. The stranger claimed to be a cop and wanted information about the death of Carvilio, a guard at the lumberyard. Do you know anything about that?"

20

I looked out on the neighborhood from the office window for a long time, and then I took a hot shower that erased the last remnants of the beating from my body. After that I made breakfast and gave Simenon a portion of the cat food that Anselmo brought him once a week. Even though I didn't really feel like leaving the office, I snapped out of my funk and prepared to take a walk around the area, just to feel like I was still a part of the city that embraced me every day.

In the street, everything continued with the usual order, if the confusion of cars constantly trying to pass one another could be called that. People walked quickly, stepping around street vendors' wares and the extended hands of drunks asking for coins to buy the wine they needed to stop the shakes. I paused in the entrance of a Teletrak branch; inside, a dozen horse fans waited for the races to start.

My attention was drawn back out to the sidewalk, where a boy pulled on his mother's sleeve in front of a store that sold used toys and clothing. I came up beside him and saw him point at a discolored astronaut that was missing an arm. Beside the astronaut was a doll with matted hair and a bear with a split stomach. I remembered the kids I had shared my childhood with in the orphanage and felt rage bubbling up in my guts. The little boy was like so many children who have to learn to accept their lack of privilege. Kids condemned to misery, to run-down schools, and later to poorly paid jobs and a life without any meaning besides pure animal survival.

When the kid insisted that she buy him the astronaut, his mother pulled him by the sleeve to move him away from the window. I looked at the toy and read the price written on a bit of cardboard that the spaceman held up with his only arm. I took a thousand-peso bill out of my jacket and passed it to the boy. His eyes brightened, and without thinking about it twice he ran inside the store. His mother observed me for an instant and then lowered her gaze. When the son returned with his toy, I stared at the astronaut, and for a second I thought I saw it smile.

I continued on my way until I came to a diner, where I went in for a beer. The waiter didn't know anyone with the last name of Zuñeda and wasn't in the mood to answer any questions. He told me that he only filled glasses and didn't want trouble with his customers, much less with the owner of the place. I left my beer half-finished, didn't leave a tip, and walked out onto the street.

Over the next three hours, I went into seven used-clothing stores, two cabarets, and a half dozen bars. I talked with some Peruvians standing together beside the main cathedral and with an old woman selling dried fruits at a stand next to the old National Congress. None of them had the slightest idea who Zuñeda was, but in order to learn nothing new, I had to listen to an infinite number of stories from drunks, dancers, street hawkers, and immigrants, which tried my patience. In the end, tired and hungry, I went to the Fish King and asked for a conger-eel broth that helped me regain my faith in humanity.

As I was getting ready for a digestif, I saw Montegón come in. He scanned the tables and came closer when he recognized me. He was agitated and sweaty, as if he had just run a marathon. I offered him something to drink and he asked for a highball glass with white wine.

"Your friend from the newsstand told me I might find you here," the detective said. "Either he saw you come in or he knows your regular dives. I don't want you to think I'm following you."

"What's the hurry? Did you just invent gunpowder?"

"It was rough, but I managed to talk with that slippery Bulnes character," said Montegón after taking a sip of wine. "I tried to get him to let me into his house, but just like you I didn't get anywhere. I took a walk around his neighborhood and talked to a few people. There's never a lack of people paying attention to what goes on in their neighbors' houses, that is for sure. A woman walking her dog gave me the key to getting to him: on Tuesdays and Thursdays, Bulnes goes to a club near his house; he plays a game of tennis and then goes to the sauna for an hour. It's difficult to get in if you're not a member, but I managed to find a pair of overalls and pass for a utility worker. Once I was inside, things were easier. I waited for him to finish playing and then followed him into the sauna."

"Spare me the details, Montegón. What did you talk about with Bulnes?"

"He's not dumb. At first he threatened to have me kicked out, but then he thought better of it. I mentioned Carvilio and said the robbery charges could have a murder charge added to them. That changed his attitude. He said all he knew was that Carvilio had been up to something and that the paid thug had gone too far in his work. He offered me a decent amount of money for my silence, and when I told him I was just trying to find the killer, he decided to give me some information."

"I'm astounded, Montegón. I never would've imagined you could be so persuasive."

"A naked man thinks carefully about what he says. Especially when he's got a gun pointed at him. Bulnes told me about his lawyer friend who'd recommended hiring the thug, using some guy named Sacotto as a middleman. In order to protect his identity, Bulnes used a fake name when he called Sacotto."

"Who is Sacotto?"

"He's a well-known lowlife in El Bosque, it seems. He owns a bar that serves as a front for drug traffickers, fences, counterfeiters, and contract killers. They say that the cops protect him in exchange for money and information about the work of other criminals in the area."

"This guy's got some initiative! They should give him the Entrepreneur of the Year award."

"Bulnes said Sacotto recommended a guy named Chito as the best person to intimidate Carvilio. He also said he didn't know anything about Chito, because Sacotto arranged everything. That was all I could get out of him. Two members of the club came into the sauna and Bulnes started screaming that he was the victim of a robbery. Things went south from there. I managed to escape the sauna, but it wasn't easy getting out of the club with only a towel wrapped around my waist. I ended up jumping over a wall naked. Luckily, my car was nearby and I had a tracksuit in the trunk that I used to wear for jogging on weekends."

"By now, Bulnes has probably made his calls, and Sacotto probably knows what happened."

"I wouldn't bet on it. I think Bulnes is probably only interested in staying afloat and doesn't think we'll ever catch up with Sacotto. Besides, I don't have any way to check what he told me."

"We should talk with Sacotto."

"Before we put our hands on him, I want to know more about him. I don't think it's as easy as just showing up at his bar. Let me ask a few questions, and I'll let you know when we're ready to visit him."

I looked around awkwardly, not knowing what else to say. I waved to the waiter and told him to bring Montegón another glass of wine.

"What's wrong? Something bothering you?" asked the detective, trying to contain a smile.

"I owe you an apology. You did a good job."

"Does that mean we're friends now?"

"Everything in its time, Montegón. True friends aren't cooked in the first boil. They need time."

"Promise me you'll think about my proposal of a partnership."

"I will," I said grudgingly. "But don't get your hopes up."

When Montegón left the restaurant a bit later, I followed him out the door. I thought about taking up my investigations again, but my steps were growing heavy, and they led me to Anselmo's kiosk. The newsstand owner listened patiently as I told him about my long trip through the stores, cabarets, and bars of the neighborhood. We had a coffee from the noisy machine that he kept inside the kiosk, and I headed toward my building feeling a bit less downcast. I walked through the rooms of my apartment without focusing on anything specific. I leafed through books, glanced out the window at the neighborhood, played with Simenon, and finally decided to get back to work.

As I went down in the elevator, I reread Cotapos's brief. I still hadn't looked up Víctor Moltisanti, and nothing in the lawyer's notes led me to expect a different result from what I'd gotten from Uribe and Tapia. Moltisanti had retired from the army at the rank of colonel, and his service sheet indicated postings in Puerto Aysén, Copiapó, Rancagua, Puerto Natales, and a short time in the Directorate of National Intelligence. The brief didn't give his current occupation, but indicated that he was a regular at the Lo Curro Military Club, where he met with other retired officers.

The little bit of information that I had about this club came from a few articles in the press. I knew that it was housed in an imposing building originally intended as a home for the dictator and his porky wife. The community was disgusted when the amount of money used to construct the palace became public. At the end of the dictatorship, this, along with the imminent arrival of Patricio Aylwin, the new president, forced Pinochet to give up the house and transfer it to the army. After some time, the institution turned it into an ostentatious club for officers. I remembered reading a report on it that described the mansion. Gardens, tennis courts, saunas, a movie theater, marble floors, crystal lamps, imported faucets, fine wood trim, and a sophisticated security system were some of the features and finishes that had bled the coffers dry, just as the thefts committed by the dictator and his supporters had.

I had some luck and managed to get into the military facility more easily than I expected. It turned out that the main ballrooms were being used that day for the wedding reception of the daughter of a colonel; I said I was a wedding guest, and the guards let me into the parking lot. Once I was inside, I parked my Chevy Nova beside a Toyota and followed the line of elegantly dressed men and women entering the ballrooms. I found myself in the middle of a room adorned with military-themed paintings. The floor reflected the light of the lamps, and off to the side an enormous marble staircase leading to the second floor drew the eye. Everything around me screamed ostentation and bad taste. I went up the stairs and entered another room where more tables had been set up for the wedding reception. Windows running the length of the room allowed one to observe the city from a distance—a view that blended into radiant flashes of light. I thought about the dictator who had dreamed of ending his time on earth watching life moving beneath his feet, unable to imagine the judicial worries and house arrest that would actually accompany his old age.

The room soon filled with wedding guests, and when someone announced the arrival of the bride and groom, I decided to make my move. I asked a waiter who was serving flutes of champagne for the welcome toast where in the building the officers met. Without stopping to consider the nosiness of my question, he pointed me toward a corridor out the main entrance to the room. I followed his directions and for a few minutes walked through a labyrinth of softly lit hallways. After some time, I discovered a series of doors differentiated by names engraved on shining bronze plaques. I continued farther, and just as I was thinking about retracing my steps, I heard voices. I kept walking with caution until I came to a door that opened into a luxurious room where I saw a dozen officers seated around tables. Beside the door was a waiter in a white jacket, accompanied by a uniformed officer, young and tall, who stepped forward and blocked my path.

"Civilians are not permitted unless invited by an officer," he said in a respectful but authoritarian tone.

"Excuse me. I must have gotten turned around," I said, feigning confusion. "I'm here for a wedding party, and I thought I recognized Colonel Víctor Moltisanti among the guests. Someone told me he had gone to have a drink in the officers' room, so I tried to find him."

It wouldn't take much to realize that my story was as fake as a plastic shark, but that didn't seem to bother the young soldier, who, after listening to me attentively, simply looked at the waiter and made a gesture for him to approach.

"This man is looking for Colonel Moltisanti," said the officer to the waiter.

The waiter observed me closely; the presence of the young officer seemed to make him uncomfortable.

"It's been months since Colonel Moltisanti has been to the club," he said. "He is barred from entering this room."

"Barred? What does that mean?" I asked.

"I would prefer that the colonel explain the reason."

"Of course. But if I can't find him here, where can I find him?" I asked, feeling my tightrope go slack. "I served under him and I wanted to visit him."

"There's a circle of enlisted men on Calle Vergara, close to the Military History Museum. I work there twice a week and he's always there at night."

"A circle of enlisted men?"

"I'm sure you'll find Colonel Moltisanti there," repeated the waiter, and to make it clear that he had no more to say, he retreated a few steps to his place beside the door.

"Would you like me to tell you how to get back to the ballroom?" asked the soldier.

"I left a big handful of breadcrumbs along the way," I responded sarcastically. "I can get back to the party on my own."

I returned to the wedding reception and spent a few minutes observing the people there. They seemed happy to eat at the expense of the bride's father. The newlyweds glided around the tables taking photographs, the planners huddled in a corner, and an orchestra tuned their instruments to play the first dance.

A waiter offered me a glass of champagne, and before I was able to try its contents, a tall, dark man came up beside me. He had the unmistakable air of a military man trying to blend in with civilians.

"Are you with the bride or the groom?" he inquired after looking me up and down and deciding I was unlikely to be on the exclusive wedding list.

"Neither. I happened to be coming through and the bride's dress caught my attention," I answered. "But don't worry. I know I don't belong here and I can show myself out."

The soldier was at a loss for words. I left my glass in his hands and said goodbye to the newlyweds with a wave.

21

It was a few minutes before midnight when I arrived at the place the waiter had told me about. The club for enlisted men was located in a house that evoked the grandeur of the mansions and small palaces that had once populated the República neighborhood and its surroundings. The place lacked the luxury that I had seen an hour before, but its more modest appearance made me feel safer and more comfortable. Nobody stopped me or asked questions when I walked into a room where a dozen tables were occupied by soldiers who appeared to be celebrating promotions in rank or transfers to other cities. The uniformed men were pleasantly drunk and happily devouring the grilled meat that had been set out on the tables in front of them. On one wall there was a Chilean flag with the chubby face of Bernardo O'Higgins printed on it. In another room, which also had a dozen tables in it, I saw more men in uniform who appeared to be drunker than those in the last room. None of them were interested in me, and so I continued on to a third room, where I found a small bar tended by a waiter in an impeccably clean and pressed white jacket. Behind the bar was a collection of military portraits, coats of arms, and a large painting of the Virgin of Carmen, patron saint of the Chilean army.

"This is a private facility," said the waiter as I approached the bar. "We only serve members of the army and their guests."

"That's why I came in," I answered, and before the waiter could think of his next words, I added, "I'm looking for Colonel Víctor Moltisanti, who I had the privilege of knowing when I did my military service in Puerto Natales. I went to see him at the Lo Curro Military Club and was told to come here. I know it's late, but I'm hoping someone will tell me where to find him."

"You should have told me you were a veteran," said the waiter in a friendlier tone.

"I only did my obligatory service, and that was a long time ago," I lied.

"A soldier is a soldier for life," affirmed the waiter, and then, as he was drying a glass, he offered, "And you're in luck. Colonel Moltisanti is in the Ignacio Carrera Pinto room. Go out of the bar, walk straight down the hallway, and don't stop until you reach the last door."

"It's been a long time since I've seen him. Maybe that's why I don't understand what the colonel is doing in a club for enlisted men."

"You don't know? If you've got five minutes, I can tell you."

The room where the waiter directed me was understated, modest, and messy. There were three tables covered with white tablecloths. Two of them were empty, and on the third were propped the elbows of a tall, thin man with carefully cut gray hair. His face had the ruddy complexion and burst capillaries of the habitual drinker, and his attention appeared to be focused entirely on the nearly empty bottle of whiskey in front of him. I approached and cleared my throat to get his attention.

"Colonel Moltisanti?" I asked.

"What do you want?" growled the colonel, looking at me without much interest.

"Do you remember me, Colonel?"

"Where do we supposedly know each other from?" he asked. His eyes were glassy and he seemed to be having trouble finding the words he needed.

"You were my instructor in Puerto Natales," I said, deciding to invent a lie to win his trust.

"I don't remember you, but it doesn't matter. Pull up a seat and have a drink," he ordered, pointing at the bottle. "I have good memories of the time I spent in the Armored Cavalry Regiment at Puerto Natales. In the morning I froze my ass off, but at night the whores were sweet and horny. What's your name, soldier?"

"Hugo Vera," I lied, remembering the name of a poet from Puerto Natales who I had met on a trip to Buenos Aires.

"I remember Canteen Vera, and Three-Tater Vera, a recruit from Chiloé who came to my office to demand that the base's soup have three potatoes and a generous amount of meat. I told him to go to hell and then sent him to clean the stables. I had a lot of recruits under me there, and it's hard to remember them all. What I'll never forget are the exercises we did on Mount Dorotea and the parades for the national holidays. Everyone in town came out to see us."

"You were hard to find, Colonel," I interrupted. "I ended up going to the Lo Curro club and they told me you preferred this place."

The mention of the military club made Moltisanti's face darken momentarily.

"Saying that I prefer this place is a crude way of hiding the truth. Most of the officers who frequent Lo Curro turned their backs on me—and a number of them were my classmates at the Military Academy," he said, taking a quick drink of whiskey. "But they can stay there if they want to keep living a lie. They taught me that an officer should always tell the truth. And sure, maybe I kept quiet for too many years, but in the end . . ."

"So it's true what they say about you testifying on human-rights violations? Believe me, I think you did the right thing."

"It's true, and because of it they accuse me of being a traitor. The truly despicable ones are those who stain the uniform. First they kept their distance from me, and then they told me it would be better if I didn't come to the club anymore. A few even threatened me. I'm alone, that's true, but my conscience is clean. I'm not a killer, or a coward, or a liar, like those miserable people who despise me."

"They also told me that you come here too much."

"If I drink one or two too many, it's my problem. Who cares? I hardly have any friends, and I haven't spoken to my wife in ten years. My two sons moved away from Santiago; I only see them once or twice a year. The older one, Vitoco, followed in my footsteps and joined the military. He's going to be posted in Antofagasta. If they don't fuck him over because of me, he'll have a fine career. My other son, Claudio, studied agronomy and went to work in Coyhaique. But I don't know why I'm telling you these things. You're a stranger, a soldier who says he knows me but who I don't remember ever seeing before."

"That's why you hide every night in this place."

"We need another bottle, soldier," said Moltisanti, not listening to me, and while he was pressing a button beside him on the wall, he added, "I don't even have to talk for them to give me what I need. I just press the button. Here they know me and they respect me."

"What made you want to testify?"

"I don't remember her name or all the details, but it had something to do with a university girl. I saw them take her dead body out of a cell and put her in a vehicle to dispose of somewhere on the road between Santiago and Valparaíso. I gave the judge the names of the officers who commanded the unit that did it."

"That was when you were assigned to the Villa Grimaldi barracks."

"How do you know?" hissed Moltisanti, grabbing on to a lightning bolt of lucidity in the alcoholic cloud that surrounded him. "Why are you interested in that?"

The waiter I had talked with at the bar came in and saved me from having to answer. After he had left a new bottle on the table and gone away, Moltisanti apparently didn't even remember asking me the question.

"I imagine that you had to detain a lot of people while you were at Villa Grimaldi."

"No one," responded Moltisanti, raising his voice. "My work was of an administrative and logistical nature."

I refilled the officer's glass and waited for him to drink.

"That's not what some of your old comrades say."

"Who?"

"Vicente Tapia and Danilo Uribe."

"Those sons of bitches lie," snorted the officer, and after coming back from another trip to the bottom of the glass, he shot back, "Who are you? Why are you asking me these questions? Who sent you to talk to me?"

"If you want answers to those questions, Colonel, let's make a deal. Your truth for mine."

"Have another drink and tell me your truth."

"I'm a private detective and I want to find two ex-soldiers who were stationed at Villa Grimaldi. Toro Palacios and Fullerton. One of them is probably responsible for the recent death of a human-rights activist."

"A recent crime?"

"There are those who never lose their taste for blood, Colonel. What do you say? Did you know those two men?"

"I knew them, but I don't know their real names. They were two scary fuckers. They used to call Toro Palacios 'King Midas,' because apart from the operations against leftists, he liked to organize bank and store robberies that he would blame on the detainees later. He was also one of the most enthusiastic when it came to torture. He had a lot of connections among the superiors—always invited to the meals and parties that they organized with people from television and the arts."

"What was Toro like?"

"Stocky and not very tall. Back then he had blond hair. He liked martial arts and was known to be a good marksman."

"Do you know where to find him?"

"I don't know if he's even still alive," answered Moltisanti. "It's strange that in all these years he's never had to answer to the tribunals, while other assholes who acted like him have been in jail for a while now."

"Maybe he left the country."

"I don't know. All I have from him are memories from the months we spent together at Villa Grimaldi. I've never even heard his name mentioned at the military club. But nobody talks about the past in that place, or at least not the past you're interested in. They never mention names unless they appear in the press—either as part of a trial or in the obituaries."

"What can you tell me about Fullerton?"

"I have only a vague recollection of him. I doubt I'd recognize him if we met face-to-face. Back then he was thin and pale. I saw him the night that an important leader of the MIR died. He spent ten or fifteen minutes at the celebration in the barracks and then he left. I never saw him again. He wasn't talked about often, but we knew he had influence within the organization."

"Did you ever hear about or know anyone named Zuñeda?"

"Who's he?"

"A guy who might know where Toro Palacios ended up," I said, taking another drink of whiskey.

Moltisanti was quiet for a moment, and I was afraid that he had gone to sleep. I filled his glass again, and that appeared to wake him up.

"I wish the past could be erased, like a misspelled word or a stain on a shirt."

"The only thing that can be erased are the echoes of memory."

"I hope that's the case. There are some who think hell is a place where one is forced to remember for eternity," said Moltisanti, and then, as if seeking relief from a sudden pain, he asked, "Is it really true that Tapia and Uribe accused me of participating in torture?"

"No. I said that to provoke you."

"I never got my hands dirty. My only crime was staying silent for too long."

"You testified in a case."

"Yes, but too long after the crimes occurred. Bravery is acting at the right time. Everything else is regret and justification."

"Do you have a way to get home?" I asked him once we had come out onto the street. We were the last to leave the house. Watching the officer's staggering steps, I could tell he wasn't capable of even getting to the next corner on his own.

"Help me get a taxi and leave the rest up to me," he responded.

"I can take you in my car."

"Why would you do that for me?" he asked suspiciously. "You want to get more information out of me?"

"It's a way of paying you back for the answers and the drinks."

"It's been a long time since I've had the chance to get drunk with another person. I accept your offer. I also want to confess that I didn't tell you the whole truth in there. I heard people talking about Toro Palacios two months ago. An enlisted man who'd worked with me told me he had seen him in the General Cemetery during the burial of a general who'd been in charge at the National Information Center. It seems he has changed his physical appearance, and during the ceremony he tried to keep his distance from everyone else."

"That means he's still alive and he's still in Chile."

"It could be. With guys like Toro you can't be sure of anything."

Moltisanti lived on the Calle Ramón Carnicer, in an old building with a view of the park and playground. I helped him get out of the car and climb the stairs to the second floor. His apartment was large and disordered. On the table were some newspapers and military magazines. One of the walls featured an enormous portrait of Moltisanti with two young men who I supposed were his sons. Moltisanti let himself fall into a sagging leather chair and spread his arms as if to breathe in more air or embrace all the objects in the room.

"Here I am, surrounded by all the wreckage of my life. Without a wife, with a meaningless career and two faraway sons," he said in a low voice.

I watched him in silence and took a few steps around the room.

"Do me one more favor," said Moltisanti. "On the kitchen table, there's a bottle of whiskey. Pour us a couple of drinks."

I obeyed the order and went to the kitchen. In the bottle, there was enough liquor left to continue getting us drunk for a couple of hours more. I opened the small refrigerator beneath the pantry and put a few cubes of ice in the glass that I found beside the bottle. I returned and passed the officer his drink. And without saying a word, I left the apartment.

While I was driving back to my neighborhood, I remembered the military parade in Parque O'Higgins that they had taken me to when I lived at the orphanage. I had liked the colorful uniforms and the sound of the bands, but in the noise of the boots and the heavy rigor of the weapons I had detected something suspicious that I didn't know how to decipher back then.

22

It felt like there was a boulder on top of my head. The bed was like a carousel that wouldn't stop spinning, and I had to wait a few minutes before the world around me recovered its normal order. Later, when I heard a knock on my office door, I remembered a poem about the poet wanting no one to come along and disturb him unless it's the dancer with diamond stars on the toes of her shoes.

The memory went up in smoke when I opened the door and saw red-faced Cotapos. His tired expression disappeared as soon as I invited him into my office. Without hurry, as if he were carefully surveying the terrain that he was treading on, he took a few steps into the office and stopped to examine some of the titles on my disorderly bookshelves.

"What are so many poetry books doing in a detective's library?"

"Someone has to read our poets," I replied in an irritated voice.

"Did you have nightmares or just wake up on the wrong side of the bed?"

"I spent a good deal of the night squeezing out the memory of an ex-military man who likes to drink."

"Did you get anything from your conversation?"

"A bit, but I'm done visiting the ex-military members in your brief," I said, and then brought him up to date on my conversation with Moltisanti.

"Now we know for sure that Toro Palacios is flesh and blood," the lawyer said after hearing my report. "To be honest, I hadn't put much faith in your investigations, but what you found out could be very useful. It's true that Moltisanti gave information in a case, but the other two officers have never been brought into the courts. We will ask for them to be called to testify, and there's always the chance that we'll get them to jump out from behind the iron wall of silence that the military puts up to protect themselves from the truth."

"Do you know a lawyer named Guillermo Zuñeda?" I asked. "They say he was quite a figure during the dictatorship."

"I don't know him. Is he related to the case we're looking into?"

"He could lead us to Toro Palacios."

"I'll ask among the lawyers I know." Cotapos went to the window and looked out at the street. "What are your thoughts on what you've uncovered so far?"

"I don't know, really," I said, "but something I can't explain tells me that there's a murky, dark motivation behind Reyes's death. Intuition, my nose, call it whatever you want. And then there are the former military men I talked with. Silence, forgetfulness, secret loyalties—a world that respects its codes and keeps itself hidden in the watchtower it has built to scrutinize civilians that it doesn't trust."

"That's why it's so hard to get justice for the crimes they committed. We have to accumulate enough proof that the truth is irrefutable. It has taken us a long time to break through their wall. Follow your instincts, Heredia. You might just get lucky and get something more than a handful of half truths." Cotapos looked at his watch and said, "I've got to go. Keep me in the loop."

Without knowing why, I thought about an old investigation where I had trailed a ghostwriter involved in the death of a literary critic. I winked in complicity at Simenon and went to the kitchen to make coffee. I put water in the coffeemaker and before it started to boil, I heard someone else knock on the door. I thought that Cotapos might have left something in the office, but when I opened it I saw the aged face of Virginia Reyes.

"Forgive me for coming by without calling first," she said, entering my office and dropping a discolored canvas bag on my desk that plainly did not match her suit.

"I'm a detective, ma'am, not a doctor. You can come whenever you want. There's no need to make an appointment fifteen days before, and I'm not going to charge you to listen to what you have to say." I was in a bad mood.

"May I sit down?" she asked, pointing at the seat in front of the desk. "The elevator is broken and I had to walk up the stairs. I shouldn't be moving so much at my age. I'm exhausted."

"If you wanted an update, you should have used the phone."

"I didn't come for that. I know you would have called me if there was any news. It's about these notebooks," said Mrs. Reyes, pointing at the bag that she had left on my desk. "Benilde sent them three days ago."

"Benilde Roos?"

"An intern brought them to me. Benilde called me and explained some things that I didn't really understand. The notebooks are a sort of diary, and she wanted me to have them to remember my brother by. I thought you might be interested in reading them."

I grabbed the bag and opened it. Inside were two university notebooks. I thumbed through them briefly.

"This is how they were when you got them? Just glancing at them, it looks like someone tore some pages out."

"It might seem strange, but despite what Benilde told me, I didn't read them. I didn't think I had the right to meddle in my brother's intimate life."

"What's in there?" I thought I heard Simenon ask from his corner of the office, surrounded by books that he had knocked off the shelf to make a bed. "Ever since Mrs. Reyes left, you haven't done anything but read, smoke, and look at the ceiling."

"I'm reading Germán Reyes's notebooks. The first has some stories from his childhood that don't help me. In the second there are a bunch of annotations from his meetings with the psychologist and some small references to his investigations. Of these, there are five that really caught my attention."

"What do they say?"

"Toro Palacios has kept himself hidden, but not just to elude justice."

"One."

"I get the impression that Fullerton was something more than just a torturer."

"Two."

"I met a person who can help me get to Toro Palacios."

"Three."

"She asked me to write everything I knew about Fullerton. At first I didn't want to, but then . . ."

"Four. Then what?" asked Simenon, impatient.

"After that the pages were torn out. It reminds me of the Scerbanenco novel that I bought in the booth at Plaza Almagro. I read two hundred pages until I discovered that it was missing the page where the name of the killer is revealed."

"Five. Your life is full of small tragedies, Heredia."

"Another joke like that and you're going to get your tail stomped on."

"Take it easy. At least now you know that you're not chasing ghosts."

"Reyes's investigations were more than just clipping out news articles, and if my intuition is correct, it seems like he got so close to the fire that he got burned."

"Who is this 'she' that Reyes mentions? Benilde Roos?"

"No idea. We wouldn't even know the notebooks existed if Benilde hadn't given them to Virginia Reyes."

"The same goes for the sister."

I picked up the phone, called Dionisio Terán, and without any explanation asked him whether Germán Reyes had had the help of a woman in his investigations.

"Not that I know of," responded Terán. "However, it's not impossible. A lot of university girls offer to help with the work of the cultural center."

"You told me that Germán was reserved when it came to his work."

"That doesn't mean no one ever helped him."

"Can you give me some names?"

"I'll have to ask the girls from the group, and even then I can't guarantee anything. Sometimes they help out for a while and then move away."

"Let me know if you find anything, and especially if a name comes up." I said goodbye and hung up.

"Now what?" asked Simenon.

"Time to see what Benilde Roos has to say."

"I noticed that there were some pages missing from one of the notebooks, but I didn't really think too much about it," Benilde said when I explained why I was calling. "Germán was very insecure and guarded, and I thought he might have torn them out. More than once I saw him write something down, then tear out the page that he had just written and throw it in the garbage."

"When was the last time you saw Germán with the bag?"

"The day before his death. He carried it whenever he was going to the library or the psychologist. He didn't have it on him the day he was killed."

"Do you know if some woman helped him with his work? Someone besides you?"

"Not that I know of." With a hint of doubt in her voice, Benilde asked, "Do you think there was another woman in Germán's life?"

"Don't let your imagination get away from you. I'm thinking of someone who could have helped him gather information. Like one of the students who visit the cultural center."

"He would have told me. He knew that I'm jealous."

"Did you read the notebooks?"

"I knew what was in them, and I thought it would be better for his sister to have them, since there are a lot of family memories in there."

"One last question, Benilde. Did you ask or advise Germán to write in the notebooks?"

"Germán always went around telling stories from his life, and one day I told him that he should write them down, because they might help him with the book he dreamed of writing. He liked the idea and began writing, but he didn't just write stories. If you read those notebooks, you'll see that he also wrote reflections and notes about his daily activities."

"So much for the clue," I muttered to Simenon when I had finished talking with Benilde Roos. "For a second I got excited, but the famous 'she' isn't a mystery anymore."

"A false clue isn't a reason to jump onto the toboggan of despair."

"So what now? A drink to ring in the night?"

My intention of having a drink evaporated at the speed of light. Just when I was ready to pull out the emergency bottle from my desk, Montegón burst into the office with the force of a bull that has seen the shadow of a matador in the ring. I growled a hello and offered him a drink.

"I'd prefer to go somewhere else," he said with a smile that didn't give me a good feeling. "I went by Sacotto's bar, and I think we should go pay him a visit."

"What do you have in mind, Montegón?"

"That we should have a few words with Sacotto and get him to tell us where we can find Chito. Do you want to go on a field trip?"

It had been at least six months since I had last been on the Gran Avenida José Miguel Carrera, and because of that, as soon as Montegón's car passed in front of the Barros Luco Hospital, I noticed that the appearance of the street had changed. Where before there had been a monument to Che Guevara, there were now some gigantic statues of the cartoon characters Mampato and Ogú; where I remembered houses made of adobe, there were enormous apartment buildings; the stadium where Los Prisioneros played their first big concert had been replaced by a supermarket whose escalators were visible from the street, making it possible to see the customers going in and out of the establishment like an interminable line of ants.

The car forged a path between buses and trucks until it was in front of the municipality of La Cisterna. From there it crossed the Américo Vespucio beltway and kept moving with the speed of a stray dog that just smelled the tastiest bone in the neighborhood.

"The restaurant is close to bus stop twenty-nine of Gran Avenida," said Montegón, breaking the silence we had maintained since the beginning of the trip. "It's nothing big. It's an adobe house with discolored walls and about a dozen tables. Sacotto isn't interested in the comfort of his customers. The bar is just a front for his illicit activity. Beside the restaurant there's a storage area where he keeps the merchandise that he buys from local thieves and then sells at the flea market on the Calle Morros. Everyone knows what they do, but nobody, not even the cops, dares to get in the way."

"If you're trying to get me excited about this, you're not doing a good job, Montegón."

"Did you bring your pistol?" he asked a bit later. "We're about to arrive at Ali Baba's cave."

The restaurant was less attractive than a rat hole, but the three customers drinking beer around a table weren't worried about the terrible state of the place or the sinister look of the waiter serving them drinks. Behind the bar a tall, dark-skinned man showed off his enormous gut without any shame. Montegón chose a table far from everyone else, and when the waiter came to take our order he asked for a family-sized beer. The fat man watched us for an instant from his trench and then went back to talking to a woman smoking at the bar.

"The fat one is Sacotto, and the chick is probably a hooker," said Montegón.

"So what's the plan?"

"Drink and wait for the place to empty out."

A skinny kid came in, went up to the bar, and asked Sacotto to sell him a tea bag. Sacotto reached into a box beside the register and took out something that he quickly passed to the kid.

"A bump," said Montegón, his eyes following the kid out of the restaurant. "Cocaine of bad quality or crack. Drugs have got the kids in this neighborhood by the balls, and nobody does anything to slow the dealers down."

The telephone beside the fat man rang and he hurried to answer it, listening for a couple of seconds and then passing the phone to his customer. After a brief exchange, the woman put some money on the bar and left.

"Someone found their entertainment for the evening," said Montegón, taking a slug of beer.

When I was growing impatient with the wait, the customers at the other table paid their check and left the bar with wavering steps. Montegón winked at me and we both finished the contents of our glasses. After that, everything happened very quickly. While I came up to the bar and showed my fake credential from the Investigative Police, Montegón quietly took out his pistol and pointed it at the waiter, ordering him to close the restaurant door.

"What's wrong with you two? Don't you know who you're dealing with?" asked Sacotto, passing quickly from surprise to rage. "You're going to regret this, motherfuckers."

"We'll ask the questions," I responded. "We know about all your rackets, and this will go better for you if you cooperate."

"Today wasn't a good day. I've only got a few coins in the register," said the fat man, trying to stay calm.

"Keep your coins. We want to find Chito."

"I don't know anybody by that name."

"Let's make a deal, Sacotto. You tell us where to find your friend, and we leave you alone."

"Why would I have to make a deal with you two? I don't know what the hell you're talking about, shit-for-brains."

"Right now our colleagues are interrogating Bulnes, the guy who paid you to intimidate Carvilio. I'm sure he's going to sing every note. It's only a matter of time before they'll be coming to get you. Do you understand the mess you're in or do I need to draw you a picture?"

"Fuck you, shithead!" screamed Sacotto. "Who do you think you're fooling with this bullshit?"

"Put a bullet in him where it hurts," said Montegón.

Sacotto tried to change his luck with a quick smack to the detective's head. Montegón took the blow on firm feet, looked at his aggressor, and almost with indifference let loose a fist to his chin. Then he grabbed Sacotto by the neck and bounced the man's head off the sticky cloth covering the bar.

"I can do you a lot of damage if you don't cooperate," Montegón said to the fat man after forcing him to sit on the floor.

"He needed to get rid of an asshole who was sticking his nose into his business," said Sacotto after a few seconds. "We met in a bar downtown and he paid me to get the job done."

"Bulnes says he contacted you by phone using a fake name."

"He's lying. I've been buying a lot of the shit he steals from the lumberyard."

"What can you tell me about Chito? What's his real name? Where can we find him?"

"How much do you want to stop fucking with me?" asked Sacotto, and after a pause to clean the blood that was flowing down his nose, he said, "It won't be the first or the last time that I grease the palm of a cop. All the ones I know smile when they smell a wad of bills coming their way."

"We're not cops, and you're in no position to be offering anything."

"And that ID you flashed me?"

"As fake as your innocence."

Montegón stopped paying attention to the waiter and came over to my side. Sacotto understood that talking was his only option for getting out of the mess he was in, and he made himself more comfortable on the floor with an irritated gesture.

"His name is Juan Lugo and he's usually at the Arco, a bar on the Avenida Carlos Valdovinos," he said reluctantly.

"Do you think he's telling the truth?" asked Montegón, looking at the fat man. It was clear that he would be more than happy to give him a second beating.

I thought about responding, but in that instant I saw that the waiter was moving toward me with a knife in his right hand. I was slow to react. I heard the whistling of the blade and prepared myself to be cut, but Montegón's left arm got into the knife's path. The waiter looked at me with surprise, and before he had time to make another attack, I kicked him in the balls and punched him twice on the chin. The waiter fell to the floor. I figured it would take him a while to regain his senses. I took a couple of steps back and ended up looking down the barrel of the gun that Sacotto was holding. He had gotten to his feet and his face was distorted with rage. I couldn't do much to change my luck. I heard a shot. Sacotto spun around and landed on a crate of empty bottles. He moaned for a few seconds and then his gaze fixed on the peeling paint of the ceiling. Montegón's shot had been good, and a thick red spring of blood flowed from the mouth of the obese man. Beside me, the detective took off his jacket and rolled up his sleeve to examine the cut on his arm.

"Is it deep? Are you OK?" I asked.

"It will need a few stitches, but it'll heal."

"You saved my life twice, Montegón."

"Maybe that will be something to consider when you think about our partnership."

"Perhaps," I said, still unconvinced.

"There isn't much more we can do here," added the detective.

"I want to put things in order before we call the police," I said, and I dragged the waiter to leave him beside his boss's body. I took Sacotto's belt and used it to tie the two men together, face-to-face. The waiter could talk with his boss until he began to stink like death.

"You think you're going to trick the cops? Our prints must be all over the place."

"Are you OK?" I asked Montegón again as I got behind the wheel of his car. The detective's face was pale, and a bloodstain covered the front of his shirt. "Do you want me to call anyone? Your wife, your kids, someone who wants to be with you?"

"I don't have anybody. My wife left me four years ago, and my kids don't want to talk to me. And don't say you're sorry, because it's not true. What I need right now is a surgeon with steady hands."

"I'll take you to the Barros Luco Hospital."

"They're going to ask me questions I'd prefer not to answer."

"Tell them you were robbed and you didn't get a good look at the muggers. People are always coming into the hospital with that story. They won't have any reason to doubt you."

"Do whatever you want, but hurry up," said Montegón. Grimacing, he asked, "What are you going to do with Lugo?"

My head began to clear after leaving the hospital. We had to wait three hours before Montegón was seen by a doctor. After sewing up his arm, the surgeon suggested that he stay in the hospital overnight. I left Montegón on a gurney in the hallway between two old people spitting phlegm on the floor and a girl who was complaining of stomach pain. I was tired and hungry, but it was too early to find a diner for a coffee and something to eat. I'd have to settle for the street vendors on the corners, with their cakes, cheese empanadas, and cookies. I surveyed my options, and when none of them seemed attractive, I got on a bus that let me off beside the Central Market. There I found a little kitchen that had begun to receive its first customers. I asked for scrambled eggs and a mug of coffee. Life had begun to show me its pleasures again.

23

On the radio they were talking about the sinking of a small fishing boat in the south, in which eight children returning to a small rural village from a private school had died; about climate change in Asia; about the latest fashions in New York; and about the scores of soccer games in Italy and Spain. It was a soup of names and numbers in which a goal, an increase in unemployment, an Italian tie, and the death of children had the same relative value. I swore aloud—to the surprise of Simenon, who had seen me come in and was rubbing himself against my legs.

Fighting the desire to go back to sleep, I picked up the phone and called Bernales. After the third attempt to get him to pick up, I managed to talk with him and tell him about what had happened in the restaurant. I told him that the shooting of Sacotto had been in self-defense, and to avoid implicating Montegón, I charged the dead man to my account. I told Bernales about Lugo, and the police officer said he would send some men to arrest Carvilio's killer.

"Besides what Sacotto told you, do you have any other information that can help us convict Lugo?"

"You've got Bulnes and the testimony of a street vendor who works in front of the building where Carvilio lived. Also, assuming my nose isn't failing me, I think the doorman there can tell us something about the murderer. I'm guessing he allowed Lugo to enter the building."

"You never cease to amaze me, Heredia. Why are you giving me this case on a platter? In another time, you would have been after Lugo yourself. What's changed?"

"I want to give you the chance to justify your salary."

"I doubt that's the real answer."

"Shootouts don't hold the same appeal as they used to. After what happened with Sacotto, I don't want any more dead people in my path for a while."

"That seems closer to the truth," said Bernales.

I called the hospital to ask about Montegón's condition, but the receptionist refused to give me information by phone and hung up before I could ask further questions. I spat out some choice words about the woman and walked back toward the bedroom.

I dreamed of trees getting pushed around by the wind. A thick liquid was trickling from their roots, and their leaves were spreading over the earth. I woke with a start, and for a second I thought I could see the blood-covered face of Sacotto. I closed my eyes and opened them again. Anselmo was beside me, regarding me with a mixture of worry and curiosity.

"What's going on with you, man? You've been tossing and turning. Who are you fighting?"

"There's always wind in my dreams. I need to have Madame Zara interpret them for me," I said, remembering the fortune-teller that Anselmo had once been married to for two years.

"Don't even mention her. Who needs nightmares when they go to sleep?" said Anselmo. He put the newspaper he was carrying on the bed. "Looks like you were partying pretty hard last night. You've slept through the whole morning again."

"I spent the night at Barros Luco with Montegón. Today all I want is to rest."

"It doesn't look like you'll be able to."

"What do you have up your sleeve, Anselmo?"

"Remember when I told you I would ask around the neighborhood about Zuñeda?"

"Vaguely."

"I've been doing it on my own, and today I hit on something. I found a messed-up guy in the Teletrak branch who says he knows someone with that last name. I came to find you so we can go talk to him."

The Teletrak was full of bettors studying the racing program, looking at odds, and discussing each horse's chances. Determined to remain focused on my job, I ignored the TV screens showing the bets and followed Anselmo to a corner of the room where five men shared a bottle that was supposedly hidden in a thick paper bag. The bottle passed from hand to hand, while the chatter about bets kept getting louder and louder. No one could agree on which horses would win. In the middle of the group, like a sitting Buddha, was the man we were looking for. He was young, and his long black hair fell onto his shoulders. His expansive flesh struggled to escape the tight black T-shirt that contained it. Anselmo came up beside him, greeted him pleasantly, and introduced me.

"How's your luck been?" I asked.

"I can't complain. I just hit on the second triple wheel of the afternoon," he replied, a smile lighting up his swollen cheeks.

"That's why you either have to know about horses or have some luck."

"Heredia wants to find the person we talked about yesterday," said Anselmo to the Buddha, cutting off the commentary that the young guy clearly wanted to make about his successful bet.

"Zuñeda?" I asked impatiently.

"I heard him say that name once," responded the Buddha. "They say he's a lawyer."

"Do you know where he lives or works?"

"I don't know, but I've seen him a bunch of times in the restaurant in front of the old National Congress. I go there with my friends when our bets go well. I've also seen him a few times in the cabaret on Calle Catedral, in the basement across from the church."

"I need you to describe him to me."

"He's about seventy years old, gray, thin, and has a red face. He comes in here sometimes and places a few bets. The gossip is that he's looking for boys that he can seduce with a few pesos."

"I'm guessing he doesn't always come here at the same time."

"He usually comes in the afternoon, and sometimes he stays until the last race. I don't know anything else. I'm interested in horses, not the guys who come to bet."

"Speaking of bets, do you have a good hunch about the next race?"

"I can't help you with that, friend. I don't give info and I don't share my hunches, since a guy tried to stab me when the horse I recommended came in last. I also don't lend money or make bets for other people."

"I guess we'd better follow our feelings," I said to Anselmo, who had been listening attentively.

"There's nothing like the feelings in one's own heart."

"At your age you should know that where women and horses are concerned, you can't get carried away with your heart's desire."

The Buddha smiled and immediately turned back to reading the racing program he was holding in one of his enormously fat hands.

"Are we going to bet or not?" Anselmo asked, impatient.

"What does your heart tell you?"

At the end of the strip I could see the flash of red neon coming from the cabaret as it blended with the signs of stores selling electronics, watches, cheap jewelry, and videos. I walked toward the door of the den and paid my cover to a shady-looking doorman who observed me closely, calculating his chances of stealing my wallet or a piece of my soul. Inside, the place smelled of humidity, air freshener, and cigarette smoke. I waited for my eyes to adjust to the darkness and moved toward a corner where I could see the whole room. On the stage, a tall, chubby brunette was dancing. Her movements were about as sensual as a drunk bum, and except for a skinny guy leaning on the thin counter that surrounded the stage, none of the customers paid her any attention. They drank their drinks and talked with the women who circulated among them like sharks ready to attack a group of distracted bathers. I lit a cigarette and looked around with the hope of seeing a recognizable face. I didn't have any luck. A woman approached and pressed her ample bust against my chest. She was wearing a cowboy hat, a tiny leather skirt, and boots that came up to her knees. Her lips were painted a furious red, and the velvet in her eyes made me guess that she had shared too many drinks with the customers. She tried to kiss me, and when I moved away she put on a hurt expression that only accentuated the grotesque aspect of her face.

"Will you buy me a drink? Do you want me to do nice things to you?" she asked, repeating an offer that she had surely made many times that day.

"I'm waiting for a friend," I said, ignoring her invitation.

"You're in the wrong place. There are only women working here."

"I'm waiting for a friend so that I can talk to him," I clarified.

"A lot of guys come in here," said the woman, suspicious.

"You can make some money if you help me."

"I've got enough problems in my life without buying more. If I've learned one thing in places like this, it's to keep my mouth shut."

"Whatever you say will just be between us."

"Will you buy me a drink?"

I assented reluctantly, and the girl walked away. A few minutes later she came back with a plastic cup in her hands.

"What's your friend's name?" she asked in a low voice.

"Zuñeda," I said, and then described the lawyer.

"I don't know anybody with that name."

"Maybe one of your coworkers knows him."

"Could be. What do I make for asking them?"

"Five thousand pesos for you, and another five for the girl who knows something about my friend. That's more than they pay you for a whole day of gymnastics on the stage, yes?"

The woman walked away without saying anything. I saw her talking with some of the other dancers, and five minutes later she came back with a small, thin woman in a tiny white bikini.

"Dalila knows your friend," said the woman with the boots.

"He's a lawyer, comes in once or twice a week. He has a few drinks and then goes to the private dance room."

"Has he told you his name?"

"No, but once he came with a friend who called him by that name."

"Zuñeda?"

"Yeah. He always comes looking for me. Says I remind him of a girlfriend he had when he was young."

"Does he always come on the same day?"

"No, but he seems to prefer Mondays."

"Has he ever taken you somewhere else? A restaurant? His house?"

"Never. But he spends a lot of money with me."

"Can you give me a call when he comes in again?"

"What do I get out of it?"

"Another piece of paper like this one," I said, handing her a five-thousand-peso bill.

"That's not a lot of money to lose a good client."

"Who said you were going to lose him?"

"Nobody comes here looking for someone just to smoke a cigarette with him."

There are places in the city that never change. Houses, sidewalks, side streets with strange names, corners, small plazas with hundred-year-old trees that remain unchanged in front of gigantic buildings that alter the landscape with their arrogant cement and metal. Bars and restaurants that no one notices and whose customers remain the same, each one faithful to the table where they rest their elbows. The blonde who smiles from a sign advertising a soft drink that doesn't exist anymore, the waiter who grows old with the cloth on his arm, the thick wine that stains the tablecloths, and above all, the memories that move among the tables like butterflies searching for meaning in their fleeting life. The Congreso restaurant was one of those places. It was located a few blocks from my apartment, close to the old parliament building and the Plaza de Armas. Its name had changed a few times over the years, but I kept calling it the same thing it was called when I'd first crossed the threshold at the end of the 1970s, during a university bar crawl to celebrate passing a course. The last time I pulled up a chair to one of its tables was in the company of an old friend from the university, during an afternoon when wine worked its magic and the stories made us chase the more impassioned trails of a past that we were condemned to remember.

I sat down at a table that allowed me to observe the tired movement of the restaurant and ordered a shot of pisco from the waiter. While he wrote down the order in his notebook, I asked about Guillermo Zuñeda. The name didn't get his attention, but when I described the lawyer, he immediately recognized him as a regular.

"He usually comes in the late afternoon."

"Every day?"

"There are weeks when he comes in every day, and others when he only comes in one or two days. He usually says it's because he's been away on a trip, but I get the feeling that it's really because he's broke. For a lawyer, he doesn't seem to be very well off. In the end, though, I can't judge. Everything a customer says is true, funny, and interesting. Everything they tell me goes in one ear and out the other."

"Your philosophy is unique, friend. Do you know where he lives or works?"

"No idea. My interest in the customers stops when they leave the restaurant."

"Maybe some other time I'll be luckier. I'll try to come in again."

"When he shows up, I can tell him you're looking for him."

"Thanks, but I prefer that our meeting be a surprise."

I returned to the restaurant that night and my luck remained poor. Zuñeda didn't show, nor did I have any luck the next two nights. I didn't turn up anything new in my visits to the strip club, where the chubby dancer continued to wear her cowboy hat and offer her dubious charms to anyone who would listen. Zuñeda seemed to be trying to stay anonymous, and the only thing that I had managed to gain during my wait for him was the friendship of the waiter. He took advantage of his free time to talk about soccer and politics. Poverty and the country's growing inequality seemed to interest him, and he was constantly finding a new reason to vent about the way the law applied to you differently depending on how much money you had. I let him talk, every now and then nodding to feign agreement, while my attention remained focused on the door. I also took advantage of our newfound friendship to borrow his cell phone and call the hospital. Atilio Montegón had been released; when I called his house he told me that the wound hadn't been as bad as it seemed at first. He offered to accompany me on my stakeout, and it took me several minutes to convince him to keep resting until he had regained his strength.

A voice inside my head whispered that the wait wouldn't be in vain, and that just like other times, I should try to have the patience of a hunter waiting for his prey. I was finally rewarded at the beginning of the fourth night, while I was drinking a glass of red wine. I had just put out a cigarette in the tin ashtray near me when a man who I knew immediately was Zuñeda entered the restaurant. The waiter came up to my table and confirmed my hunch. I told him to stay quiet and not tell the lawyer about me.

Zuñeda sat at a table where two other men dressed in gray were eating. The lawyer was taller and thinner than I had imagined. He had a prominent jaw, and when he smiled, folds appeared in his skin. His years seemed to weigh on him, and despite his tidy appearance, I guessed that he wasn't someone who went through life satisfied.

"Aren't you going to talk to your friend?" asked the waiter as he passed my table on his way to the kitchen.

"I'll wait for him to be alone and then give him the surprise of his life."

"You might be waiting a while." He shook his head to indicate that he didn't understand my behavior.

Zuñeda continued his animated conversation, and much to my disappointment, his companions didn't leave once they had finished eating. They asked for a bottle of rum and several Coca-Colas, and drank until the waiter moved around the tables to announce that it was closing time. It was two in the morning, and I had been fighting sleep for the last half hour. I just wanted to go home and go to bed. The lawyer and his friends left the restaurant, and I followed them until they said their goodbyes at the beginning of Paseo Puente. Zuñeda crossed the Plaza de Armas, and I followed behind him like a serpent. From one of the corners of the Portal Fernández Concha, I saw two prostitutes appear, along with a bunch of boys looking for a john. The kids surrounded Zuñeda, and after a few minutes the lawyer entered the Portal building accompanied by a young boy in a stained blue shirt. I quickened my steps and saw them go through the doorway of some apartments on the other side of the courtyard. I climbed a bronze-colored stairway and followed Zuñeda until he and his companion got to the third floor. I stopped in the stairwell landing, and while I caught my breath I saw them go inside one of the apartments. I felt for the pistol in the right-hand pocket of my jacket and waited five minutes before following through with the plan I had just come up with.

The door didn't offer a lot of resistance, and no one saw me push it in with my right shoulder. Pistol in hand, I entered a small living room with a bookshelf and a bunch of paintings on the walls. I took a few quick steps, and without excusing my bad manners, I entered the bedroom from which I could hear the sound of a television. Zuñeda and the kid were lying on the bed. The lawyer had his shoes off and his chest was bare. Neither of them seemed to have noticed the noise I had made pushing through the door; they were engrossed in the pornographic images playing on the screen in front of the bed. Zuñeda tried to get up but didn't succeed. My fist was quicker and hit him in the face, heavy with rage and contempt. His head hit the backrest of the bed, and I figured it would be a few minutes before he came to. The kid got onto his feet looking scared.

"Take it easy. This doesn't have anything to do with you," I told him, hoping to gain his trust.

The kid jumped up on the bed, and before I could stop him, he jumped over Zuñeda, burst past me, and bolted out of the room with the agility of a street cat. I imagined him running down the stairs and wondered if he would ever escape his life on the street. I sat on the foot of the bed and watched the screen as a busty blonde endured the buffeting of an enormous cock with exaggerated pleasure. I quickly grew bored with her moaning and shut off the TV. I lit a cigarette, looked out the window onto the Plaza de Armas, and sat waiting for the lawyer to wake up. The plaza looked deserted, far from the secret heartbeat of the city.

24

"Police?" Zuñeda asked while he buttoned the shirt that he had grabbed from the floor. "No, definitely not—if you were a cop you wouldn't be alone. You also don't know the mess you're getting yourself into by tossing my apartment."

"Cut the bullshit, Zuñeda. You and I both know you're in no position to threaten anybody."

"Let's fix this without a big fuss. I'll give you some money and you can go back to your house and forget what you've seen."

Zuñeda's speech was rapid-fire, and I asked myself if it was the effects of the alcohol, the situation that I had found him in, or the empty little paper beside the bed. Beyond the aggressiveness of his speech, he was tense, and my silence seemed to make him just as uncomfortable as the pistol pointed at his heart.

"What happened to the kid?" he asked in a low voice.

"He flew the coop, and I doubt he'll escape the other sons of bitches like you." I lowered the gun and said, "I've got some friends on the force who'd be happy to learn about your hobbies. Pornography, pederasty, drug use."

"Who are you?" insisted Zuñeda. "How much will your discretion cost?"

"Don't worry about my discretion. I know how to keep my mouth shut if you cooperate with me. I need to find a certain former military man determined to stay hidden. Javier Toro Palacios is one of the names that he uses. And don't tell me you don't know him. I know you're friends and that you get together frequently. I also know about your past. Your legal problems in the 1970s and your collaboration with the dictatorship. Just so you don't have any delusions that you're going to get out of this situation, let me assure you that I've got more than enough to fuck up your existence."

"Why do you want to find Toro?" asked Zuñeda.

"I want him to start paying his debt to the truth, and I want to see him live out the rest of his days behind bars."

"What's the point of digging around in the past? Do they pay you for every bone you find?"

"Be careful what you say. I'm in a bad mood and don't have much patience. The time when you could knock on the doors of the powerful has passed. Today you're nothing more than a shyster trolling the streets to satisfy his perversions."

"Where do you get this stupid shit from?"

"People have seen you skulking around the alleys here. I also checked some of the lowlife places you visit."

"Do you really think you can pin something on me?"

"I can make you really unhappy, don't doubt it. But what I'm most interested in is finding Toro so he can pay for what he's done."

"Sure, I know him, but I'll never give away anything about him."

"Did you meet at Villa Grimaldi?"

"I don't have to answer that."

"I have six reasons in my pistol for you to answer my questions. I'm also sure I can find some crime to pin on you, Zuñeda."

"You might be doing me a favor by using that pistol," said the lawyer, who added with resignation, "I worked in the Ministry of the

Interior and coordinated the information we had on the Marxists who were detained by the security services. The minister received letters from international entities and offices of the courts, asking about people who had been detained. It was my job to answer them, so I needed to know if the detained persons would be set free or if I had to deny that they had been detained."

"Where do I find your friend?" I insisted.

"I can tell you some things about my past, but I'm not going to betray Toro."

"I can wait. I know that in a few hours you're going to need a drink or a few grams of coke."

"Get out! You've already done enough."

"The clock is ticking, Zuñeda," I said in a low voice.

The lawyer's face became rigid and then suddenly exploded with a mocking laugh. It surprised him when I punched him on the chin. He closed his eyes and slid down softly until he was spread out on the bed. I took his belt off his pants, tied his hands behind his back, and left him facedown. Then I picked up the phone beside the television and called Montegón.

"How are you feeling? Can you do me a big favor?" I asked, and then told him about my night with the lawyer. "I need you to help me with Zuñeda until he tells us where Toro is."

"Leave me alone with him for half an hour."

"You're not in any kind of shape to be handing out beatings. Let him feel the time passing and the lack of alcohol. Keep him in the dark. Let him think about his past and remember. Every now and then make him think about whiskey or a cold beer. I'm sure he can't take abstinence."

Montegón replaced me at dawn. The floor where Zuñeda's hole-in-the-wall was located was mostly taken up by a brothel posing as a massage parlor, a few apartments used by hookers who worked in the Plaza de Armas, and a few others apparently occupied by people who were careful not to stick their noses into other people's business.

The detective was happy to help me watch Zuñeda, but he was a little bit too happy, and the way he looked at the lawyer for the first time made me worry that leaving them alone together might not be such a good idea. It was temporary, though. Whether or not the detective broke the scumbag's neck didn't matter to me one iota. Zuñeda was a tough nut to crack, and knowing that there were at least two of us interested in his words would make him think about the consequences of his silence.

Once I was outside, I breathed in the sleepy air blanketing the street, and I only needed to close my eyes to imagine the angry voices, the tumult, the gushing blood of the city that embraced me as a stubborn witness to the life that flowed through its veins. I stopped in front of a newsstand to read the front pages of the papers. I looked out at the plaza, and at the people walking toward the metro entrance and down the neighborhood streets. Life stayed its course, ignorant of my desires and the exhaustion that was sticking to my skin. I went into the Haiti for a coffee and then started the short walk to my office.

"The rat's in the cage and we just have to wait for its tongue to loosen," I told Simenon while I filled his bowls with food and the water that he usually drank with the zeal of a Bedouin.

"And then?"

"I'll keep looking in other hideouts."

"And then?"

"There's always something to be entertained by," I responded as I dragged my body toward the bedroom.

I woke up a little after noon. I took a shower and then, as I was frying a steak I planned to share with Simenon, Inspector Bernales appeared, accompanied by a twelve-pack of beer that he put on the desk. I finished cooking the meat, cut it in small pieces, and left it out for the cat.

"One eats while two watch. It's not ideal, but given the size of the steak, there's not much that can be done."

"We could order pizza or Chinese food."

"Beer, pizza, Chinese food. Did you just rob a bank?"

"We've got reason to celebrate. We found Lugo. It wasn't easy to bring him in; he greeted us with a gun in his hand, and we were forced to put a couple of bullets in him. Nothing fatal. He lived to confess to Carvilio's murder."

"Just out of curiosity, does Lugo have white hair?"

"Like snow. Why do you ask?"

"I think I told you that a street vendor saw a man with white hair coming out of the building where Carvilio died."

I walked out of the apartment while Bernales took a nap, brought on by the beers and the pizza he had scarfed down like a teenager. The sun was hitting hard on the Plaza de Armas, and I noticed a lot of people hiding under the shade of trees and restaurant awnings. I was always surprised by how many people congregated there. Old folks, young lovers, Peruvian immigrants, preachers, comedians, and unemployed people who stared at the sky looking for a drop of hope.

I thought about Montegón and felt guilty for taking so long to go back to Zuñeda's place. I went into one of the restaurants in the Portal Fernández Concha and bought him a steak sandwich and two beers.

The detective didn't complain about my lateness. He simply drank one of the beers and then devoured the sandwich while he finished watching one of the lawyer's movies.

"I've seen some moves that I didn't even think were possible," he said, pointing at the screen. "Perversion has no limits."

"Speaking of perversion, how's the man of the house?"

"He fell asleep an hour ago. He screams, he hallucinates, he threatens, but he still hasn't talked. I had to gag him so he wouldn't get the neighbors interested."

"Has anyone come asking for him?"

"Nobody. No phone calls either."

I took a couple of steps through the room and lit a cigarette.

"Bernales came to visit me in my office. They got Lugo and closed the investigation into Carvilio's murder. I told him what you did to find the hit man," I said, and then, seeing the bags under Montegón's tired eyes, added, "Go out for a while and come back later. I know how to deal with Zuñeda."

The bedroom was covered with shadows. Zuñeda was breathing with difficulty and seemed to be having a nightmare. I came up beside him and tore off the gag in one stroke.

"Do you still not know where I can find your friend?" I asked him, not expecting what instantly came out.

"Son of a bitch!" he shouted in a muffled voice, glaring at me hatefully.

"Time is flying and the chance to talk is growing short," I told him before gagging him again and leaving the bedroom.

The clock in the living room struck midnight. All day long we had waited in vain for Zuñeda to talk. Montegón played solitaire with some cards he found in the kitchen, and I was looking out the window at the Plaza de Armas.

"You haven't told me what your plan is," said Montegón.

"The idea is for Zuñeda to lead us to Toro Palacios."

"If you give me an opportunity to make him talk, Zuñeda will give us what we want."

"I've thought about that, as well as some other things," I said, going over to the table where the bottle of whiskey I'd bought that afternoon was sitting.

I filled a glass and walked into the bedroom. Zuñeda was awake and staring at the ceiling. He was shaking, and his face was covered in sweat. I took the gag off and forced him to smell the whiskey. I drank a sip of the liquor and felt the lawyer's hate spread through the room like a toxic cloud.

"A good whiskey at the beginning of the night is priceless," I said.

"You're going to pay for this."

"This is your last chance to talk, Zuñeda. After this, I'm going to leave you in the hands of some friends. They're good guys, but sometimes they get a bit rough."

"What friends?"

"People who know how to use weapons against the military and would love to have a lawyer who collaborated with torturers in their hands."

"You're just trying to scare me."

"If you don't talk in the next few minutes, I'll give them a call."

"I don't know where Toro lives, but I have his cell-phone number," said the lawyer after taking a desperate look around the room.

"I'm happy that you are starting to see reason."

"We worked together at Villa Grimaldi, and years later, when the political situation changed, we ran into each other again and he invited me to have a few drinks. I thought he was going to ask me for help with some legal matter, but he just wanted to talk. Since then we've seen each other pretty regularly. He has never told me what he does these days, but it's clear that he's not lonely."

"Do you have a place where you meet?"

"No. Toro changes the place every time."

"Call him and tell him you want to get together tomorrow at eleven."

"And if he can't come then?"

"The day and the time don't matter to me. You and I will go to the meeting together, my friend. Without making a scene or doing anything smart, all you have to do is finger Toro."

25

The meeting with Toro was at noon, and the first thing that caught my attention, when Zuñeda told me where they were meeting, was how close it was to my home.

"Toro always wants to meet downtown. I imagine he does it to make it easier for me. I've also seen him walking on Paseo Huérfanos and Calle Estado," said Zuñeda when I made a comment about the place, taking care not to mention that it was close to my office.

"I suppose you understand that there's no point in playing dirty," I told him later, as we were leaving his apartment.

The lawyer stopped, looked me in the eye and made a scornful face.

"My friend will be following us," I warned him. "He's carrying a pistol and he's got good aim."

"I only hope that you keep your word and leave me alone once you've seen Toro."

"I'll leave you alone, but before that you'll have to put up with my friend's company for one or two more days."

"Are you going to kill Toro?"

"I haven't invested this much time in finding him to just kill him. I want to unmask him and make him confront his past."

Zuñeda smiled and continued on his way.

"Can we get a drink before we go to the restaurant?" he asked.

"Once we're done, you'll have time to drink all you want. You can drown in a pool of alcohol and I won't lift a finger to stop you."

The Chinese restaurant was located on Calle Bandera, in between a bunch of used-clothing stores and a telephone call center. I used to pass by the chalkboards that advertised their food, but I had never bothered to go down the dark gallery that led to the restaurant's main entrance. The place had one big room with two dozen tables covered in red tablecloths.

"Be careful what you do," Montegón warned Zuñeda as we were stepping across the threshold of the restaurant.

Zuñeda stopped and observed the room. Only five tables were occupied. At one of them an older couple was eating lunch. Another table was taken up by two men in black, and the rest had men sitting alone. Two of them had their backs to the door. The third, young and dressed somewhat sloppily, looked up at us when he sensed our presence.

"Which one is he?" I asked Zuñeda.

The lawyer shrugged his shoulders and seemed to think for a moment.

"The man in the blue jacket at the right-hand back corner," he finally said, and, as if it were a social occasion, "Gentlemen, I would like to introduce you to Colonel Javier Toro Palacios."

I looked at Toro's back and immediately made a signal to Montegón. The detective grabbed the lawyer by an arm and forced him out of the restaurant. Once I was alone, I advanced toward the table occupied by the man Zuñeda had identified as Toro, and when I was almost at his side, he turned his head and looked toward the entrance. When I saw his face, something froze inside of me, and before he noticed me I turned back and took a seat at a distant table. I had a hard time responding when the waiter came to take my order. I asked for a shot of pisco as an aperitif and told him I would have a look at the menu. Toro went back to his meal. I observed his face from a distance and smiled at all that had happened over the last few weeks to bring me to this hole-in-the-wall. Was it just a coincidence, or was there something that pulled the past into the worn streets of my neighborhood? I drank a sip of pisco, and when the waiter came back to take my order, I told him that I had lost my appetite, threw a few bills on the table, and went out to the street. I wanted to think about my next step. I looked for Montegón and Zuñeda but couldn't spot them. If they were following the plan we had made a few hours ago, they should be back at the lawyer's apartment.

From my spot on the corner, I saw Toro Palacios leave the restaurant. I followed him with my eyes until he was lost among the pedestrians walking down the Calle Bandera to the north. The old man at the Chinese restaurant didn't match the image I had of the notorious torturer from another time. I couldn't let myself be fooled, though. I knew exactly who he was and where to find him. I lit a cigarette, and after getting to the Calle Aillavilú, I stopped at Anselmo's kiosk and asked him for a pack of cigarettes, which he refused to charge me for.

"I wanted to thank you for the info you got for me," I said.

"I don't remember talking about horses with you."

"I mean the info about the lawyer. It wasn't easy, but in the end, he cooperated."

"Glad to hear it. Do you remember the neighbor that I told you about the other afternoon? The one who's married to a prison guard but showed up at my house telling me she was alone and needed an understanding man?"

"Honestly, I don't know who you're talking about."

"I invited her in for a piscola, let her lean on my shoulder, and a half hour later I had her in bed. It wasn't bad, but the next day she came back to tell me that she had never cheated on her husband and she wanted to leave things like that."

"So you made her another piscola and she fell into your arms again."

"It's not just that. She came back a third time, complaining about how she regretted everything, and how she wanted to tell her husband."

"And?"

"I've been waiting for two days for the prison guard to show up, and I can't sleep. The other afternoon I saw him when he was getting home, and the guy looks like one of those wrestlers on TV. What should I do, man?"

"Buy another bottle of pisco. She'll be back again."

"Don't mess with me, man. I'm really afraid."

"Of the husband or the wife?"

"Both, I think."

I left the newspaper vendor with his worries and went into my building. At the doorman's desk I found Feliz Domingo. He had some envelopes in his hands that it seemed he didn't know what to do with.

"Bad news?" I asked him.

"Two letters for Mr. Hernández, your neighbor."

"So what's the problem?"

"I have to deliver them to him, and the last time I went to his apartment, he swore at me. That man has no manners."

"You're drowning in a glass of water, Feliz."

"Félix, Mr. Heredia. Félix."

"I can give Mr. Hernández your letters."

"Would you do that for me, Mr. Heredia?"

"It's on the way to my apartment."

"Maybe you can talk to him about his bad manners."

"That's not a bad idea, Feliz."

"Félix, with an *x*."

The mirrors in the elevator showed me the face of a man who had stopped thinking about the future. I touched the gun inside my jacket and waited for the elevator door to open. From my office, I called Campbell, my journalist friend, and told him that I had managed to find out some things about Toro Palacios. I told him to wait twenty-four hours, and if he hadn't heard from me, to call Bernales and Cotapos, the lawyer. Then I took the letters that Feliz Domingo had given me, and with more resignation than excitement, I went to deliver them.

The hallway was full of shadows, and from the neighboring apartments came the murmurs of televisions. I stopped in front of my neighbor's door and looked at the letters. For a second I felt the temptation not to intervene and to just go back to my office and read a good book. It was a fleeting thought that I put out of my mind. It was time to finish my job. I pushed the doorbell a couple of times and waited. Just like the first visit, after a time, my neighbor opened the door and showed me part of his face.

"I've got mail for you," I said, holding up the letters. "The doorman was busy and I offered to bring them up."

"Give me the letters," ordered my neighbor.

"I'd like to have a few words with you about the doorman."

"You're the private detective that has the office on this floor, right?"

"I see you're not as distracted as you act. Heredia is my name, and I would like a few minutes of your time."

"I don't have time. Pass me the letters," he insisted.

I passed the letters through the crack of light in the door, and when Hernández was getting ready to close it, I put a foot in the way to stop him and pushed in on it with all my weight. The chain holding the door to the frame broke noisily, and my neighbor fell to the floor. I didn't give him time to recover. My first punch was to his chin, and the second was a few inches above his waist. I pulled out my pistol and forced him to get on his feet, take a few steps back, and sit on the only chair in the room. I breathed deeply until I could feel my heartbeat slow to its normal speed, while I waited for him to recover.

"What do you want me to call you? Hernández? Colonel Toro Palacios? Or do you want to tell me your real name?" I asked him.

"What the hell are you talking about?" he spat back, angry.

"Or do you prefer I call you King Midas? Do you remember? Your prisoners trembled when they heard that name mentioned."

"How dare you?" he asked, defensive.

"You can't keep running. And in case you're thinking of doing something to me, let me tell you that I'm not the only one who knows your real identity."

"You're confusing me with someone else. My name is Desiderio Hernández and I can show you my ID to prove it," said my neighbor in a low voice, as if that would make his words true.

"I'd prefer to put you face-to-face with some of the people who survived your torture," I said, and then, as if talking to myself, added, "I followed your tracks through a good bit of this city, and in the end, we were only separated by a couple of doors."

"What do you want?"

"To talk about the past."

"I'm telling you again, you've got the wrong person."

"Guillermo Zuñeda. Does that name mean anything to you?"

"Nothing," he responded quickly, but a nervous tic in his right eyelid gave him away.

"Do you remember the meeting you were supposed to have with Zuñeda? Didn't it seem strange that he never got there? The truth is that we came together, and he didn't waste any time identifying you. Now he's been arrested and the police are interrogating him."

"What does that have to do with me?"

"You know exactly what I'm talking about. Sooner or later you'll have to accept that the time for hiding is over. Think about it. Depending on what you tell me, we might even be able to make a deal. You're up against a wall, and I doubt anyone is going to make you a better deal than me."

My neighbor looked at his hands and then at his surroundings. Finally, he crossed his hands over his stomach and looked me in the eye.

"Miguel Pastrana Gándara. That's my real name. It's been years since I used it," he said with exhaustion in his voice.

"It's also strange that those who were working under you didn't know it. Víctor Moltisanti, Vicente Tapia, and Danilo Uribe. None of them could tell it to me."

"There are still people who believe in loyalty."

"No, they just didn't know your true name."

"I was always careful to hide my name. It wasn't just part of my job, it was common sense. From the beginning, I knew that safety wasn't eternal, and that one day they would catch up with us. And I prepared for that moment. I invented false identities and opened bank accounts, fabricated passports, credit cards, university degrees, credentials of every kind. Later, when we left the government and they started chasing us, we created clandestine networks to keep ourselves safe and hidden."

"Now the time has come for you to answer for your crimes."

"You're digging up a past that very few want to remember."

"If that were the case, you wouldn't have tried so hard to stay hidden."

"I've never wanted to be meat for vengeance or get dragged through the tribunals."

"Or maybe you never stopped doing your old job."

"Why do you say that?" asked Pastrana, his right eyelid moving with more insistence.

"The murder I'm investigating isn't from another time. Germán Reyes. Does that name mean anything to you?"

"Nothing," responded Pastrana.

"Reyes was trying to locate ex-military members involved in human-rights violations. He found one of his torturers, and it cost him his life."

"You have an active imagination."

"Reyes was detained at Villa Grimaldi. There, he heard the names of some of the men who tortured him, and once he got out, he spent a good part of his time locating those responsible for what happened to him and his friends. Finally, after many years of diligent work, he uncovered the true identities of the torturers who had called themselves Toro Palacios and Fullerton." I noticed that on hearing the name Fullerton, Pastrana made a new effort to look nonchalant.

"Just out of curiosity, where do you want this story to end?"

"I've been asking myself one question this whole time. What is an officer of your rank doing in a dump like this? Alone, hiding, running around with a drunk pederast of a lawyer, forced to use a fake name. It sounds like a story with gaps to be filled in. A story about an officer with dirty hands trying to protect himself from those who can judge him. The plan works for years, until you figure out that the past you have spent your life trying to hide is about to emerge, like a giant wave in a peaceful ocean. I don't know how you found out about Reyes or the progress of his investigation, but one day you decided to remove the danger, and with the help of some old comrades, you killed the interloper."

"You don't have any proof to back up that absurd story."

"There are other questions bouncing around in my head. What were the names of the guys you used to kill Reyes? What is Fullerton's real name? Who told you that Reyes knew your real name and Fullerton's?"

"I'll ask you one more time. What do you gain from digging up these things?"

"I want to silence the echoes of the past that I can't stop hearing."

"I don't know what they're paying you, but we can make a deal. How much do you want to stay quiet?"

"I don't think you have any intention of keeping up your end of the bargain. You just want to buy yourself enough time to plan your next move."

"You seem like a stubborn man."

"There is no way out this time, Pastrana. Even if you eliminate me, you'd only buy yourself a few days' head start."

"A goddamned stubborn mule, just like Reyes," said Pastrana with disdain.

"Was that why you killed him? Because he was trying to find his torturers?"

"You're wrong. I had other ways of evading Reyes's investigations. But I'm a soldier and I follow the orders I'm given."

"Your answer isn't very original. With people like you, the other guy is always responsible," I said. "Was Julio Suazo also on your list of stubborn people?"

"Who is that?"

"Another person who passed through Villa Grimaldi. He gave testimony against you in court, and very soon after that, he died in a street accident. It was a long time ago now, but the daughter of the deceased continues to think it wasn't an accident."

"They may have mentioned me in a lot of trials, but I'm not responsible for all of the dead people in this country. When are you planning on wrapping up your interrogation?"

"When I hear the answers I came for."

"Few things hurt as much as loneliness," he muttered. "But I'm not complaining. They taught me to obey and be loyal."

"From now on you won't be alone. Cops, lawyers, and the families of the people you killed are very interested in hearing from you."

"Is that the only option you're offering me?"

"You'll find some old friends in jail," I told him, ignoring his question. "A jail with a lot more amenities than most."

"Why are you doing all this? Why are you getting yourself mixed up in things that are more complicated than you can imagine?"

"I'm one of those people who pay attention to the lives of their neighbors. A nosy guy who will do whatever he can so that you don't get away again."

Pastrana lowered his gaze and kept it there for some time, thinking.

Perhaps it was time for me to call Bernales, I thought, so he could take charge of the officer. Maybe he'd be able to get more information out of him and then take him to an honest judge. I looked at the pistol in my hand, and for a moment I imagined the sound of a gunshot in the room.

The temptation didn't last long. Everything happened quickly. Pastrana took advantage of my distraction, grabbed a glass ashtray within reach, and threw it at my head. The strike wasn't violent, but it made me lose my grip on the situation. I fell to my knees and was unable to defend myself. Pastrana pressed his advantage, punching me in the chin. When I came around, he had left the room. I chased him and managed to see him disappear into the elevator, which must have taken some time to reach our floor. I ran down the stairs and arrived at the ground floor at the same time that Pastrana was closing the building door behind him.

Out on the street, I saw him running away among the throngs of people. Even from a distance, I could make out his green shirt. He tried to run, but it was clear that time had slowed him down. He crossed the street, dodging the oncoming cars, and after looking behind him, walked toward Calle General Mackenna. I saw him stop and look at the cars that were passing in front of him. I figured he would try to hail a taxi, but I was wrong. He fixed his shirt and went into the sales office of a building that was under construction a few steps away from the Cal y Canto metro station. I took a deep breath and walked toward the sales office. Inside I found a saleswoman busy with a client. I waited a few seconds and asked her about the man in the green shirt who had come in just moments before.

"He went up to the display apartments. Tenth floor," answered the woman, who then turned her attention back to her client.

The building was in its final stages of construction. At the end of a hallway covered in plywood, I found the elevator. Its doors took time to open, and when they finally did, I entered a box whose walls were protected by plastic and cardboard. An improvised paper sign announced that the only stop the elevator would make was the tenth floor. I pressed the button and the box began moving. On the tenth floor a sign pointed toward the apartments that could be visited by prospective buyers. I began my search with the biggest one. It was dominated by the odors of paint and glue. I quickly moved through the living room, kitchen, and dining room. In the bedrooms I looked in the closets, and in the bathroom I swept away the shower curtain. I didn't see anyone. I took a quick look at the balcony and walked to the next apartment, where a couple was arguing about the size of the rooms. Not a trace of Pastrana.

The last of the apartments was the size of a dollhouse. The kitchen, living room, and dining room had all been shoehorned into one small space where I didn't think more than three guests could stand at the same time. The bathroom and bedroom were like two matchboxes. I didn't see any sign of Pastrana, but when I was ready to leave I heard shouts coming from the street. I remembered something that I had seen in the bedroom that I hadn't paid enough attention to. I retraced my steps and stopped at a glass door leading to a small balcony. I went outside, and the vertigo made me step back. I controlled my breathing, looked for a second time at the base of the building, and knew immediately that the chase had come to an end. In the middle of a circle of workers who were shouting and looking up, I saw a body wearing a green shirt. I left the apartment and got into the elevator with the couple who had been arguing about the size of the rooms.

I went back to the office and asked the saleswoman for permission to use the phone on her desk. It took a few rings for Bernales to answer his cell phone, and when he did, he told me that he was inspecting a dump where a rotten cadaver had been discovered, probably stabbed by members of a gang of neo-Nazis. I told him about Pastrana, and we agreed to meet at La Piojera later in the day. Upon leaving the office, I approached Pastrana's corpse and contemplated it for a few seconds. Just another mass of body parts on the pavement. I lit a cigarette and began to walk back to my apartment.

26

The door to Pastrana's apartment was still half-open, and without any reason other than curiosity, I went into the room where our last conversation had taken place. The ashtray on the floor made me remember the lump on the side of my forehead.

The apartment's layout was similar to mine. A big living-dining room, which in my case was used as an office. Two bedrooms, the same number of bathrooms, and a big, well-lit kitchen. One of the bedrooms was unoccupied, and the other had only a bed and a nightstand in it. Beneath the bed I found a pair of black shoes, and on the nightstand a Tom Clancy novel, two pens, and a packet of aspirin. In the closet hung a blue suit with four miserable ten-peso coins in one of the pockets. Nothing that laid bare any feature of Pastrana's personality or gave a clue about what he had been doing since he'd gone into hiding. I thought about a commando surviving behind enemy lines. A man who had given himself over to luck with no resources beyond his instincts and his knowledge of killing. I asked myself if his conscience could have bothered him or if he really was nothing but a mastiff trained to obey the orders of his master. A creature devoid of feelings who opted for suicide when cornered—not out of regret, but to cut off all connection to the source of his orders.

Before leaving the apartment, I inspected the kitchen. In the pantry were a can of instant coffee and an unopened bottle of Absolut. Above the sink I found glasses and a teacup. I grabbed the bottle and walked out with it under my arm. Nobody would miss it, and Pastrana had no reason to celebrate anymore.

Back at my place, I sat beside my desk and for a few minutes scratched Simenon's soft, hairy belly. There was something incomplete in my investigations, something that remained hidden. I couldn't put my finger on the cause of my unease. It was like a jab in the middle of my gut or a premonition of bad news. I opened the bottle of vodka and poured a few drops into a glass. Simenon smelled it and moved away. He went down to the floor and started scratching the side of the desk that he usually sharpened his claws on. The vodka didn't do much to sharpen my thinking, but it did help me remember that Montegón was still in Zuñeda's apartment.

The voice of the detective revealed his irritation. I asked him about Zuñeda and he told me that the lawyer was fast asleep, hugging a bottle of whiskey that he had emptied in no time.

"You can leave him alone," I told him. "When he wakes up he'll probably think the last few days were part of a nightmare. He might not even remember what we look like."

"I'm not really excited about the idea of letting Zuñeda go free."

"He did what he said he would and helped us find Toro Palacios."

"OK. I'll leave Zuñeda passed out," grumbled Montegón without a hint of excitement, and then he asked me how things had gone with Toro.

"Toro, who also went by Desiderio Hernández, and whose real name was Miguel Pastrana Gándara, is likely on a slab at the Legal Medical Service," I replied, and then gave him a detailed account of my neighbor's one-way flight.

"Case closed," declared Montegón. "Now what are we going to do?"

"Probably go back to what I always do."

"And our partnership?"

"My business barely covers the cost of my food."

"That's not the answer I was hoping for, Heredia."

"We can always get together to have a few drinks. I'm not forgetting that I owe you more than one favor."

"Maybe at some point, after a few drinks, you'll change your mind about a partnership."

I spotted Bernales sitting at a table from which he could watch the customers coming in. La Piojera looked basically the same, but upon closer inspection, it was clear that some of the tables and chairs had been replaced. The rest was the same as it always was, with mason jars of *chicha* and *pipeño* on top of the bar, a couple of cats passing through the customers' legs, university students drinking their "earthquakes," and the same old paintings on the walls. Most people were more preoccupied with looking for the bottom of their glasses than with their surroundings.

"Why do you like this place?" inquired Bernales, a bit irritated from waiting for me.

"It's got life to it, local color, and nobody cares what their neighbor is doing."

"It reminds me of when I was new on the job. My boss used to come here to find informants."

We ordered a few pieces of *arrollado caliente* with boiled potatoes and tomato salad. When the mountain of food arrived at our table in a large earthenware baking dish, Bernales attacked it with an uncontrollable appetite.

"Nothing all that surprising," he commented when I had finished telling him about Pastrana. "He couldn't take being exposed and chose suicide instead. We see the same thing sometimes with common criminals, especially when they've spent some time in jail before."

"Pastrana wasn't a common criminal. Nor was he a thief who stabs himself when he's about to be arrested. He was an army officer who specialized in intelligence work. He must have had a reason. I think he was trying to hide something from us."

"The guy's dead. Why keep thinking about it?"

"I was hoping to see him in jail."

"And what about Zuñeda? He also deserves to spend some time behind bars."

"If you put one of your men on him, it won't take him long to mess up. Drug trafficking and pedophilia. He'll give you a reason to lock him up."

"A few days from now that bird will be in the cage, I promise you," said Bernales, and after gulping down a piece of arrollado, he added, "We worked Lugo and Bulnes against each other. By the second question they were already contradicting each other, and the rest was just putting the pieces together."

"Aren't you sick of stomping around in the shit all the time?" I asked Bernales. "Murderers, drug dealers, rapists, guys who throw their daughters out of the apartment window. Something is wrong with people. Frustration, debt, young people with no options other than unemployment and misery, people working day in and day out to pay off their loans. Little or no happiness. It makes me want to lower the curtain and start history all over again."

"I try not to think about it too much."

"There must be another way to live, Bernales."

"You're a bit old to change the world."

"Is there an age for that? I'm still holding on to the dream of living in a world where our profession is a useless thing, a relic of the past."

"I'm a cop and I just do my job. Not like you, always looking for five legs on a cat."

"Maybe you're right, Bernales. Reality won't let me unwind."

◆ ◆ ◆

Five legs on a cat. That was just it. Looking for a hidden sign, the truth behind appearances, the answer to the question no one dared to ask aloud. I had said goodbye to the policeman in front of La Piojera and was on my way back to my office, without much to do except mull over what Pastrana had said. *Orders.* He had talked about orders that he had to obey. But was he referring to the past or the present? Something didn't fit. I looked at the bottle of vodka on the desk but left it where it was.

"What's got you worried?" asked Simenon. "You're going to die trying to figure out what's on the dark side of the moon."

"And what if that's what life is all about? Imagining, asking, dreaming, with your feet on the earth and also far from it."

"Come on, Heredia. You're giving yourself too much credit. A few loose threads, the sensation of having left the investigation half-finished. So what? Pastrana ordered Reyes killed. Carvilio was killed by Lugo. What else do you want? Two crimes for the price of one, like an end-of-season clearance."

"Doubt kills—or opens doors. I still don't know who killed Reyes."

"Don't push your cheap philosophy on me."

"Reyes discovered Pastrana, and instead of changing safe houses like he had for years, Pastrana killed him. Why did he do it? Why didn't he just lie low and wait for the storm to pass?"

"Maybe Reyes discovered something more than Pastrana's name and location."

"Now I think you've got something, you nosy cat. Finally you say something that makes sense." I picked up the phone.

"What's it about this time?" asked Campbell, after a long yawn. "You never call to talk about the weather or the fate of Atlantis."

"I'd like to, but I know you're a busy man and have more important things to worry about."

"Tell me about it. I have to write three articles by tomorrow. In addition to that, I was hired to write fifteen ads, two radio scripts, and six talking points for a senator's campaign."

"You know, it is possible to say no. 'I can't. I don't want to. I don't have time. I'm not interested.'"

"And pass up a handful of cash?"

"Money, money. You're going to get to your last day and keep thinking that you've got to pump up the numbers in your checking account."

"Stop busting my balls and tell me what you need," the journalist growled back.

"I need information about the location of agents from the Directorate of National Intelligence and the National Information Center."

"Don't you think that's a bit of a broad request? Some of them stayed in their jobs, others were reassigned, and a good number retired. Of that last group, the majority live in silence, and a small number, the most obvious ones, have ended up in the tribunals."

"I don't want information on all the agents. Just ones you've come across in your work. I need some of the cases that caught your attention because they mentioned a name you hadn't heard before."

"I wrote a lot of pieces like that. You could check my archives, but you'd probably just spend a couple of weeks digging around in my papers and contaminating my office with your disgusting cigarettes. I'll send you some articles by email, and if something grabs your attention you can check in the archives."

"I don't have email. I have more faith in the postman who rings twice."

"You can read them on my blog."

"I don't have a computer, and the only café in the neighborhood with internet was closed for not paying their taxes."

"Next you'll tell me I have to write them with ink and a quill."

"The best thing is a modest black pen."

Anselmo came into the office carrying a pile of papers that looked ready to fall out of his hands. He indelicately tossed them onto the desk blotter.

"Your friend Campbell's gone crazy, man," he said, wiping his shiny forehead with a kerchief. "He sent a guy with all these papers. I don't know why, but the messenger left the delivery with me. What's this about?"

"I asked Campbell to send me some of his articles."

"And couldn't he have sent them to my fax machine?"

"There are too many pages."

"It would have made use of the machine, because up until now, it's only been good for receiving religious chain letters and ads."

"You could always donate it to a museum, together with the photo from your first communion."

"Give me a break. I'm thinking about exchanging it for a toaster to go with the coffeemaker. What do you think?"

"Every day your brain shrinks a bit more, Anselmo."

"You've got to keep up with the times, man."

"At this rate, you'll only be keeping up with the rhythm of debts. You'll end up like most Chileans, indebted and stressed—or maybe you'll end up like a friend who remembers the milestones of his life by when he bought the appliances in his house. When I talk with him he tells me things like: 'My oldest daughter was born two months before I bought the computer' or 'My wife had an appendectomy the same year that I bought my first VHS.'"

"I want to enjoy some comfort in life."

"A book, a nice bed, food on the table, and a bit of music to soothe the ears."

"Don't terrorize me, man. As far as books go, just looking at a library makes me tired. I prefer to tune to the horse-racing channel and open a couple of beers. Like my dear mother used to say, 'God has a place in heaven for everybody to wear the shoe that fits them best.'"

"There's no point arguing with you, Anselmo."

"Nor with you."

I read Campbell's stories carefully and didn't find any information that shed new light on the investigation. Toro Palacios was mentioned in one of the pieces as being responsible for the torture of a professor who had filed charges against him, but the case stalled for lack of proof. Most of the stories focused on cases that made it to trial, and whose guilty parties either served their sentences or died during the judicial process. Other pieces highlighted how ex-military men of different ranks were supposedly involved in illegitimate activities like arms trafficking, drug trafficking, and the disappearance of people. The only constant in all his articles was the cruelty with which so many lives had been ended, and the apathy demonstrated by the judges. It took until the 1990s for many magistrates to do the work of pulling back the veil of secrecy hiding the guilty.

I set aside the papers for a while and didn't do anything but contemplate the piece of sky I could see through the window. Some clouds moved slowly by, far removed from my musings on the work remaining on Germán Reyes's case. I would have to talk with his sister and girlfriend, and then, if I still felt like it, go back to Terán's workshop. After that, I could return to my office, sit down, and wait for more clients to arrive.

"You should be used to discovering half-truths," I heard Simenon say as he left the pile of books he had been sleeping on.

"Things don't always turn out like one wants. I would've liked to have gotten more out of Pastrana."

"The biggest truths are hidden in plain sight."

"I've got the feeling that I missed at least one clue," I sighed, barely hearing what Simenon had said.

"You need to take a walk around the neighborhood and think about other things."

"And maybe drink a glass of wine."

"You've always got an excuse for drinking."

"My friendship with wine doesn't need an excuse."

27

My friendship with wine was fragile. After walking around the neighborhood and going into a couple of dive bars with not many customers and too many hookers, I came back to my apartment and gave my body over to the caress of my sheets. I was tired, I missed Griseta. I let sleep throw its net over me, and without wanting to keep fighting, I fell asleep.

In the morning, I was awakened by Anselmo's voice. He seemed especially interested in reintegrating me to the poorly lit reality of my bedroom. He was wearing a bright lime-green T-shirt and shorts that left his skinny, hairy toothpicks visible.

"I thought you'd want to read the news today," he said, passing me a paper whose top story showed the silicone implants of a television floozy. "There is something in there about your neighbor's death."

The story occupied a whole page and featured an old photo of Pastrana, dressed in uniform. The article was based mainly on supposition and contained only a few certainties. It said that the ex-officer had suffered through a prolonged depression, attributed to his retirement from the army and having been named in multiple legal cases. The story quoted his younger sister, who said she hadn't seen him during the last five years, since the burial of their mother. The woman had thought he'd been living outside of Santiago and gave no comment when asked about the accusations against her brother. There was also a statement from a colonel, the spokesman for a retired officers' organization. He lamented Pastrana's death and attributed it to the aggression of those seeking vengeance for their defeat at the hands of the military. This, in turn, was juxtaposed with a note about the recent suicide of a woman who had been a jailer in the "Sexy Blindfold," a DINA torture center. The woman had hanged herself from a tree in the backyard of the house where she lived alone, overwhelmed, according to her neighbors, by problems with alcohol and drugs.

"God punishes, but not with beatings," Anselmo said when I had finished my reading.

"You can't escape the pressure of memory. Sooner or later, whether we like it or not, we've got to keep our appointment with her."

"The news in the paper didn't help much, did it?"

"The investigation is done, and it's time to inform the interested parties of the results. After that I'm going to sit down and watch the pigeons."

"The possibilities seem pretty limited."

"I'll always find something to entertain myself with. Crime is always lurking just outside our doors," I said, somewhat dejected, while I leafed through the paper for the simple and morbid pleasure of confirming that the world kept spinning with the same clumsiness.

Anselmo returned to his kiosk. I drank a coffee, and a bit later, as I was getting ready to leave the apartment, I heard the grating sound of the telephone. The caller asked about my fee to work as a bodyguard for a singer who would be on a long tour throughout the country. I gave him a King Kong doppelganger's phone number and hung up when the guy started to insult my family. Three seconds later, the phone chirped again. I thought the guy was still worried about the origins of my ancestors, and I picked up the phone ready to give him hell.

"Finally, you answered," I heard Griseta say. "I've been trying to call you for days now and you never answer the phone. What's going on? How are you?"

"As good as someone about to be unemployed can be," I responded.

"That's all you have to tell me?"

"Simenon and I miss you. When are you heading back?"

"I'll be back in Santiago in two or three weeks."

"You'll have to say goodbye to the fresh air and leisure."

"No leisure here. I've spent the last two days reading things written by the women that I'm interviewing. I gave every one of them a notebook so that they could write whatever they wanted."

"A notebook?"

"It's not something they teach us to do in the university, but it can be useful. I ask my patients to write down their life experiences and everything that they might not want to tell me during our sessions. When I read the notebooks, I usually get valuable information."

"Can the patients write about their jobs?"

"Anything that influences their behavior or their feelings," said Griseta.

"Do other psychologists ever use that method?"

"It's not standard, unless they're working with children, who are sometimes asked to make drawings that can then be evaluated by a specialist. In the case of adult patients, oral expression is usually privileged. And, of course, there is the notebook that the psychologist uses to note down what her patients say."

"I don't think that's the case," I thought aloud.

"Why the sudden interest in my work, Heredia?"

"Maybe when you come back I'll be able to give you a good answer to that question. Right now I have to go to a client's house," I said, trying to end the conversation.

But I didn't go to Virginia Reyes's house, because as soon as I had hung up with Griseta, I called the medical clinic where Benilde Roos worked, and asked to speak with her.

"I'm still looking for the men who killed Germán," I told her, asking myself if I was telling the truth or lying to gain her trust. "I need to ask you a few questions."

"What do you want to know?"

"Did Germán write in his notebooks every day?"

"Why does that matter?"

"Frankly, I don't know. But I'm interested in hearing what you can tell me about it."

"He wrote stories every once in a while, depending on whether he wanted to and if he had time. In terms of his investigations, he wrote pretty much daily, every time he read something that interested him."

"Do you know if he wrote about his therapy sessions in that one?"

"He had a special notebook for that. I learned about it one day when he couldn't find it and called me to ask if it was at my house. In the end, he never found it, and I guess he must have written the therapy notes in the notebook that he used for his investigations."

"You mean what he was writing a day before he died."

"No. The notebooks were in the psychologist's office the day he died. I guess Germán forgot them there and she wanted to have a look at them."

"There's something that doesn't fit, Benilde. The last time we talked, you told me that you had found the notebooks in your house."

"I must have been confused," said the nurse, lowering her voice. "Ana Melgoza sent me the notebooks after Germán's murder, two days before I decided to give them to Virginia. When I got them, I was busy with something; I left them in my bedroom and forgot about them until the next day, when I was cleaning the room. At that point I remembered Virginia. She had never been in favor of our relationship, so I thought that by sharing the notebooks with her I could show her that there was a real relationship between the two of us."

"Did you notice that there were pages missing?"

"No. What pages are you talking about? Blank pages?"

"When I was checking the notebooks I discovered that there were some missing pages in one of them. Some of the notes had been torn out."

"I didn't notice when I read them. Do you have any idea what Germán could have been writing on those pages?" Benilde asked.

"Not at the moment," I replied, just then remembering a name that I had read in one of Campbell's articles.

28

The Chevy Nova didn't want to start, even with the help of Anselmo and two neighbors pushing it. I left it parked and got into a taxi to go to Ana Melgoza's office. On the way, while the driver complained about rising gas prices, I reread Campbell's pieces until I found the name that I had remembered during my conversation with Benilde Roos.

The psychologist's waiting room was full of patients, and I had to rely on a number of lies to get her secretary to put me on the list of appointments that day. I sat down beside a young man with dyed-red hair and a woman who chewed her nails compulsively. On one low, square table there was a pile of pamphlets about diets that seemed specifically designed to torment fat people. I picked up one of the pamphlets and the woman asked me if I was seeing the psychologist for bulimia.

"I'm a serial killer," I responded, hoping to avoid conversation with the woman. "My problem is that no one takes me seriously. I've gone to the police a few times to confess my crimes, and they won't believe me."

The kid let loose a cackle upon hearing my answer; the woman, disconcerted, ate her fingernails and didn't say another word. Two hours later, as I was questioning the intuition that had led me to the clinic, the secretary told me that I could go in to see the therapist.

Ana Melgoza looked just as attractive as during our first conversation, but something in her tone of voice and disengaged manner told me that she was tired of her patients' misery. I sat in front of her desk and remained silent for a moment, trying to decide upon the most suitable way to begin my questions.

"My secretary told me you would like to talk about a matter outside of my specialty," she said.

"You don't remember me? Only a few days ago, I was here to talk to you about Germán Reyes, one of your patients."

"The detective?" asked Ana Melgoza, showing surprise that didn't seem authentic. "Excuse me for not recognizing you, but I get confused with so many people coming through this office."

"For your patients' sake, I hope you don't tell them the same thing."

"I remember my patients perfectly," she said in an irritated tone.

"If you want to smoke, feel free."

"How do you know I want to smoke?"

"You've seen three people in the last two hours, and during our last meeting you told me that you don't smoke in front of patients."

"You've got a good memory," she said as she took a pack of cigarettes out of her blazer, and then asked, "What can I help you with, Mr. . . . ?"

"Heredia," I responded, then I summarized my work from Virginia Reyes's visit until then.

"I suppose that with Pastrana's suicide you will have completed your investigation. I congratulate you for being so efficient," she said when I had finished my story.

"I'm not sure I deserve your congratulations."

"No?" asked Ana Melgoza, sounding nervous.

"I get the impression that I've left a few loose threads, and I need you to help me tie them up. Since you told me I could come and bother you with any new questions . . ."

"What questions?"

"Do you use notebooks in your work with patients?" I asked slowly, calculating the effect that my words might have on her mood.

"Why are you interested in that?"

"I already told you, there are a few loose threads. What can you tell me about it?"

"I use notebooks to record what they say in the sessions."

"I'm referring to notebooks used by the patients."

"Sometimes I use them with children, or with adults who have trouble communicating. A key aspect of therapy is getting patients to talk about their problems."

"Did Germán Reyes use notebooks?"

"I'd have to look at his file to be able to answer that."

"Don't mess with me. You told me a couple minutes ago that you remember your patients perfectly."

"Maybe I exaggerated and there are some details that I forget," said Melgoza with apparent indifference.

"You also sent the notebooks to Benilde Roos."

"That's true. How could I forget about that?" the psychologist added, accompanying her words with a nervous smile. "Germán took notes about what he wanted to tell me and used them in our conversations. It was a sort of memory aid for him. But neither of those two notebooks was the one that he used in our sessions. That one got lost on the bus or left in a restaurant."

"Just the same, you asked him for the two notebooks to read them more carefully. Why did you do it? Because Germán, when he didn't have the usual notebook, wrote some notes for his therapy in one of them? Or because you were interested in some of the notes that he had made during his investigations?"

"Are you accusing me of something?"

"What was it that caught your attention?"

"Did you read the notebooks?" asked the psychologist, dodging my question.

"Almost every page," I responded, and then, as she was lowering her eyes, I reminded her that Germán was dedicated to unmasking former military men involved in acts of repression.

"We talked about that during your first visit."

"Yes, and it has me wondering why you still haven't answered my question about why you kept the notebooks."

"They contained useful information for therapy. As for the rest, once they stopped being important to me, I sent them to Benilde Roos."

"And she passed them to Germán's sister."

"I didn't know where they ended up. I also don't know where you're going with these questions."

"Did you notice that some pages were missing in one of the notebooks?"

"No, I didn't notice any missing pages."

"Perhaps you gave the notebook to someone else?"

"How dare you? What my patients say and write is confidential, and covered under physician-patient privilege."

"If that's the case, can you tell me why you tore pages out of the notebook?" I insisted, prepared to confront her with the idea that had brought me to her office in the first place.

"I've had a long day and I'm tired," sighed the psychologist, lighting another cigarette. "I don't have the patience to put up with your rudeness."

"I want you to be honest and help me find out the truth."

"A moment ago you told me that you were done investigating Germán's killing."

"I still don't know who was behind the crime. I know that Pastrana organized the murder, but I have a feeling that someone else ordered him to do it," I said.

"Are you accusing me of taking part in that crime?"

"You had privileged access to Reyes's notebook, and unless I am wrong, you are the sister of the retired brigadier Tulio Melgoza Imbert."

"Tulio is my older brother. Why does that matter?"

"Reyes unearthed his dark past. Tulio Melgoza, when he was a young and promising lieutenant, worked in various positions for the poorly named intelligence services. Fullerton was the alias that he used then. Despite his young age, he stood out for his ferocity in interrogating prisoners. Until Germán's discoveries, nobody had been able to uncover Fullerton's real identity. You should know that your brother's name is mentioned in numerous judicial cases."

"Where did you get that story from? I haven't heard that much nonsense in a long time."

"The imagination helps in some cases. In novels, crimes are usually complex and represent a challenge for the sharpest wits, but in reality, they follow a much simpler pattern. A motive or a good clue is usually enough to bring the detective to the killer's doorstep."

"You can't force me to continue with this conversation," said Ana Melgoza, raising her voice.

"I can be rough if I have to. But I don't want to do that to you. Something tells me that you're the victim of a game that you never wanted to play."

"What makes you think that?" she asked, a look of contained sadness on her face.

"The first time we talked, you told me about your work recording testimony for the National Commission on Political Prisoners and Torture, created to identify and recognize the victims of repression. This, I suppose, motivated Reyes to come to your office."

"You win, Heredia. Like they say, you can't cover the sun with your finger."

"I have time and patience. Tell me your story."

"I'm the black sheep of the family," said Ana Melgoza. "Or better put, the red sheep. While I was studying at the university, I was a member of the Christian Left, and since that time I have never been in favor of the military government. The only one, besides my father, in a family of businessmen, soldiers, and right-wing priests; the only ones who didn't breathe easy when the armed forces began to kill and jail the rebellious scum, as my family called the supporters of the Popular Unity party. When they offered me the opportunity to participate in the work of the commission, I felt I would have the chance to contribute to the reparation of a lot of injustice."

"Tell me about your brother."

"I had heard the rumors about his work in the security services. I also heard, like most people, the stories about what happened in Villa Grimaldi, the National Stadium, Dawson Island, Chile Stadium, and other torture centers. Before accepting the work with the commission, I talked about it with Tulio. He denied everything and told me that his work at the time consisted only of processing the information gathered by agents embedded in the unions and Catholic organizations. I wasn't surprised to hear him say that, but I didn't believe him."

"When did you figure out that your brother was Fullerton?"

"Germán told me that he had made progress in his investigations and read me part of his notes. I told him I wanted to analyze them and asked for the notebooks. While reading them, I remembered the testimony from Villa Grimaldi that I had heard during my work. Even with proof in my hands, I couldn't accept that he was the same Fullerton that the prisoners had accused of so much wickedness. First I felt disbelief, and then shame. How could someone so close to me, someone who had been raised with the same values by our parents, have committed so many atrocities? I met with Tulio and he told me that I shouldn't pay attention to Communist lies. I haven't talked to him since I gave him Reyes's notes."

"I want to believe what you're saying, but I don't understand why you ended up helping your brother."

"For my father and my husband," said the psychologist, who then took a nervous drag on her cigarette. "There are two long stories."

"I came to hear everything you have to tell."

"My father is an old army officer who was forced into retirement after the military coup. At that time, he was one of the officers who, like the assassinated General Schneider, believed in the army's obligation to adhere to the constitution. He never agreed with the coup and agreed even less with the crimes they committed afterward. One of his great sources of pride was seeing my brother go into the army and become an officer. My father is old now. If he finds out that Tulio participated in the crimes that he hated so much, it will be his death. What he understands as military honor has ruled his life since he began his career in the armed services. Tulio made sure to make me see what kind of an effect it would have on my father."

"That's your father's story. What's your husband's?"

"It's a story that only my brother and I know. In a few words, it's that the father of my oldest son isn't my husband but an old classmate from the university who I had a brief affair with after getting married. Immaturity, weakness, call it whatever you want. What is true is that I love my husband, and to save my marriage, I chose to keep it quiet. Tulio discovered the truth when he found a letter in my office that had been sent by my lover. He used his power to detain my classmate and interrogate him about our relationship. He never told me until I talked with him about Germán's investigations. In that moment, he reminded me about my father's health and revealed what he knew about my son Eduardo."

"So you decided to give the notes to your brother."

"I let him intimidate me, but I never thought Tulio would commit murder to hide his past. I'll regret that until my last day."

"Why did you tear the pages out of the notebook? You could have given your brother the whole thing or photocopied the important parts."

"I wanted to make a copy, but Tulio demanded the original. I also thought that Germán would ask for the notebook back, and only after

I tore the pages out did I realize that he could tell they were missing. I got nervous and acted recklessly."

"I also don't understand why you gave the notebooks to Benilde Roos."

"I thought that someone else might find out about the notebook's existence, and in that case, it would be better if it were with someone else. Once it was in Benilde's hands, nobody could accuse me of tearing out the pages."

"That's the only reason?"

"No. After Germán was killed, I understood that I should have turned my brother in. I thought that giving away the notebooks might lead to him being discovered without my involvement, and that seems to be the only thing I didn't get wrong. In everything else, I was naive. My brother knew that Germán, with notes or without them, would reveal that he was Fullerton. That's why Tulio decided to kill him. For that, and because Germán knew about his other crimes."

"What other crimes?"

"The ones mentioned in the pages I took out of the notebook."

"Do you remember what they said?"

"I don't just remember them. I can give them to you to read. I copied the pages before giving them to Tulio."

"An ace up your sleeve?"

"My brother's reaction when he learned about the notebook scared me, and I decided to keep a copy for protection."

"You did a good job," I said, and after looking the woman in the eye, I added, "Now you'll have to answer the police's questions."

"That's something I've been ready for since Reyes died. It's time for me to take responsibility for my part."

"You'll have to tell your story many times."

"I should have told Germán the truth, and should have known that Tulio wouldn't stand around with his arms crossed just because I had given him the pages. I also don't know why Germán never noticed that my brother and I had the same last name."

"We all make mistakes. You know which were yours, and maybe Germán noticed too late that the last names coincided, and didn't have time to amend the error."

"What are you going to do?" asked Ana Melgoza.

"Read the photocopies and call some friends."

"Tulio will have to pay for what he has done, and my father will find out about it."

"It's always better to bet on the truth."

"I just have one question, Heredia. What made you ask about the notebooks?"

"You're not going to believe me, but I did it with the help of a psychologist."

I closed the door of the office and smiled at the thought that I finally knew who the mysterious "she" that Reyes had mentioned in his notes was. I went out onto the street and started walking without any real direction, watching the people on their way home. Made-up faces, dyed hair, dark glasses. Appearances. All appearances, trickery, masks, hiding, and lies.

29

Germán Reyes made two mistakes. First, for reasons that no one would understand, he didn't realize that the last names of his psychologist and the brigadier were the same; and, second, he entered his most important discoveries in the wrong notebook. As I read the photocopies that Ana Melgoza had given me, I saw that in addition to the identities of the torturers, Reyes had also made a list of all the cases in which they were mentioned. But that wasn't all—a large part of the notes was dedicated to recopying the confessions of Bernardo Aliaga, an agent of the Directorate of National Intelligence, who had been given a twenty-year prison sentence for the kidnapping and murder of a student activist in 1982. Reyes wrote in one section:

> We saw each other for the first time in ten years, when I visited him in the penitentiary hoping to obtain information that would allow me to locate Fullerton. He didn't tell me anything at that time, but I took the risk of giving him a telephone number he could reach me at in case he changed his mind. I didn't have any hope that it would happen, so I was surprised when I received a call seven months later. When I visited him for the second time, I could see immediately that Aliaga was ill. He had lost more

> than forty pounds and could barely walk. He told me that he had liver cancer, and that treatment hadn't worked. Without any prodding from me, he talked about his relationship with Toro Palacios and Fullerton. Aliaga had been a subordinate of both officers during his time within the security services. Due to his close personal as well as professional relationships with both men, Aliaga was one of the few men to know both of their real names. Aliaga remembered a surprising number of names of the prisoners who had gone through Villa Grimaldi, and he talked in great detail about how the different offices within the DINA and the CNI operated. He also, without my asking, talked about the work of the Directorate of Army Intelligence, DINE, the military agency that had succeeded the DINA and the CNI. I went back to visit him a third time, and it was then that he talked about the organization that Fullerton had created, with the help of other officers and the complicity of high-ranking functionaries in both the Business and Materiel Manufacturing Unit of the army and the Logistics Branch. It was difficult to believe what he was telling me was true, but by verifying his information against media reports and court documents, I understood how powerful the information I had in my hands was.

The last part of the notes reminded me of what Pastrana had said about having orders that he had to follow, and I now had no doubt what had motivated the murder of Germán Reyes. I prepared my next steps, but before moving the pieces on the board, I thought about covering my back, and called Marcos Campbell to let him know about the new information I had on my desk.

Finding Tulio Melgoza was more difficult than I had imagined. It took me a full day just to figure out where he lived, and another two days following his movements to find out that he spent most of his time in his office, which was located close to the Ministry of Defense. He had been retired from the army for three years and managed a security-consulting business that specialized in providing guards, drivers, and personal bodyguards to a clientele that included financial companies, supermarkets, universities, and private schools. During the stakeout, I saw him leave his office a number of times, always accompanied by a muscular young man who I guessed was his assistant or bodyguard. Melgoza was blond, of medium height, and had kept himself in good shape. He was married to a lawyer who worked in the Ministry of Foreign Affairs and had two children. The oldest had graduated from the Military Academy one year ago, and the other was studying at the Naval Academy.

On the fourth day, I discovered that Melgoza had a routine that could help me. Every morning on the way to his office, he went to a church six blocks from his house. He prayed for a few minutes and then went on his way. This first stop of his day was made alone, without his guard, and in his own car. The church was small. It had a main door, and one on the side that led to the parish house where two older priests lived. It was the ideal setting for a talk with the retired officer, and without thinking about it any more, I spent a few hours briefing Anselmo, Campbell, and Atilio Montegón.

"You're crazy, man!" exclaimed Anselmo when I told him my plan.

"You're a condemned man who wants to put the noose around his own neck," responded Campbell.

"Where and what time?" asked Montegón with enthusiasm.

After rereading Reyes's notes, I made my own summary of the information and left the apartment to have a drink and go over the details of the plan I intended to carry out the next day.

Except for the old women praying at the front altar, the church was empty. Melgoza arrived at the same time as he usually did. He was wearing a gray jacket and blue pants. A shiny black briefcase hung from his left hand. He looked over the interior of the church and sat in a pew close to the door. I left my hiding place in a confession booth, caressed the Beretta in my right-hand jacket pocket, and walked toward the soldier.

"Good morning, Brigadier Melgoza. I want you to know that I'm pointing a gun at you, and that behind us I have friends ready to use their weapons," I said, sitting down beside him and nodding toward the main door of the church, which Campbell and Montegón had walked through.

"A kidnapping?" he asked with apparent calm.

"If you look ahead you'll see another one of my friends," I said, pointing at Anselmo, standing beside the door that led to the sacristy.

"Your friends look a bit nervous."

"It's well known that appearances can be deceiving."

"What do you want?" he asked.

"For right now, to have a conversation."

"Whatever reason you have for bothering me, you still have time to change your mind. Leave the church now, and I promise you that I won't even go to the trouble of remembering this incident," said Melgoza with a mocking look in his eyes.

"I don't think that you're in a position to negotiate, Fullerton."

The mention of his old alias briefly robbed Melgoza of his composure. He made a disdainful face and looked behind him again to make sure that Montegón and Campbell were still in their places.

"That's what this is about?" he asked with a hint of annoyance. "I should have guessed. Who are you? Former FPMR militants out after a bender? MIR? Or some new group of trash that can't accept defeat?"

"Watch your words, Fullerton. My pistol is sensitive to harsh language," I said, and without giving the soldier a chance to answer, I added, "Trust me, the temptation to shoot is strong, and there are a lot of people who would thank me. But I'm not here to take justice into my own hands. I came to verify a few loose ends in a story, and to tell you that it's time for Fullerton to show his face."

"What do you want to talk about?" asked Melgoza.

"About the investigation that Germán Reyes was undertaking. And don't waste time pretending you don't know who he is. I read the notes that he wrote for his psychologist and I've seen some of the information he had gathered over the last months."

"Did Ana tell you about those notes?" asked the soldier, not bothering to lose time with useless evasion.

"If you're thinking that she ratted on you, you're wrong. She only turned over the evidence and we talked, the same as we're doing now."

"What's your relationship to Reyes? Are you part of the same group?"

"I'm a private detective. I was hired to investigate his death."

"A private detective? Don't make me laugh. You look like you just got out of jail. Private detectives investigate adultery and small-time robberies, they don't go digging into the distant past."

"As I already told you, appearances can be deceiving. But what can I tell you about deceiving people, when that's what you've done for your whole life." I looked around and added, "I know what I'm getting into, and even though I'd like to see you behind bars, at the moment what I really want is to know the names of the guys who killed Reyes."

"What makes you think I'm going to discuss that with you?"

"I talked with Pastrana a few minutes before he threw himself off a building. He said that he was a soldier obeying orders. I figured out that those orders must have come from you."

"I see you've discovered a few things, but you don't know how they fit together. With Pastrana dead, you don't have anything to use against me."

"That may be true, but my story will get the attention of certain lawyers and civil-rights advocates. Reyes's notes and what I learned from Pastrana will be more than enough to get you in front of a judge."

"Then why take the risk of coming to talk to me?"

"Stubbornness, vanity, whatever you want to call it, but I want to know that I've filled out the crossword puzzle right. You decide, Melgoza. Do we talk here with the protection of the saints, or would you prefer someplace like where you used to interrogate your victims?"

"We can talk, but I'm warning you that you won't come out well from the mess you got yourself into by coming to this church."

"Let me worry about that. What do you have to tell me?"

"Sometimes, the way we've done things over the last years, you can let the enemy advance, so they feel a misguided sense of victory."

"Are you trying to tell me that Reyes was a danger to those you represent? It seems like you're exaggerating, Melgoza."

"He was a danger to me."

"So you ordered Pastrana to kill him and make it look like a robbery. Too bad it ended up not being very convincing."

"Missions aren't always executed the way they're planned. I told Pastrana that when we analyzed the results of the operation."

"You must feel some nostalgia for the time when you could kill someone and go have a beer with your accomplices."

"Save your irony, Detective What's-your-name," said Melgoza, looking around. "As time went by, I thought I didn't have anything to worry about. The police accepted the motive of a robbery, and everything appeared to be going down the right path, straight to forgetfulness."

"What are the names of Reyes's killers?"

"That's information Pastrana took with him to the grave."

"You were Pastrana's superior, and he would have informed you of every detail of the mission. Or am I wrong?"

"Pastrana was an obedient soldier."

"The two of you met at Villa Grimaldi."

"Correct."

"And since then, up until his death, he kept working under your orders."

"Even if that were the case, it's not something I'm going to tell you."

"Reyes figured out that Pastrana was in charge of protecting the ex-soldiers who were sought by the courts. His work permitted him to hide some officers and send others to foreign countries. Also, and this is my theory, Pastrana was in charge of eliminating people like Reyes who turned into annoying pebbles in your shoes."

"You don't think I'm going to confirm or deny that, do you?"

"You'll have a chance to deny it all later, but while we're here in this church I want you to tell me the truth. When did you make the decision to kill Reyes?"

"What makes you think it was my idea?"

"Everything. Your past, your relationship with Pastrana, your sister, and Reyes's notebooks. Cut the bullshit, Melgoza. You and I both know what we're talking about."

"There's nothing better than knowing the stream you're swimming against."

"When did you decide to eliminate Reyes?" I asked again.

"Why do you insist that it was my idea?"

"I suppose you made the decision when your sister told you about the notebooks, or after investigating Reyes and realizing that the notes were the tip of the iceberg. Reyes wanted to get to the bottom of things, and you don't have to be very sharp to figure out that he had more information than he wrote down in the notebook. Up until now, your real name has never been mentioned in any investigation."

"You're right about my name."

"Luck or caution?"

"We made a pact—if one of ours ends up in court, he will not name any others of us who have not been identified in other cases. The important thing is to prolong the judicial investigations. The agreements negotiated since 1990 assure us that pending cases will be closed—a few of them with prison sentences and the rest with amnesty."

"Your sin is optimism, Melgoza. These days there are a number of judges willing to wade in the swamp. The brownnosing magistrates of the past are either dead or enjoying the comfortable retirement their complicity bought them."

"There's always the opportunity for new negotiations, and the truth is that the cases about what they call human rights don't have me very worried."

"No. Your fear comes from somewhere else. What you're worried about is arms trafficking."

"What do you know about that?" he asked cautiously.

"Everything," I lied. I smiled, knowing I had finally hit the nail on the head.

The officer looked at me with daggers in his eyes and then glanced at the old women praying in front of the altar.

"What do you say? Should we keep talking, or would you like to play some more-violent games?"

The idea to begin trafficking in arms, according to Melgoza, came up when the end of the military government became an undeniable reality. Melgoza and many other officers foresaw difficult times ahead, so they arranged a series of operations that would bring in resources for their future and those of some of their superiors who didn't want to leave the government empty-handed. They needed a plan that would bring in large sums of cash. Something different from the bank robberies of the past. Operations of a greater magnitude. Someone, maybe even Melgoza, thought arms trafficking could be a lucrative business. There were already a number of armed conflicts going on in our part of the world, with others about to start elsewhere—which meant the existence of people interested in buying weapons at any cost. They received approval for the project from their superiors, including the aging dictator, and for its execution a group formed made up of officers from the Business and Materiel Manufacturing Unit of the army, the Logistics Branch, and the Intelligence Directorate. This new organization acquired weapons, both new and used, and then resold them at far higher prices. The group made its first deals with Colombian narcotraffickers who needed weapons for their ongoing conflict against their country's army and the guerillas of the Revolutionary Armed Forces of Colombia (FARC).

"The opportunity to truly make an enormous windfall came in the form of the Balkan War of the 1990s," said Melgoza, emphasizing his words as if he were delivering a public speech and not exposing his guilt before an ordinary detective. "When the breakup of Yugoslavia happened, the majority of the munitions in that country ended up in the hands of the Serbs, which gave them a clear advantage in their war against Croatia and Slovenia. The Croats declared their independence in 1991, and to defend themselves, they needed to strengthen the National Guard, a police body that didn't even come close to the Serbian forces' war-making capabilities. Because of the United Nations prohibition, the Croats weren't able to buy directly from arms-manufacturing countries, so those in charge of acquiring weapons had to find providers that operated outside of the legal channels. It was a race against time for them, in which any weapon or provision they could get ahold of was useful for defending the new republic."

"And so that's how you were able to negotiate with the Croatians," I said, briefly interrupting Melgoza's monologue.

"The information came to us from Argentina, where there is a large Croatian expat community, and among them a lot of Ustasha nationalists who fled there after the victory of Marshal Tito at the end of World War II. Initially, the Croats did business with functionaries from the executive branch and the Argentine military. But when the demand for weapons couldn't be satisfied there, the Argentinians offered to help them acquire arms and supplies from Chile. Our intelligence services had been collaborating secretly since Operation Condor in the 1970s."

Melgoza explained that the final deal with the Croats had materialized through a European arms manufacturer that participated in the aeronautical fair every year it was held in Santiago. "The negotiations were very quick and convenient for us," he said. The sale of eleven tons of arms was finalized for more than six million dollars. Rifles, rockets, grenades, and ammunition began to be dispatched to countries where it was easy to pass off the cargo to the Croats. The shipments were made to look like the transport of medical devices from Chile as humanitarian aid for countries in conflict, and everything was fine until one of the deliveries was discovered in the Budapest airport. The local police confiscated the materiel and the press didn't take too long to break the story. The Chilean government at the time confronted the scandal, and after negotiating an investigation with the army, some of the officers who participated in the sales were forced to retire. The business began to get shaky, and it became necessary to design a strategy to avoid the larger part of the organization being discovered.

At the beginning of 1992, things got increasingly complicated for Melgoza and his group. The head of foreign purchases in the army's Logistics Branch was accused of having a role in the operation. The officer, who had not participated in the deal but who was aware that it had occurred, got nervous and threatened to make a statement to the tribunal investigating the case. His superiors put pressure on him to keep quiet, but the officer decided to move forward with the statement anyway. It was at that moment that Melgoza went to Pastrana and ordered him to take the rogue officer out of circulation. First they kidnapped him and tried to convince him to remain silent. When that didn't work, Pastrana killed him. His body was found in a park outside the city, and the evidence pointed toward a suicide. The army staged a perfunctory investigation and confirmed that the cause of death was suicide. A doctor said in a formal statement that the officer had suffered from severe depression, and a story was leaked to the press that was intended to bury the scandal for good.

"The government asked for a visiting minister to be named in order to reactivate the investigation," added Melgoza. "The judge subpoenaed a lot of officers, and despite all our efforts to keep a united front, little by little, contradictions began to appear in our stories. Even though a number of officers were formally accused of arms trafficking, we have managed to control the situation. From the time the magistrate was brought in until today, more than ten years have gone by, and the judicial investigations are still stalled."

"And that whole time, you lived in absolute comfort," I said.

"*Comfort* isn't exactly the right word. For the last years, I have had to work hard to keep them from discovering the activities of our organization. Fortunately, all of those involved know how to behave, and any who get caught keep quiet. It hasn't been easy to keep the nucleus of the association hidden," said Tulio Melgoza. He paused and looked toward the church entrance once more. "At first I thought that Reyes's digging around would be the start of an uncontrollable avalanche that would bury us all, but the way he worked, alone and without sharing his findings, betrayed him. If Reyes's information and Aliaga's confession had gotten out, the minister in charge of the investigation would have had enough evidence to convict the officers they had already detained—and to identify me. That was why Pastrana went to his collaborators."

"Everything seems so simple and logical."

"I've only told you the main facts. Knowing too much could put you in danger," said Melgoza. "I'm not the only one who would like to remain anonymous."

"If you're considering giving me the same treatment you gave Reyes, forget about it. The police already know what Pastrana said before he died, and Reyes's notes are in the hands of a lawyer who will release them if anything should happen to me. And don't even think about going after my friends either."

"I don't suppose there's any point in asking you if we could arrive at an economic understanding."

"*Blood Money.* That's the title of a Dashiell Hammett novel. Remember it when you're on your way to jail."

"It's not as simple as you think. Justice is slow, and every day that we delay the investigation helps us destroy evidence and cover our tracks."

"I know that's true, but your name will still come out into the light, and you'll have to answer for what you've done."

"I'm just a part of the machine, and it is my duty to protect the more important pieces. I am not afraid to face anyone," Melgoza said arrogantly. "Now, if you don't have anything else to say, get out of here."

"I just have one last question for you, Fullerton."

"Tulio Melgoza Imbert is my name," the officer interrupted me.

"Why do you come to this church every day? To look for the forgiveness that your victims can never give you?"

Melgoza looked down and stared at the lines on his hand.

"I don't have to ask for forgiveness," he finally said. "I wouldn't think twice about doing it all again."

I got to my feet and went over to Campbell and Montegón, at the church door. We got in the journalist's car, where Anselmo was waiting for us. I lit a cigarette and smoked in silence until we saw Melgoza leave the church.

"What do we do now?" asked Montegón. "Do we follow him? Put a bullet in him? Call the cops?"

I threw the cigarette out the car window and fixed the knot in my tie.

"I'm going to buy you all some beer," I said.

"Beers?" asked Anselmo.

"Or whatever you want," I replied. "And we should invite Cotapos too. I'm sure he'll be interested in hearing the story I have to tell."

30

"Did you hear about what happened to Mr. Hernández?" Feliz Domingo asked as soon as he saw me come out of the elevator. "I don't wish to speak ill of the dead, but that man always made the hair on the back of my neck stand up. His bad attitude, his nighttime outings, his constantly asking whether anyone had come to visit. He was obviously hiding something."

"I read about it in the papers," I responded, not wanting to encourage the doorman, who seemed especially affected by what had happened to Pastrana. "They said he was a retired army officer mixed up in drug trafficking, and that his rivals threw him from a building."

"Do you believe everything you read in the papers?"

"The racing forms and soccer scores are usually right, but as far as op-eds, literary criticism, and political news, I have my doubts."

"With respect to Mr. Hernández, I have a different theory from the one that appears in the papers," said the doorman. "I think he was a con man who got caught in one of his scams."

"It doesn't matter. Nothing we say will change our neighbor's luck."

"I can't say I feel very bad about it."

"Easy there, Feliz Domingo. Haven't you heard, all of the dead are good?"

"Félix, Mr. Heredia. With an *x*."

"*X* as in *xerograph*, *xiphoid*, and *xylitol*. If I keep messing up your name, I'm going to run out of words in the dictionary that start with *x*."

"Memory, Mr. Heredia. The important thing is to exercise your memory."

"I'll keep that in mind, Félix."

"Thank you, Mr. Heredia. I can tell that you're a gentleman." Still blocking my way, the doorman continued, "They're going to rent out the apartment that the dead man lived in. Yesterday the owner came with some workers and had them retouch the paint. I hope the next renter is a decent person. Not a drug trafficker or a con man—"

"Nor a private detective," I jumped in, interrupting him. "The neighborhood can't take two people sticking their noses into things at the same time."

Cotapos and Terán were waiting for me in the workshop of the Cultural Center of the Americas. It had been two weeks since my conversation with Melgoza, and a lawyer had called me the night before to set up the appointment. For a few days, the press had covered the arms trafficking constantly, but after the first week it had been given secondary importance until it was completely replaced on the front pages by the discovery of a cut-up body on the outskirts of Puente Alto. When I arrived at the workshop, I found three young men painting pickets and banners. One of the banners bore the words **GERMÁN REYES BRIGADE**.

"Did you read any of the papers this morning?" Cotapos asked as soon as I sat down.

"No. What happened? Did world peace break out?"

"They all ran stories about an army communiqué in support of the work of the tribunals to bring the arms traffickers to justice. It doesn't seem like a big deal, but it's more than anyone expected from the military."

"What your friend wrote probably played a role," Terán intervened, pointing at the bulletin board where Campbell's story had been posted.

"Don't put too much stock in their words. They've just gotten to the point where they can no longer cover the sun with their finger," I replied.

"I did some asking around in the tribunals, and they're coming after Melgoza hard," Cotapos continued. "They're going to open an investigation into Reyes's death, based on evidence I submitted. If Pastrana's accomplices are identified and talk, Melgoza will probably be found guilty of being the mastermind of the killing. His name has also been added to those being investigated for arms trafficking. The case is advancing. The instructing judge is expected to present charges in the next couple of days. A number of prominent military men are already under house arrest, and Melgoza will be added to that list. And then there are the human-rights cases in which he's mentioned. They will bring him to testify, and I don't think he's going to escape this time. Reyes would have been happy with the results of his work, and you should be happy too, Heredia."

"I got lucky. That's all."

"Don't deny yourself credit," said the lawyer, and then suddenly, his expression hardening, he asked, "You haven't had any problems?"

"What kind of problems?"

"Melgoza hasn't tried to get even?"

"I think he's got other things to worry about."

"You should take precautions," added Terán.

"It's not necessary. If they try to do something to me, it won't be for a while, and it'll probably work."

I stopped in front of Anselmo's newsstand, and he gave me a fax that Griseta had sent with the details of her return to Santiago. I invited him to eat at the Fish King, and while we caught up over some grilled pomfret fillets with celery salad, I told him about the meeting with Cotapos and Terán.

"Who would have imagined that we had someone so evil for a neighbor?"

"We're surrounded by people with dark pasts. That's why so many are still afraid to express their opinions."

"Félix told me that the police inspected Pastrana's storage space in the basement. He had a collection of handcuffs, pistols, and knives. What do you think about that?"

"You have to pay attention to your neighbors. You never know what's behind a friendly smile."

"I read that the army isn't going to lift a finger to assist Melgoza."

"The time when they could defend the indefensible has passed."

"There are some people who think the military has changed."

"They keep their mouths shut and salute courteously now, but in the future they could show their teeth again. I don't have much hope for them. They're trained to keep order for the powerful. Our history is full of examples."

"Anyone who heard you would think you hate them."

"Mistrust, Anselmo. One time they fucked up our lives, and I haven't forgotten about it."

In the afternoon, after a nap that helped me scare away the ghosts of the fish and white wine I had shared with Anselmo, I visited Julio Suazo's daughter, Yolanda. I found her in the tailor's shop and, taking advantage of the fact that her boss was out buying materials, gave her an update. It couldn't be proven that Suazo had been killed by the officer or any of his men, but Melgoza would at least be held to account for what he did in Villa Grimaldi. The woman listened in silence and then let loose a few tears that she wiped away with a handkerchief. She thanked me for the information and went back to her work. It seemed like she had submerged herself once more in the world of memories and pain that she inhabited.

I said goodbye to Yolanda and then walked toward Virginia Reyes's house to make the visit that I had thought about making ever since I'd discovered there were pages missing from her brother's notebook. Just like during my first visit, I found her in the garden, tending to her flowers and plants. She offered me a soft drink, and we sat together at a table beneath a pergola and talked about her plants and a trip to the south that she was planning with some friends. I could tell that she didn't want to immediately touch on the real motive for my visit, or perhaps that she needed to talk with someone to drive away the loneliness that surrounded her.

"I found out who was responsible for Germán's death," I told her when I felt that too much time had passed.

"I know, and I figured you would come. I read the articles about arms trafficking, strange business deals, and deaths—they mentioned my brother's name in passing. What's all that about, Heredia?"

"It's a long story, and full of details that I haven't been able to completely figure out. It's the tip of an iceberg, and I can only guess how deep it goes."

Virginia nodded her head slowly, listening to my report.

"One of those responsible is dead, another will face charges, and the other two are still unknown, but I haven't given up hope that the police will catch them."

"I never thought that Germán could get mixed up in something so scary," Virginia Reyes said.

"We never know just how close we are to the horror."

"Now I only want justice to be done."

"I can't do much about that. All I can do in this case is to find a bit of truth."

"Isn't that the same thing?"

"Sometimes truth and justice move in opposite directions."

"I wish my brother were here, so we could talk about all those things we never had a chance to discuss."

"That's something that can't be fixed."

"All of a sudden, we find that time has passed, and we have done very little to be happy."

"The problem is that no one teaches us the business of living."

Virginia Reyes breathed deeply to stifle a sob, and looked at the patio where her plants and flowers grew. I felt for my cigarettes in order to give her a private moment.

"I'm sorry. I forgot I didn't hire you to listen to me complain," the woman suddenly said, and as she brushed the hair off her forehead, she continued, "You must have other things to do. It's time for us to talk about your fee."

"It's not much, but it's better than eating rats," I said to Montegón, passing him eight ten-thousand-peso notes over the table we were sharing.

We were in the Rimbaud restaurant sharing a bottle of wine, with the entire night ahead of us. From the window at our side, we could see the lights of Plaza Bulnes and the presidential palace. The darkness winked at us from the street, and every now and then we could hear the steps of someone hurrying to get home.

"I admire the ice in your veins," said the detective. "If I'd been in your place, I would have shot Melgoza right there in the church." He put the bills away in a worn bluish leather wallet.

"His death would have meant more silence around his crimes. Now he'll have to face a judge and the media, and maybe even his victims."

"Your words make sense, but they don't completely convince me."

"The case is out of our hands now, Atilio," I told him, speaking to him more informally than I had since we'd met. "And thank you for your help. The job would have been a lot harder if I'd had to watch my own back."

"It's been a long time since anyone thanked me for anything."

"I think we deserve a toast to our health," I said, raising the glass of wine to my lips.

"I've decided not to work for any more companies that snoop around in their employees' lives. I rented a storefront on the Gran Avenida. It's in a sort of strip mall. Nothing big. With a couple of cases a month I should be fine."

"Write a couple of novels and you'll be like Hammett."

"Who's that?"

"A guy who worked as a strikebreaker for the Pinkerton Detective Agency in the US. He got sick of that work and wrote some stories based on his experiences. He did really well."

"It's a shame you don't want to have a partner," said Montegón, showing no interest in Dashiell Hammett. "In any case, if you ever need help or have too many clients, remember me."

"Don't worry. I won't forget your help," I said.

Montegón brought his glass close to mine and we toasted our health.

"What do you feel when you solve a case?" he asked a bit later.

"I turn the page and collect my wage."

"Come on, Heredia. What do you really do?"

"You bang your head against a wall for a few days, and then all of a sudden the mystery is gone. You don't have anything else to think about. Victims, evidence, suspects, criminals. It all forms a fuzzy picture of the past that may or may not be decipherable."

"When you put it that way, it doesn't seem like a very attractive occupation."

"But it is, especially when the doubts make your heart skip a beat. Afterward, the mystery evaporates, transformed into a series of more or less reasonable explanations. Without doubts and mysteries, the job, like life, ends up being a lump of repeated days."

"Do you like your work?"

"Very much, but lately I've been thinking about taking a break."

Montegón picked up his glass of wine and raised it with a ceremonious gesture. "Let's drink to the partnership that never was."

"And to death, which never tires of working and keeps us busy."

31

I couldn't remember exactly when they had dragged me to that place. I was blindfolded, tied to a chair. From the other room I could hear the sounds of a military march being played, insistent and demanding, and the screams of a woman who was being asked questions that she didn't want to or couldn't answer. I wanted to sleep, but the punches to my chest kept me awake. My lips were dry, and the pressure of the blindfold on my eyes grew as the hell went on and on. Nobody knew where I was, and the few people who would worry about me would have doors slammed on them or lies told to them should they try to find me. I wanted to stop hearing the military march, the voices in the cell, the near-imperceptible whistle of the fist that plowed through the air before hitting my face. I seemed to be reliving the testimony of other victims of the warriors against forgetfulness. Liberal beatings, immersion in foul water, electric shocks, simulated executions, rapes, genitals being torn off, pleading that reason would reassert itself. Perhaps I would survive, but my steps would become ghostly. I would fear the gaze of strangers, the quick braking of a vehicle in the middle of the night, and terror would be imprinted on my senses like a brand made by molten iron. Nothing would be the same, but all the same I wanted to keep holding on to the sliver of light that the blindfold allowed me to see. To live was all I wanted.

Suddenly, the sun lit up my room, and everything around me seemed calm with the silent peace of Sunday morning. But the nightmare continued, ferocious and merciless, reminding me that the horror was still there, sitting around the family table, inside of certain words, or in the arrogance of a uniformed guard watching the entrance of a supermarket. Its echo was reborn in the call to forget the past. The horror was in my body, in my battered conscience that forced me to relive the nightmare while I watched some dogs walk by from my window.

I took Simenon into my arms, and as the nightmare became more diffuse, I managed to remember the moment when I'd said goodbye to Montegón.

"For a second I thought I was in the hands of Melgoza or one of his men," I told Simenon.

"You're at home and nobody has come looking for you. You're tired and hungry. Nothing you can't fix with a good breakfast."

"You're right. I'm tired, and it wouldn't be bad to sleep for a couple of weeks."

I had eaten breakfast and was at my desk looking over late bills and newspaper articles that I had saved for some reason I could no longer remember—the crimes and news items that took up a few lines in the papers. I tried to go through the clippings, but after a while I gave up and left them on top of the desk. I walked around the apartment, opened a couple of books, and lay down to listen to a Ben Webster CD that I'd loved ever since listening to it with Griseta during a long afternoon of reconciliation. My hangover from the night before came back, and I allowed myself to be lulled to sleep by the music.

I woke up a little before the time that Griseta had told me her bus would be arriving. I grabbed my jacket and closed the door of the apartment with more violence than necessary. The Chevy Nova started as soon as I turned the key, and I took off in a hurry toward the Los

Héroes Terminal. I got there half an hour before the bus parked on platform number seven. Griseta was sitting toward the front. I saw her face against the window and waved to greet her from a distance. She was carrying two bags that she dropped on the ground when she saw me come up beside her. The city roared behind me, the past nested in my memories, and I wasn't sure I wanted to hear what the next person who came into my office to hire me had to say. Anything could happen in the future, but right then the only thing that mattered was kissing the woman I had in my arms.

The next day I went back to the City. I said hi to the waiter who always took care of me and moved toward the table where the Writer was sitting, reading *Hombre Muerto* by Guillermo Riedemann.

"What's up? What's so important?" he asked. "Do you have a good story to tell me?"

"On the contrary. I wanted to tell you that I decided to put an end to our deal. Myra and Patricia, two friends that you don't know, wrote me to point out some inconsistencies in your books. For example, in one of the novels you say that Griseta is a brunette, and in the next, a redhead, like she is in real life."

"Women usually dye their hair."

"In one of the novels, she is a psychology student, and in another she works as a psychologist."

"If I remember, at some point you told me that she had changed majors at the university."

"In one place you say that Anselmo retired from horse racing because he broke his arm; in another because he broke his right knee."

"As far as I know, he suffered fractures in both extremities. Let's not worry about medical details."

"They also tell me that you're not very precise about my age or Griseta's."

"You know that time is relative."

"In one of your first novels, the priest who took care of me at the orphanage was named Jacinto, and in the most recent, John Brown."

"I suppose you didn't meet more than one priest in the orphanage."

"I'd prefer not to keep going with my complaints, Writer."

"All of this can be fixed in the future, Heredia. What do you think about working on some other cases? I've heard about a drug ring that operates out of a horse racetrack, and also about a television executive who's the victim of extortion."

"I'm not interested. I'm taking a break."

"Singing that song again, huh? You've said the same thing a hundred times. There was even that one time when you went to the beach. Six months later, you came back with your tail between your legs." He impishly added, "I've got a good thing for you to investigate. Someone who lives in Temuco contacted me and said they want to find out who killed their cousin. The victim was part of a group of Mapuches who were fighting to recover their land. It sounds like he was killed by the guards of a logging company that was cutting down the forests in that region."

"It sounds like a good case, but—"

"Don't retire, Heredia. Guys like you—"

"Die old or with a bullet in them. I've read that phrase in at least thirty-three novels."

"Why would you close your office? Why do you want to retire?" asked the Writer, worried. "You're the best detective in Santiago."

"Who said anything about closing the office? Have you heard me mention the word *retirement*?"

"You talked about resting . . ."

"I'll put a sign up on my door that says *No clients for the next five weeks*, and then I'll shut myself in and read twenty novels that I've got sitting on the nightstand."

"So you'll get back on track and come to tell me stories?"

"Don't get your hopes up about the stories."

"We'll discuss this later, after you've read your novels. You'll have something to tell me in the future."

"Don't bet anything on it, Writer," I responded, watching a brunette with seductive curves come into the bar.

ABOUT THE AUTHOR

Photo © 2016 Paulo Slachevsky

Ramón Díaz Eterovic is one of the best-known writers of crime stories in Chile, where the adventures of his private investigator Heredia are enormously popular. They've been adapted into the graphic-novel series *Heredia Detective* and a TV series, *Heredia y Asociados*. In 2009, Díaz Eterovic became the subject of the documentary *El rostro oculto en las palabras* (*The Face Hidden in the Words*).

Díaz Eterovic is also the author of *The Fires of the Past* and *The Music of Solitude* and has published forty novels, short-story and poetry collections, graphic novels, and children's books. He has received Gijón's Salón Iberoamericano del libro *Las Dos Orillas* prize, the Chilean National Cultural Board Prize, the Santiago Municipal Book Prize, the Francisco Coloane National Narrative Prize, and the Altazor Arts Prize. His work has also been published in numerous countries, including

Chile, Portugal, Spain, Greece, Croatia, Argentina, Mexico, France, Holland, and Germany.

Díaz Eterovic lives in Santiago, Chile, with his wife, Sonia, and their three children.

ABOUT THE TRANSLATOR

Patrick Blaine is an associate professor of Latin American cultural studies at Morningside College in Sioux City, Iowa. He earned his MA and PhD in comparative literature from the University of Washington. He specializes in Chilean and Argentinian literature and film and has written extensively on these subjects.

In 2000, Blaine moved to Santiago, Chile, where he taught English at the Instituto Chileno-Norteamericano de Cultura and worked as a commercial translator and interpreter. Before returning to the United States, he studied in the Universidad de Chile's graduate literature program. Blaine frequently returns to Chile with his wife, Mónica, and son, Sebastián.

As a translator, Blaine has published English translations of essays by Angel Guido and Jorge Ruedas de la Serna, as well as a Spanish translation of his own essay on Chilean filmmaker Patricio Guzmán. *Dark Echoes of the Past* is his first novel translation.